I SAW YOU IN BEIRUT

Science Traveler Series

Book 5

I SAW YOU IN BEIRUT

Science Traveler Series

Book 5

J. L. Greger

Bug Press

New Mexico

I Saw You in Beirut

Bug Press
An imprint of IngramSpark
Bernalillo, New Mexico 87004
http://www.jlgreger.com

Copyright, second edition © 2019 by J. L. Greger
First edition © November 2015
Cover design by Barbara Hodges for Got You Covered Bookcover
Design © 2019

ISBN (paperback): 97809600285-4-2
ISBN (EPUB): 97809600285-5-9
Library of Congress Catalogue Number: 2019907776

DEDICATION

To my Iranian graduate student who was the model for Farideh
and
to my ever faithful Bug.

ACKNOWLEDGMENTS

I want to thank:

Barbara Hodges for designing the cover,

The late Billie Johnson and Oak Tree Press, publisher of the first edition of *Malignancy*,

Zelda Gatuskin and reviewers of all my books in the Science Traveler Series.

MAP: Locations in *I Saw You in Beirut*

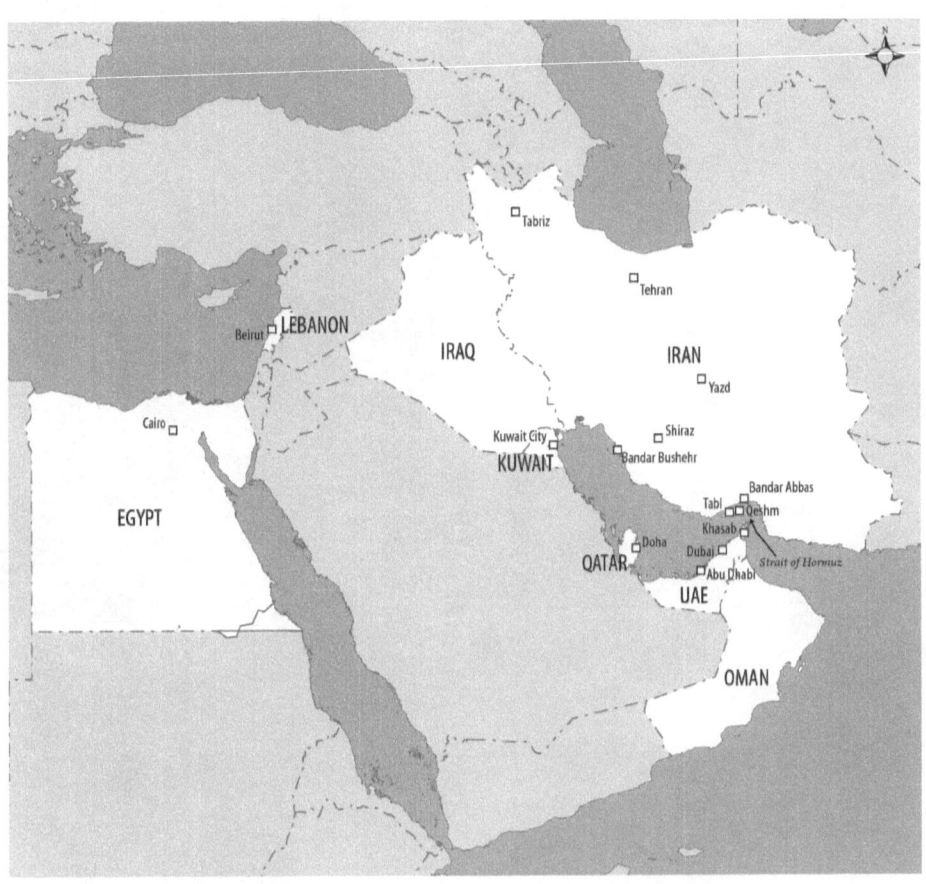

CHAPTER 1: Sara Almquist in Washington, D.C.

Sara Almquist wondered whether her romance with Eric Sanders was cooling as she read his email:

> *Please be at my place by five thirty?*
> *Sanders*

He usually stopped by with dinner invitations and didn't send emails.

They met six months before when he engineered her rescue from a drug lord in Bolivia where she was assessing public health problems for the U.S. Agency for International Development, better known as USAID. Not long after they worked on a demanding assignment in Cuba, and they had learned to trust each other and discovered mutual interests. The last four months had been fun, and both had adjusted their lifestyles.

Sometimes she wished their relationship was based less on shared challenges in difficult environments and intellectual interests, and more on... She didn't know what she wanted. Certainly not an irrational passion that generated knots in her stomach. She didn't need more of those kinds of lover's knots.

The fiftyish, tall blonde looked over at Bug, her Japanese Chin, who pretended to snooze on a table by the printer. He studied her with his big brown eyes and emitted little mumbling noises until he noticed she was staring back. Then he averted his eyes to the floor. After seven years, she couldn't decide whether the sounds Bug uttered were groans of disgust or sighs of satisfaction. Funny, Sanders was a lot like Bug. Smart and independent. Sara valued those characteristics in the man and in the dog, although she wished both were more demonstrative at times. But that was unrealistic because she wasn't effusive either. She hadn't even developed a pet name for the man and called him Sanders, like everyone else.

She and Bug had been in Washington on and off for four months. Although most of the paperwork for her part-time position at

USAID could be done from her home in La Bendita, about twenty-five miles north of Albuquerque, USAID required her to attend several face-to-face meetings each month in Washington. Part of the deal struck to entice her out of early retirement from Michigan State was permission to bring Bug to work, provided he was "unobtrusive at all times." Bug, like the good pet therapy dog he was, never barked, didn't have accidents, and sat calmly for hours. However, he wasn't exactly unobtrusive. He perched in obvious places in her office and greeted all visitors by standing and waving his plumed, black and white tail.

During her stays in Washington, she and Bug stayed in a bed and breakfast in Georgetown. She and Sanders had agreed if she stayed in his spare bedroom it would hamper both of them and be a source of gossip.

Today, she had led a conference call with Bolivian public health officials, leaders of environmental test laboratories in Bolivia, and a chemist from Johns Hopkins University. The Bolivian laboratories were unable to consistently analyze water and soil samples for certain pollutants, especially mercury, in mine runoff. This was problematic. Mercury had been used for almost five hundred years to extract silver from the ore from the mines near Potosí. The ultimate test of the success of the passive water purifications systems, which USAID was constructing around the silver mines in Potosi, was the removal of mercury from mine effluents and soil. Everyone was relieved when the chemist from Johns Hopkins agreed to spend two weeks in Bolivia to train laboratory staff. Sara had included funds in the USAID contract for this contingency, even though the Bolivian officials had assured her five months ago their laboratories were up to the task.

With this key hurdle handled, she was returning tomorrow to Albuquerque and hoped this would be a romantic evening. She wanted to introduce a bit of fun into her reply to Sanders's email, but recognized others might see it. She thought of the new red silk chemise in her suitcase and typed:

I'll bring something red.

Sara

She was pleased Sanders suggested an early dinner. She was always hungry by five thirty and ate a bit, which frequently was more than bit, when she knew dinner would be after seven. She didn't ask for a reason for the early dinner because she understood him well enough to know he was also cautious about what he included in emails.

At four, she and Bug jumped out of a cab in front of a gray, stone-faced building in Georgetown. She let go of Bug's leash as they climbed the four stairs to the enameled blue door, sailed past the unmanned reception desk, and hurried up the carpeted stairs to their room on the second floor. Strange. A do-not-disturb sign hung on the door. She never used the sign because she was thankful to have her room tidied daily.

She unlocked the door and gasped. Her suitcase lay on the queen-sized bed with her clothes and papers littered over the rumpled bed and the floor. She wasn't neat, but she never left the room in chaos.

For a second, Sara debated what to do. She picked up Bug, locked the door, ran down the steps, and knocked on the owner's apartment door. "What happened?" she exclaimed as a young woman opened the door to reveal a room cluttered with children's toys.

The young woman, with her cornrowed hair pulled back from her face, blinked. "What do you mean? At breakfast, I told you today was a bad day for me with two guests checking out, and another wanting to check-in by noon. I was thankful you posted the do-not-disturb sign, and I never entered your room." Her voice became louder as her two-year-old son banged on a toy drum, and her daughter tooted on a red plastic kazoo.

Sara took a deep breath and decided not to display her alarm. "Was anyone in my room?"

"Of course, not. It was locked." The woman scooped up her two-year-old. The noise level was reduced, but the four-year-old girl continued to play her instrument. "I could come up in ten minutes."

She didn't wait for Sara's reply. "Oh, you got a delivery this morning. Where did I put it?" She motioned Sara and Bug to enter, closed the door, and sorted through neat piles of papers on a desk. She pulled a small white envelope from the bottom of the pile. "It was hand delivered right after you left at seven thirty by a gentleman in a suit."

"Can you describe him?"

The woman rolled her eyes and bounced her son her hip. "Not young. Dark, thin, straight hair. Not Hispanic. More likely, Greek or Middle Eastern. Yes. That's right. He spoke with a slight accent when he said, 'Important. Give to her immediately.' Pretty nondescript." She smiled nervously and cuddled her son as he emitted chirping noises. "Except he walked with a limp and used a cane."

Sara debated her options. The landlady could barely handle her own problems. She suspected the envelope and the break-in were connected. Mainly, she wanted to get away from the noise. "Thanks. Don't bother to clean my room."

Bug ran up the steps in front of Sara. She thought he was eager to get away from the noise too.

She unlocked the door, pulled on her outdoor gloves, and sat on the blue chintz chair, the only piece of furniture not covered by her tossed garments and papers. She turned the envelope over. *Dr. Sara Almquist* was neatly printed on one side. When she held the envelope up to the light, all she saw was a small card. No signs of powder. She slit it with a nail file and laid it on the TV so Bug couldn't sniff it.

The card was a business card for an antique shop on a side street near Dupont Circle in Washington, D.C. She thought she'd been in the shop when she followed Sanders on one of his "antique runs." He was into mid-century modern furniture and items. She wasn't, but she enjoyed the challenge of spotting cracks, chips, stains, and repairs on vintage pieces. On the back of the card was printed:

Claim your bracelet today after four. Don't be afraid.
We need your help.
A friend

She muttered to herself, "Sanders, what have you gotten me into this time?"

She'd brought only one bracelet with her on this trip. It was a vintage scarab one, a gift from Sanders. Although most scarab bracelets contained stones or tiles in multiple colors, this one was carved green jade scarabs set in gold. She'd spotted it in a store, perhaps the one mentioned on the card, in December. Sanders had surprised her with the bracelet at Christmas. She pawed through the clutter on her bed. Three pairs of earrings — gold stars, navy Bakelite balls, and black glass buttons — were still in her turquoise silk brocade pouch with a string of navy Bakelite beads. The bracelet was gone.

The thief had taken her best piece, but it wasn't worth enough to file a report with the overworked Metropolitan Police Department. A call to the police would mean she'd have to skip dinner, spend a miserable evening filling out forms in a noisy police substation, and be less likely to retrieve the bracelet than if she went to the shop as indicated on the card. Besides, she was curious. She wondered whether they really wanted her help or thought she was a conduit to Sanders.

She glanced at her watch. If she hurried, she could retrieve the bracelet and get to dinner on time. One of Sanders's "associates" could learn more from the mess in her room, if she didn't disturb it. She placed the envelope and card in a clean plastic bag and laughed. "One advantage of always having poop bags handy," and announced to Bug, "Let's go."

Once she and Bug were in a cab, she realized perhaps it wasn't smart to go to the shop alone. She figured going into a shop in a busy area during daylight hours wasn't dangerous, but texted the address of the shop to Sanders anyway. Thought a bit, and emailed him a few details about the break-in and suggested he have one of his so-called "associates" check out her room. She seldom asked him about these men from the dimmer side of his international activities. She wondered if maybe she should.

She was lucky and traffic was moderate. In less than fifteen minutes, the cab stopped in front of a slightly run-down antique shop. She hesitated as she departed the cab because she suddenly realized the environs were perfect for a mugging. The shop looked deserted.

The cabbie growled, "Lady I haven't got all day. This is the place."

For almost a minute, she clutched Bug's leash and peered through the front window, wondering how bad could it get. She'd been a professor in a university department that had finally split into two departments — epidemiology and statistics. Now, *that* was a hostile environment.

A bell tinkled when she finally pushed the shop's door open. A middle-aged man, shorter and lighter than herself, at five foot eight and one hundred and fifty pounds, approached. He nodded and smiled as if he recognized her. "Wait here." He disappeared behind a black velvet curtain.

She eyed the place for exits and spotted only one — the front entrance. She edged backward toward it. Bug must have sensed her nervousness because he didn't sit as he usually did in businesses. The man reappeared in less than a minute. He limped toward her. "Let me put this bracelet on you."

"No, I'd rather you put it in an envelope."

"As you wish, but it's not wired or poisoned. We wanted to give you this card."

Another business card. She flipped it over. Hand printing:

Trust your memory, not those in authority.
Allah will bless you.

She pointed at the lines. "What does this mean?"

"You'll see." He looked nervously over his shoulder when a piece of glass crashed behind the black curtain. "Go quickly."

CHAPTER 2: Sara at Sanders's home

At five thirty, she pounded the brass ring attached to the black door of Sanders's red brick, three-story townhouse on Capitol Hill. A broad-shouldered, grim-faced blond in a Marine Corps uniform answered. She stepped back in hesitation until a tall, lanky man, with thin brown hair hurried down the gray marble hallway toward her.

Sanders brushed a kiss onto her cheek, pulled her inside as he closed the door, and whispered, "I apologize. I brought you here under false pretenses." He stepped back and said more loudly, "Major Jones can show you an official badge, but…"

"I won't learn anything." She pulled Sanders toward her and whispered, "Did you get my emails?"

"He nuzzled her ear and said, "Yes, one of my associates is at your room now."

She gave him an exaggerated kiss and shoved the plastic bag with both cards and the envelope with the bracelet into his jacket pocket. "When I retrieved the bracelet at a store, they gave me the second card with the odd message."

She pulled away, forced a smile, and extended her hand to the Marine, "What did I stumble into this time?"

"Ma'am, this is a routine clearance check for one of your past graduate students."

The officer had read her wrong. Her father had instilled in her a basic distrust of the military, and she'd caught him in a lie. "I didn't fall off the turnip truck yesterday. I've been interviewed before on past students who sought high-clearance jobs. Those interviewers didn't have a major's oak leaf on their shoulder. What do you want?" Before he could answer, she strode to a Barcelona sofa in black leather and stainless steel. Bug settled on the large wine-colored Persian rug that anchored the mid-century modern furniture in the living room.

Sanders waved for the Major to be seated on a less comfortable chair of steel and white leather, switched on two Tiffany lamps that cast a rosy glow in the room, and uncharacteristically retreated to the kitchen where Sara, but not the Major, could see his face over the counter.

"Hmmf." The Major maintained his perfect posture as he sat and opened his briefcase. "Information on your past students and employees from the Middle East, particularly Iran and Iraq. You must agree to not discuss anything that we speak about with anyone, even Mr. Sanders."

As he droned on with his officious comments, Sara pulled a pad of paper from her purse and began to write. "I was the major professor for only one grad student from the Middle East. A Palestinian woman on a Fullbright Fellowship. Here's her name." She ripped off the page and handed it to him. "All my technicians and programmers were U.S. citizens. None had Arab or Middle Eastern backgrounds."

"We know that."

Sara wanted to say again, "Tell me what you want," but she faked a smile instead.

He pulled a thick file out of his briefcase and leafed through it. "You consulted in the Middle East twice on major projects. We need details." He peered at her with cold, blue eyes.

"Major, I assume you know the dates of my travel to the Middle East better than I do."

He placed a device on a side table.

"Thanks for admitting others are listening to our conversation."

He blinked and recited another memorized set of warnings.

Sara half-listened as she jotted a few words on her pad. "Perhaps you missed my first consultation. In seventy-one, the U.S. shipped seed grain treated with methyl mercury fungicide to Iraq during a drought. Peasants in the northern provinces of Iraq ate the grain because the planting season was over. When the mistakes were recognized, the farmers dumped the grain into streams and polluted the much of the water in Iraq. The net result was over five hundred Iraqis died due to methyl mercury poisoning. Thousands suffered neurological symptoms. In the mid-eighties, a WHO official asked me to statistically analyze follow-up data on neurological symptoms in children born in the area during the early seventies. I never met the WHO official in person. So, I don't know his ethnic background."

"Wait."

"What didn't you understand? WHO is a subunit of the United Nations. It's full name is World Health Organization. I doubt I was cited in the WHO report because it was at the start of my career. I was paid a nominal consulting fee, which I would have put in a university account for my research. I don't remember the name of the official."

The Marine continued to scribble. "Our experts missed it. I'm sure we'll be able to identify your WHO contact."

Sara picked up Bug and rubbed spots behind his ears. He closed his eyes and seemed to relax. "It would be helpful to know your goals?"

Sanders kept chopping vegetables. "I warned you and your boss. She's had a lot of vague contacts with the Middle East and will need honest answers from you to focus her thoughts. If not, you'll be here until midnight. Moreover, she could get a high security clearance easily. Tell her."

The Major stared at the device on the table. "I guess."

Sara waited thirty seconds. "And?"

"We received an SOS from an operative… an important one for us in Iran early this morning." He squinted at the pages in his hands. "I'm told this individual is… secretive, never shows panic, rarely sends emails."

After another thirty-second pause, Sara put Bug on the floor and leaned forward. "What did the email say?"

"It was from an account our operative uses only in emergencies, actually only once before. The message originated from a public café in Tabriz."

Sara showed her impatience as she leaned within a foot of the Major's face.

"Hmmf." A long pause. "Help. Contact Almquist."

Sara gasped and leaned back. "There are thousands of Almquists."

"But few have ever visited the Middle East or had contacts there. Our analysts examined your contacts for four hours. Several items interested us." He glanced toward the kitchen. The savory aroma of sautéed onions and mushrooms wafted from a pan on the range, while Sanders cleaned the counter. "Mr. Sanders was contacted for information on you. He suggested we meet directly. We thought your office and your room at the bed and breakfast were too public. He suggested a long conversation here would go unnoticed because you often stay overnight."

"I see." She smirked at Sanders. He kept his head down. Coward. She cleared her throat. "What was interesting? That will help me focus my thoughts?"

"I'd rather not say. This operative has been undercover for over thirty years."

Sanders sauntered from the kitchen, handed Sara a Diet Coke, and gave the Major a choice of beverages. "She'll be kinder if you admit the truth instead of making her guess. I can leave for an hour, if you don't want me to hear your conversation. My *coq au vin* is almost ready for the oven."

The Major gulped. "Your security clearance makes it unnecessary for you to leave, but I'd prefer time alone with her."

Sanders glared at him. "Fine, provided you admit your problem to her. Dr. Almquist's good at untangling knotty problems."

The Major sorted through the papers in his briefcase and made no attempt to respond to Sanders.

Sara figured the Major didn't like being outranked by Sanders or being reminded of her background. Must have an ego problem. "Major?"

"You see, our operative, who has never failed to deliver accurate data, well… we don't know who he is. The contact delivers scientific data and often gives the odds on events occurring. Hence, we assume he is comfortable with statistics. The sentence, actually phrase, structure in communications suggests extensive exposure to American, not British, English."

"When did you get the first message?"

"In eighty-three."

"Oh," Sara leaned back and kneaded her forehead. "Puts a different slant on this interview. I only considered my experiences after graduate school when I answered before. I may have met this individual while I was an undergrad or grad student." Sara straightened. "Better make no more assumptions. Give me specifics on the data received. Who receives it? And most importantly, are you sure your so-called operative isn't safer if he or she remains anonymous?"

The Major puffed his chest. "You don't need to know."

Sara motioned toward the monitor on the table. "Let's try to find answers quickly, instead of standing on protocol. I'm sure that's what your boss wants."

The Major seemed to debate options internally as he gave her a dull stare.

"Look at it this way, you're more apt to get your eagle wings if we find your agent alive."

The Major sighed. "Surprisingly diverse. Mainly alerts on Iran's nuclear efforts, but several on Iran's germ warfare efforts. Warnings about bombings on American constellations in Beirut and Iran." He stopped. "We know you've consulted at the American University of Beirut. Our operative might be linked to that institution."

Sarah swallowed a slug of cola. "I had no contact with American University of Beirut until the nineties. Are you sure there was nothing more to the email?"

"He said, 'Contact Almquist. Tell her to remember a-g-r-o.'" The Major smirked. "What do you think a-g-r-o means?"

She shrugged.

He sneered. "We heard you're not much into social networking. Kind of surprising for a statistics junkie. I mean, as an epidemiologist you must know a little about computers."

Sara wanted to tell the Major to stop being a jerk, but decided she wouldn't lower herself to his level. "I like my privacy. Now, what do you think a-g-r-o means?"

"It's a term used on the internet to mean hostile, angry, or trouble."

He seemed to stall as he watched Sanders put his yellow Le Creuset casserole into the oven, don his coat, and leave. "We're pretty sure he's based in Iran. Start with any Iranian contacts — no matter how minor."

Sara closed her eyes and thought of her experiences after high school. "Got it. When you asked me about my first contact with someone from the Middle East, I forgot… I forgot my undergrad years. There were lots of Iranian grad students at the University of Wisconsin-Madison when I was an undergrad. I was a farm girl and found all the protests and marches pretty amazing, but I'd promised my parents to never get involved." She shook her head. "Can't believe, now. I was so compliant. I've spent much of my career since defying authorities. Anyway, in seventy-eight and -nine, someone was always protesting the Shah, but no one…" She gasped. "Wait, could it be?"

"Anything?"

"I worked for Dr. Otto Steinhaus, a statistics prof. We called him Doc. He was based in the college of agriculture. That's a-g-r-i not a-g-r-o. Let's see," she closed her eyes, "I started in the fall of seventy-eight, when I was a sophomore, and worked there until I graduated early in December of eighty and left to study biostatistics at the University of North Carolina-Chapel Hill. I entered data for Doc and his grad students onto large campus computers. Then I carried the printouts back to Doc and the grad students. Slow. Two of the grad students I helped were Iranian women. One was there when I began. The other when I left." She opened her eyes and saw the officer had lost his steely composure. He was leaning towards her.

"Names?"

She fiddled with her pen. "I'm thinking. The first one's name began with F."

The Major flinched, but remained silent.

She mumbled, "Fa, Fari, Farif, no. Last name Osten, Ossein. Not right." She continued to write and cross out names.

The Major looked worried. "The professor — What was his name? — could supply their names."

"Might be hard. He died over fifteen years ago, but the Statistics Department at UW-Madison will have records." She wrote *Otto Steinhaus* on a page and shoved it toward him.

He punched a button on his phone. "Check out Iranian female graduate students in Statistics at the University of Wisconsin-Madison between seventy-eight and eighty. Major professor will be." He spelled the name on Sara's note.

Sara suddenly stood. "Farideh Hossein."

CHAPTER 3: Sara's memories of Farideh Hossein

Sara looked around Sanders's living and dining rooms as the Major went to the kitchen to engage in a muffled, but seemingly intense, conversation on the phone.

She thought it must be nice to come from a family with money. As a mainline Philadelphia family, Sanders's great-great-grandparents had collected works of the Ash Can artists before the artists became famous. His great-grandfather participated in negotiations for oil rights in Iran during the nineteen thirties. His grandparents scoured Iran, from Tabriz to Yazd, for antique Persian rugs in the early sixties. Thus, a smattering of lesser-known works by Sloan, Luks, and Glackens and exquisite rugs, mainly with maroon or navy backgrounds and flower medallions, covered the walls.

Wait. Was there any chance the Iranian contact mentioned her because of Sanders? She suspected Major Jones would be annoyed if she interrupted his phone conversation, but this was important. "Sanders's grandparents were in Iran in the sixties. They bought these rugs." She waved her hand at the rugs.

His nostrils flared as he gawked at the rugs. "Another complication."

She decided she'd think better if she was seated at the dining table. It was easier to write and organize notes there. Finally, he ended his call and sat down across the teak table from Sara. "We're interested in Farideh Hossein. Tell me every detail you remember. Nothing is too small. Start at the beginning."

He placed the monitor on the table and drummed his fingers impatiently. Sara tried to organize her thoughts but was distracted. She guessed the person listening through the monitor would like to ring the Major's neck for tapping on the table like that.

"I don't remember how I met her." She noted the Major continued to tap the table. "I only remember... three incidents with Farideh." She gulped. "I guess I'm ready. I'll start with the most revealing. I hadn't worked for Doc Steinhaus long. So, it must have been a Saturday in September or early October of seventy-eight."

***

The day was hot. I heard a roar of the crowd at a football game in Camp Randall Stadium as I entered the almost empty, red brick Horticulture Building.

Four of Doc's graduate students were in the workroom when I delivered printouts from the computer lab in a nearby building. Three hardly lifted their heads to acknowledge me. I knew why. Danny was yipping in his high tenor voice about inconsequential departmental gossip as he looked at his near empty desk. The other three politely refrained from telling him to shut up.

I sat down by Mike and waited for instructions. I had a bit of crush on Mike. As was the fashion then, he had a thick unruly beard. He muttered, "Think of a way to shut the fool up. Doc should be here shortly. He wants you to enter data for me at the computer center."

I got up and sliced a thin sliver of chocolate cake for myself from a tired-looking birthday cake on the table in the center of the room. The grad students had celebrated Mike's birthday the day before. Most of the cake was gone, but wax candles were strewn on the table. "Danny, do you want a piece of cake. It's still moist."

Danny drew a freckled hand through his carrot red hair and blinked his brown eyes at me in apparent surprise. "The baby talks."

I ignored the insult and placed a big slice of cake on a napkin and was handing it to him when Farideh slammed into the office. As usual she wore hip-hugging, frayed blue jeans, the bell-bottom type. An off-white knit ribbed top, which showed her slim waist, clung to her torso. Despite her dark hair and black eyes, I doubt most would guess she was from Iran. She was about five-seven and moved with long, smooth strides.

Danny talked as he stuffed cake in his mouth. "Did you do your daily protest march against the Shah around the Bascom Hall?" Chocolate cake dribbled from his mouth. "From what I hear, he's been good for Iran. That's why you and your husband are in grad school here."

Mike kept his head down. "Danny, leave her alone."

Farideh plunked in her chair. "We were followed today by men in suits. I think from SAVAK, the Shah's secret police."

"You're hallucinating," said Danny.

"Don't display your ignorance." Farideh strode to the table and sliced the cake.

The three other grad students kept their heads down, as though they expected a blow-up.

"Hey, doll cut me another piece," said Danny as he swallowed the last of the cake I'd given him.

Surprisingly, Farideh did. As she cut the cake, Danny rose to stand behind her. He rubbed his hands from her waist to her hips. "What a waste to cover this with a burqa, or I guess you'd say a chador in Iran."

She dropped the slice of cake and rammed her elbow into his gut. Hesitated a second, before she picked up the knife. "Don't touch me."

Mike ran from the office. The mouths of the two other grad students hung agape.

Farideh turned the knife in her hand.

Danny, who about three inches taller than Farideh and quite muscular, laughed, "Doll, you know I can take the knife from you."

Everyone gasped as the door opened and Doc rolled in, followed by Mike. Doc was obese, and he panted when he walked at a normal speed. Today he gasped from having hurried in the heat. "Farideh... come... to... my... office."

Danny squealed, "You're in trouble now."

She gripped the knife and lunged at Danny.

"Farideh!" Doc howled.

She stabbed the knife so hard into the cake that she broke its blade on the table. Then she stalked out of the office.

As he closed the door, Doc said, "Danny, try to keep your mouth shut until I return. And Sara, here's what you need to do." He handed me a stack of papers.

During the next ten minutes, Danny repeated over and over, "tee-hee."

***

"In hindsight, I suspect Danny was attempting to cover his insecurities. But at that time, I was surprised a macho guy had such a high-pitched laugh."

"So, our girl had a temper."

Sara frowned. "Major, don't imitate Danny with sexist comments. She was a woman."

The Major's lips stiffened. "What else?"

"No one ever talked about the incident, at least in front of me, but afterwards Doc was more pensive and stopped telling stupid knock-knock jokes. Danny lost his desk in the grad office and left the program in January without a degree. Mike finished his dissertation in March and accepted an assistant professorship in statistics at the University of Tennessee. Somehow, he never seemed sexy to me after the incident. I thought he looked juvenile as he ran from the office."

"No, about Farideh."

"I'll get to her. I assume you'll contact Mike and even Danny for info, so all the details could be useful."

He shrugged. "We'll see what the boss thinks."

Sara thought his response strange, but launched into her next remembrance. "Perhaps, you'll find this exchange more helpful."

***

We were walking on the icy path to the back door of the computer center. The sidewalk was treacherous because the snow had partially melted and refroze before groundskeepers could shovel it. I think it was probably in January of seventy-nine.

Suddenly Farideh stopped. "You don't talk much, but you're always watching me."

I figured in the cold my blush wouldn't show. "You… fascinate me. I think… I'm learning about Iran in a way I never could from watching TV at home on the farm."

She snorted. "Have you figured out why all the men from Iran major in physics or engineering? Or why I'm studying biostatistics?"

I shrugged. "Because Iran needs the practical skills of engineers and statisticians. But I was surprised by all the interest in physics. Seems kinds of impractical."

"You'll figure it out eventually." She trudged forward. As she pulled the door open to the computer center, she said, "Iranians who want to study in the U.S. are assigned majors."

"So, what did you want to major in?"

Her mouth twisted. "Doesn't matter. Now, I'm afraid of how I'll have to use my skills in Iran as run by the Shah, but I don't want to stay in the U.S. like my sister. She's a grad student in nutrition here."

***

"That's all?"

Sara found it hard to imagine that the Major had successfully interviewed many witnesses. He was so negative. She tried to not be equally negative and smiled before she said, "Here's the last set of

J. L. Greger

incidents. In January of seventy-nine, the Iranian students in Madison were on high alert. After the Shah left Iran, the protests changed. Fewer students participated in the demonstrations, and they carried pictures of the Ayatollah Khomeini. In late February, Farideh announced she wanted to quit grad school and return to Iran immediately to welcome the Ayatollah to Iran. She and Doc argued loudly every day for a week. Doc must have won that argument, and Farideh stayed through May to complete her master's thesis. During those three months, they argued less. Guess she was too busy writing, and he was too busy editing her thesis to squabble with her."

"That's not an incident." The Major drummed his fingers on the table again.

Sara felt annoyed. "You know when you drum your fingers on a table with an audio monitor, it irritates listeners."

He continued to tap the table and smiled.

Maybe, he wasn't an inexperienced interviewer. More likely he was just inconsiderate. "Okay, I've got two small incidents. Sometime in April, I asked her. 'Will you have to wear a burqa when you go back to Iran?' Even as naïve farm girl, I thought her glee at the return of the Ayatollah seemed misplaced."

"She bristled. 'Of course not. We call the black robes chadors, not burqas, in Iran. The Ayatollah is a smart man and knows the educated women of Iran will never go back to wearing chadors.' I never mentioned Iran to her again."

Sara noted the Major looked bored. "One day in May as I sat at Mike's vacated desk and crammed for a final, Farideh came into the grad office and slammed the box with her dissertation on her desk so hard, the seams at the sides of the box split. 'No freedom in the U.S. Doc wants me to change the dedication for my thesis. He doesn't think it should be in Farsi. His crazy wife claims only revolutionaries use the phrase that I put in my dedication. How would she know?' I think these two occurrences demonstrate Farideh was politically naïve and ill prepared to return to Iran."

The Major seemed more interested in the last incident and continued to type on his tablet's keyboard for a minute. "What did the dedication say?"

"I don't remember exactly. Something about those who sacrificed their lives for others."

"Did she remove the phrase from her dedication?"

"I don't know, but the thesis might be on file in the university library or in the departmental library for Statistics."

"Describe her husband and his friends."

"Not much to tell. I occasionally saw Farideh among the marchers circling the campus with signs calling for the overthrow of the Shah. Someone in the group would often address the crowds in the library mall before they marched, chanting, toward the state capitol. She was generally with the same man. I assume he was her husband. He was about her height, equally thin, and clean-shaven, with piercing black eyes and a full head of black hair. Obviously, I couldn't identify him in a crowd of Iranians."

The Major squinted as he stared at her. "That's all?"

She thought he should learn another phrase besides: That's all. "You might be able to get more details from her husband's fellow students. She told me one of the grad students in nuclear physics had dropped out of the program in February of seventy-nine. He was the one whom her husband suspected was a mole for SAVAK. The guy should be easy to locate. Not many advanced students drop out in the middle of a semester. I doubt he returned to Iran."

The Major scanned the notes on his tablet. "Is that all you know about Farideh?"

Sara again was surprised and insulted by his curtness. "Look, I'm no spy. I liked, actually admired Farideh — her zeal." She winced because she realized he was correct. She didn't know much about Farideh. "I feel like a traitor revealing her secrets, especially since she's probably dead."

The Major turned beet red. "After all of this," he waved his tablet, "you tell me she's dead. How do you know?"

Sara secretly was pleased to have at least aroused the interest of this egotistical officer. If Farideh's life depended on this incompetent, she was in trouble. "You told me to tell the story in chronological order."

"My fault."

Sara took the insincere-sounding comment as an apology and nodded. "About six months after Farideh left the UW, Doc told the lab group that Farideh's sister had asked him to help her gain political asylum in the U.S. The sister reported Farideh and her husband had been arrested in Iran. She believed her brother-in-law had been executed, and Farideh had barely survived a public flogging. The evidence must have been good because the sister was granted permanent residency in the U.S."

"Aha, Farideh could be alive."

"Doubtful. Neither her sister nor Doc ever heard from her again. I asked several times."

The Major cursed as he strode to the kitchen.

CHAPTER 4: The countdown begins

A little before six thirty, Sanders returned with a loaf of French bread under one arm. He murmured into Sara's ear, "Got some answers. A guest is coming to dinner."

"What?"

He put his fingers to his lips. "Later." He took one look at the Major who was huddled over his phone in a corner of the kitchen and pitched his voice louder. "Anything useful?"

The officer shook his head without turning to look at Sanders. "No."

Sarah reddened. "He's a pessimist. I suspect I've remembered a couple salient details, but there's no way to tell without a lot of legwork."

When Sanders removed the lid from the cast iron Dutch oven, a rich, meaty aroma filled the room. Sanders beamed. "My version of *coq au vin* is as good as Julia Child's and a lot easier."

As he sliced the French bread and tossed a salad of mixed greens with aged balsamic vinegar and lemon-infused olive oil, Sara set the table for four. She nudged the Major. "I think better on a full stomach. Bet you do too. Why don't you take off your jacket, get comfortable, and join us?"

"Too busy. I've wasted too much time on literally a dead end."

Sanders winked at Sara as he poured iced tea. "My associates examined the cards you gave me and your luggage."

"And?"

"Lots of fingerprints on the luggage. Probably yours. The individual who tossed your room most likely wore gloves. Now, the cards and the bracelet are another story. Fewer prints. They're running them through systems now."

"I'd guess the owner of the shop and I made the prints. He made no attempt to not leave prints."

"Our guess, too."

"But he limped. I don't think he could climb the stairs quietly without my landlady noticing. Course, her house is a three-ring circus."

A knock on the door. Sanders answered. The Major, who'd been quietly cursing, snapped to attention. "General Purcell, sir, what are you...."

"At ease. I'm here to have dinner with my old college roommate. Then too, after I listened to most of your conversation with Dr. Almquist, I wanted to talk to her." He offered his hand to Sara. "Sanders always liked smart ladies."

Sanders shepherded the General to the table. Sara noticed the Major suddenly found time to eat and stopped grumbling about her useless comments.

Sara dipped a piece of bread into the dark meat sauce, and tasted a bit of chicken. The flavor of onion, garlic, carrots, and mushrooms, and bacon with red wine had transformed the chicken thighs. "I like a man who can cook."

Sanders coughed and blushed slightly as he lightly kicked her foot under the table.

The General laughed. "I figured he went into foreign service after Princeton to sample world cuisine, but he was assigned to Afghanistan, the Soviet Union, and Paraguay — hardly gourmet centers."

The Major began to tap his fingers on the table.

The General swallowed a mouthful. "This is good, but no need to avoid the eight-hundred-pound gorilla at the table. Major, you're wrong to want to give up on Sara. The rest of us — well, as our source would say, at the point zero one level — are sure Sara's the right Almquist."

She thought the Major looked confused as his jaw hung slack. "He's using jargon used in statistics. He means there's a ninety-nine percent chance I'm the right Almquist."

"Hmmf. I've taken a statistics course, but so far all you've given me is useless fluff."

Sara remained silent, even though she thought the Major rude and dumb. If the email was real, the investigation was more important than her ego.

The General may have sensed her contempt for the Major. "The Major expected you to be a gold mine of information because you were such a popular woman on the internet today. Lots of hits and chatter on you, especially from Beirut and Iran. Mainly, the chatter shows several people want to find our source. He must have been desperate to send an uncoded email. He's only done that two other times in thirty years."

The Major frowned. "I thought only once before."

The General ignored the comments. His eyelids drooped, and he lost his perfect posture. "I admit my staff felt let down when you said Farideh was probably dead. The Major didn't tell you one intriguing detail. Our source signed off as F."

Sara straightened. This was the second addition to the message. "So, the message was, 'Help. Contact Almquist. Remind her of a-g-r-o' and signed 'F.' Anything else?"

The General gulped. "I apologize if the Major was slow to give you all the details, but he was being cautious."

"Okay, I'm willing to keep dredging up memories of Farideh and others with Middle Eastern connections from my past, but I hope someone has contacted the other people I mentioned. That is Mike and Danny. I bet my main purpose is as a decoy so this F can get to better contacts." Sara gulped her iced tea. "Gee, I don't want to be a decoy again, like I was in Bolivia," she stared at Sanders, "as you captured a drug lord."

The General scratched his chin. "You might not appreciate your value to F. He, perhaps I should say she, has always been more secretive about her methods than most agents." He shook his head. "You must have forgotten a detail — trivial to you but important to F."

She shrugged. "It was a long time ago. I need to think, and I do my best thinking when walking Bug."

As Bug lunged out the door, the Major said to Sanders. "Is she always this difficult?"

Sara lingered in the doorway to hear Sanders's answer.

Sanders rose and immediately began to clear the table. "I warned you that you should have let me prime her when I sent her the email, because she would need time to think before this meeting."

The Major said, "Protocol dictates..."

"Protocol is for hostile witnesses or witnesses who have something to hide. It's not the best plan with organized, cooperative witnesses."

The General sighed. "Time is short, Major. Work with her."

Sara closed the door and took a deep breath of cold air. She was pleased Sanders had defended her, but the Major was right. She couldn't focus. She'd had a low-grade headache and a runny nose the whole week, probably a cold.

Bug headed for a clump of bushes at the edge of Sanders's property. A tall, heavy man stood in front of the townhouse across the street. He wasn't smoking, but he stood and played with items in the pockets of his trench coat, like a husband forced to leave the house when he smokes. She'd never noticed him before when she walked the neighborhood at night with Bug.

Bug headed left. She followed along the rough brick sidewalk. The bricks were pretty but treacherous, especially at night. That's why she always carried a small flashlight. As expected, Bug turned left again at the corner, watered one of his favorite bushes, and did a U-turn.

A shadowy figure stood twenty feet in front of her. She beamed her flashlight at his face and suppressed a scream. The man from the antique shop. She didn't see his cane. Had he faked lameness earlier?

She heard a cough behind her. She turned and saw the tall heavy man, she'd seen across from Sanders's home, was moving toward her. The antique shop dealer let out a squeal and crossed the street. The tall man sped after him.

She tightened her grip on Bug's leash and let him do what came naturally — run for Sanders's house. Sara was panting more than Bug when she saw Sanders's door swing open. "I... I'm being followed."

Sanders peered down the street as he pulled her and Bug inside and closed the door.

Sara looked though the peephole in the door. "See those two men at the corner. The shorter one in a trench coat is the man from the antique shop."

Sanders lips straightened.

"There's more. The tall man was watching your house and followed me."

Sanders paced into his dining room. "Major, do you have my house under surveillance?"

The officer swallowed hard, and his Adam's apple bounced. "No, should I?"

"Sara is being followed. The antique dealer again and someone new." He stormed into his study and began to slam drawers open and shut.

Both the officers grabbed their phones, but stopped their conversations as she told them about her earlier encounter with the antique dealer. The General maintained his broad, "meet the crowd" smile throughout, while the Major became more and more animated. She guessed Sanders had told the General about the antique dealer to gain his cooperation, but the General hadn't bothered to inform the Major. Either the General didn't trust the Major or he didn't think the detail important enough to relay.

She continued to eye the strange pair until Sanders, wearing a coat and whistling "Home on the Range," emerged from his study and stormed out his front door. Sanders didn't whistle much. She guessed he was telling her he had gotten his gun because he'd taken her several times to a shooting range to learn basic marksmanship.

The General lost his fake smile and motioned to the Major. "Give him a sixty second lead."

After the Major slammed the front door, the General sat down at the table by Sara. "I didn't have a chance to tell the other two. Our experts found new chatter on the internet. One message was repeated several times. 'F will be dead ina little over thrity-six hours.'" He looked at his watch. "We don't know how or why."

Sara gasped.

The General nodded. "Yes, it appears we're on a tight timeline. We assume the threat is based on an estimate of how long it'll take Iranian Police to find F."

"Any chance F planted the message as a hint to her plans?"

The General lost his smile and gaped at Sara.

CHAPTER 5: Thirty-six hours and counting

"We located your Doc's widow — Elvira Steinhaus." The General changed his focus from his phone conversation to Sara. "Although FBI agents are already on their way or at the homes of the other people you mentioned, I think you should question Elvira."

"When? Where?" Sara tried to hide her uneasiness and leaned over and picked up Bug, who had snuggled at her feet.

"She's in Madison. A United flight leaves Reagan Airport for Chicago in a little over an hour."

Sara took a deep breath. "Okay. Who will travel with me?" She hoped not the Major.

The General looked down. "I should tell you a bit more about the recently discovered chatter. People, we don't know who, are interested in you because F named you in the email." He cleared his throat. "They think you are a source of information on F."

Sara wanted to run from the room screaming. She stroked Bug's fur. "Any details on these people? They're going to be disappointed when they get me because, as the Major discovered, I don't know much about Farideh, and it's doubtful she's F. *I'll* be dead in *less* than thirty-six hours."

"Let's think positively." The General flashed his fake smile again. "We know there are at least two camps. One group wants to protect F and accordingly you. The other intends to stop F's escape from Iran with critical data. Both groups have spotted you in Washington. If we do this right, you'll be safer out of here, but you need to be disguised. Susan, a Marine lieutenant, and Mary, an FBI agent, will accompany you. They will act as your daughters, and you'll be in a wheel chair."

"If I'm in a chair, I won't be able to run or duck. Is that wise?"

He laughed. "You are more experienced than most of our civilian witnesses. But you can wear body armor, and we can take you in a wheel chair through special security clearances without arousing suspicion. Woman guards can accompany you into bathrooms, males can't."

A rap on the door.

"That's them" The General answered the door but kept on talking. "Mary and Susan will fill you in on all details in the cab, which is a secure vehicle."

Susan, a brunette with a short practical haircut, was about Sara's height and looked athletic underneath her dowdy, navy polyester pant suit. She saluted the General, unzipped a suitcase, and began to strap body armor over Sara's torso. Mary, a blonde pixie in a pale pink velour jogging suit with a pink bow holding her ponytail, adjusted a knit black cape over Sara's armor.

Sara was caught off guard by the speed of her transformation. "What about Bug?"

The General stopped peering out the peephole. "We can't disguise you enough if you take the dog. I've been told he attracts more attention in a crowd than most senators or Cabinet members. Sanders can care for him."

Another rap on the door.

The General coughed as he opened the door. "Look what Sanders found."

The antique dealer hobbled in with Sanders behind him. Sara was pretty sure Sanders was pointing a revolver at the dealer's back. "The Major decided to take the other character directly to headquarters for serious interrogation, but we decided to give this one a chance to talk in friendly conditions." Sanders winked at her. "So far, he hasn't spoken."

The antique dealer looked more wizened than before and shook violently.

She decided to play good cop to what she assumed was Sanders's bad cop. She forced a smile. "Why were you watching us?"

"Only you. Do you understand the message you received?"

Sara blinked. "Let's start with a simpler question. Who are you?"

"Abid Jahanbani." The man shivered and dropped his gaze to avoid looking at Sara.

"Why are you following me?"

"I was in Evin Prison... in seventy-nine and eighty." He whimpered. "They questioned me for hours. I was so tired that I hallucinated nooses dangling from a wooden beam. They yelled if I closed my eyes."

"Why were you following me?"

He droned on as if he hadn't heard her. "We watched guards cane the feet of women students. They admitted anything to end the pain. One woman never spoke. Afterwards she crawled from the site. She could no longer walk. One of the men said proudly, 'My wife Farideh.' I never knew his name, only that he was a student like me." Abid emitted loud wails.

Sara believed he was in emotional turmoil, but she wasn't sure of his story. She put her hand on his shoulder. "What did you study in the U.S.?"

The man twitched. "Political science."

Sara frowned. "Did the Shah's government approve that major?" She heard Sanders and the General whisper as she put her hand under the Abid's chin and made him look in her eyes.

He sighed. "F chose wisely." He seemed to think for a couple of seconds. "My father was wealthy. I wasn't good at math. So, my father bribed officials. They still forced me to apply to schools in Washington, D.C and insisted I attend embassy parties regularly."

Sara doubted his story. "What were the majors of your cell mates?"

"They didn't say."

Susan whispered in Sara's ear, "Hurry."

Abid looked around the room before he focused on Sara. "You know. They studied physics and engineering. Most came back to Iran after the Ayatollah returned from exile."

Sara pursed her lips. "Why were you allowed to leave Iran?"

The man hung his head. "The pain. The humiliation. They suspended me on a pole, almost like a lamb ready for slaughter, and caned my feet. At first, my soles felt as if they were on fire. The pain grew. I was delirious — more nooses. Each time was worse." He chanted to Allah.

He hadn't answered her question. She tried again. "Why were you released from prison?"

"The caning was bad. Worse still, we were forced to help with the punishments and executions of other prisoners. We were all covered with blood, urine, and feces. We huddled together on cold winter nights. Soon we all were coughing. Our guts ran. My limp is not from the caning, but from tuberculosis that settled in my bones. I got medicines too late."

He obviously didn't want to answer her question. "So, how did you escape?"

Tears dripped from Abid's eyes. "I was weak and gave them what they wanted."

"Which was?"

"Information on the other students."

"That's all?"

"I knew a bit about... about several staff members at the U.S. embassy. I'd met them when I was a student in Washington. In seventy-nine, they were taken as hostages."

The General began to cough.

Abid blanched as he focused on the General's face. "It was wrong. I wanted to live. I was rewarded with an assignment in Beirut. When I sought asylum in the U.S., I answered the questions of a young American lieutenant. I deleted a few details. Was I wrong to save my life?"

The General looked at the ceiling. Sara thought his response was strange, but deemed that little mystery unimportant. "What happened to Farideh and her husband?"

"I swear I do not know."

Sara thought his watery dark eyes looked like those of a pathetic beaten dog.

CHAPTER 6: Sara thinking about Souri Fekri

"General, we're out of time." Susan moved toward the door.

"I know. Try to interview Sara on the other Iranian graduate student on the way to the airport. I'll question this pathetic traitor."

Abid sank to the floor and cried.

Sara scooped up Bug and cuddled him before she handed him to Sanders. "Take care of my baby."

Sanders kissed her and whispered, "Don't take any unnecessary risks. Call me, if you can, when you reach Chicago."

Mary grabbed Sara's arm and guided her to the waiting cab, while Susan peered in all directions as she sprinted ahead. As soon as Mary and Sara were in the back seat and before Susan had closed the front door, the cab roared off.

Mary handed Sara a short gray wig. "Put it on. Here's your travel documents. We're your two divorced daughters."

Susan fiddled with a device on her lapel. "Major Jones should have completed this interview, but I listened in as you talked about Farideh. Tell me about the second Iranian graduate student. Judging by traffic, you've got ten minutes."

Sara winced. "Okay, here goes. Souri Fekri was everything Farideh was not. She was talkative, but she said little of consequence. She expressed no interest in Iranian politics, but she liked to gossip about famous people in Iran. She was jovial and, on the surface, seemed open, but she never looked at me directly and often sat at her desk staring into space for hours. I guess, I didn't trust her, but I can't say why."

Susan nodded. "I know it's hard, but can you give specific details about Souri?"

Sara paused. "Her father had been, I think, a physician for the Shah's family. When the Shah left Iran in January of seventy-nine, Souri's family followed after a few months. Once she told me her older sister had dated the Shah's brother. Souri had no such hopes with a big mole on her lip and her squat stature."

Susan squirmed in her seat. "Can you think of details about Souri's experiences in Madison?"

Sara nodded. "I can't remember any specific stories. Hopefully, this background info will give analysts a couple of clues. Maybe jog my memory." She paused, "Souri became a grad student in Doc's group in the spring of eighty. Not a good time for Iranians in the U.S. because of the Iranian Hostage Crisis. Maybe that was why Doc introduced Souri to the rest of us in his group as coming from Egypt. Wasn't exactly a lie. She had spent several months in Egypt after fleeing Iran before she came to the U.S."

"Like many beginning grad students in Doc's group, Souri served as a stat consultant in the college of agriculture. Doc had a part-time appointment in the ag college but his main faculty appointment was in the Statistics Department in the College of Liberal Arts and Sciences. His duties in the ag college were to create and manage a statistical consulting service. As part of the deal, the ag college paid for three grad assistantships per semester for Doc's graduate students. The students on these assistantships, such as Souri, answered questions about statistics from students and faculty in agriculture. That meant each of these graduate student spent twenty hours a week at the computer center in the ag college. Most of the consults were quick and easy. When in-depth advice on the designs and analyses of studies was needed, Doc joined the discussion."

"Why is that important?"

Sara shrugged. "Suggests Souri had diverse and hard to trace contacts. Perhaps she learned a few secrets along the way. Whenever I went to the computer center to run programs or to pick up printouts for Doc, I saw Souri gabbing to anyone and everyone in sight. I also heard several profs complain about Souri's lack of attention to details. However, Doc never reprimanded her like he did other students. Seemed strange then, still does."

Finally, she remembered something useful. "She particularly liked one gangly, pockmarked grad student. He must have suffered terrible acne as a teen. He shouldn't have needed Souri's services because he was at the writing stage, which means most of the statistical analyses for his dissertation were done. One time I heard Souri tell him that she saw Farideh in a chador shortly before she left Tehran. They both thought the sight of Farideh in a chador was funny. I was annoyed

J. L. Greger

because I thought how proud Farideh had been about the revolution and how ashamed, most likely afraid, she must have been to wear a chador."

The cab cruised toward the entrance to Reagan Airport. Sara perceived she hadn't said anything important yet. "Wait. That's it. The a-g-r-o in the message from F is for agronomy." Sara repeated louder this time, "Agronomy."

"Huh" The voice of the Major boomed from Susan's lapel device.

"Major, what did you learn from the tall guy?"

"Forget him. Concentrate. We're almost out of time."

Sara snapped. "I know. The grad student Souri talked incessantly to was from the Department of Agronomy. He studied... the effects of water restriction on new varieties of wheat in field trials in... the Middle East." She scrunched her face. "Let me think. U.S. researchers used experimental farms near Tabriz before the hostage takeover in seventy-nine. Seems reasonable. I bet he did his dissertation research in northern Iran."

"Finally, something that makes sense." The Major yelled to someone with him, "Follow these leads."

Sara tapped her fingers on the armrest. "One complication. Farideh might have worked on his original study design."

"Least of our concerns now. Name of the agronomy student?"

Sara shook her head. "If I knew, I would have told you. Should be traceable. Not that many U.S.-born grad students in the Agronomy Department did their thesis research in Iran in the late seventies."

"Where is Souri now? Don't tell me she's dead, too." The Major's voice almost sounded plaintive.

"Not sure," Sara felt guilty about intentionally annoying the Major, but the dolt deserved it. "Doc finally came to his senses and encouraged her to leave the UW with a master's degree. She left Madison after I began graduate school in North Carolina. I saw her ten years ago at a conference. She was based in New Jersey and was a consultant to pharmaceutical start-up companies on clinical trials. I remember thinking I wouldn't base my business on her advice. However, all those I talked to seemed satisfied with her knowledge of how to get clinical trials done at cut rates in Egypt, Turkey, and Lebanon."

"Good. She has continued to have ties in the Middle East."

"Major, I don't want to burst your bubble, but I can't see Souri taking risks for her beliefs. On the other hand, I suppose a good undercover operative would hide her real emotions."

The cab swung into a spot in front of the United terminal. Mary jumped out and began to pull two small suitcases and a foldable wheelchair out of the trunk.

Susan motioned for Sara to stay put. "Major, we're out until we get to Chicago. Sorry."

CHAPTER 7: Thirty-five hours left

Sara felt uneasy on the two-hour flight to Chicago. Not because of any problems at Reagan National Airport. She had cleared security as a disabled sixty-year-old mother with her two adult daughters at lightning speed. Susan had rolled the chair like a driver on the Washington beltway. She had bounced in and out of lanes of traffic at a breakneck speed, never slowing, and often forcing others to stop. Mary had trotted behind pulling one suitcase, while the second bag set on Sara's lap. They boarded the plane within a minute of arriving at the gate, ostensibly because Sara was in a wheelchair.

One of Sara's problems was her head itched from the wig, and she couldn't scratch without attracting attention. Another was she was nauseated from her breakneck ride. Those were minor.

Her uneasiness stemmed from the incongruities and gaps in her memories of Doc Steinhaus and his group. For example, the relationship between the agronomy grad student and Souri didn't make sense. They were from different backgrounds. Souri was already married and not a beauty, like Farideh. Of course, the agronomy grad student wasn't much to look at either.

Sara was also acutely aware of the potential unknown challenges ahead and tried to think of pleasant activities, such as petting Bug or spooning with Sanders on the Barcelona sofa. They often did that when one of them was trying to sort through a problem. Pretty soon, they found the solution or forgot the issue. She wished Sanders was holding her now. At least she didn't need to worry about Bug. Sanders would keep him safe.

She wondered where Abid was now. He knew too much about her plans to be put in contact with other prisoners. At least, she hoped the General came to that conclusion. She decided she didn't need to worry about this detail. Sanders would act, if the General was remiss.

She yawned. This could be a long night. Then it hit her. She pulled out a pad of paper and began to scribble. Could it be? How would she prove it?

The same two hours were frustrating for Sanders. Evidence dribbled in. Abid's fingerprints were on the cards and jewelry. No surprise.

Sanders was tired of the General's ineffectual questions and Abid's singsong babbling. He interrupted them with a clear question. "Abid, when did you first meet the tall man?"

Abid spit phlegm into a soiled white handkerchief and looked at the General, who started to speak, but Sanders waved his palm toward the General and said, "Abid?"

"Not until two days ago. He came to my shop. He asked me to send a message. I did." Abid hiccupped. "He came to my house," Hiccup. "early this morning. He was angry. Claimed I must not have sent the message."

"Why?"

Abid's lips trembled as he glanced at the General, who merely shrugged. "He drove me to Georgetown. We watched Dr. Almquist and her dog leave. He told me to talk to the landlady while he searched Dr. Almquist's room." Hiccup, hiccup. "He told me I was a 'dead man if Dr. Almquist or F died.' He told me to watch your house tonight. I didn't expect him to also be here."

Sanders suspected Abid had told the truth, but with key facts deleted. "Why did the tall man come to you?"

The General responded before Sanders could stop him. "Abid has delivered data from the Middle East to the Marine Barracks several times during the last thirty years. Never the complete story, but always verifiable, eventually."

Sanders figured no one completely trusted Abid, but many Iranians realized he had contacts in Washington. He guessed the General was one of Abid's contacts. But why had the General feigned not to recognize Abid? He partially sensed the answer. The General had been a bit of a used car salesman in college and never told the whole story. He hadn't changed.

The General's phone rang. "It's the Major."

Sanders requested the General put his phone on speaker mode.

The Major's voice blasted out. "My prisoner has refused to talk, but we identified his fingerprints. He was a member of SAVAK. When the Ayatollah came to power, the Iranian Revolutionary Guard hunted down and killed members of the SAVAK. Few escaped. This man disappeared from Tabriz in late seventy-nine, reappeared in Istanbul in eighty-one, and obtained a green card in the U.S. in eighty-two. He's a valuable asset."

"Keep questioning him." The General glanced at Abid. "Oh, by the way, send a car for me and Abid. We probably should keep him for an hour or two."

Sara's phone, setting on the dining room table, rang. Susan had insisted Sara leave it behind because a clever terrorist could use it to trace her location. Sanders rushed to answer it. He recognized Gil Andrews's western drawl. Sara trusted Gil, the police chief in her hometown, implicitly. He had rescued her from gang members in a fiery shoot-out. Sanders also realized Gil was a better tactician than most generals. Five months ago, he'd watched Gil, Sara, and Ulysses Howe, the section head of the Albuquerque Office of the FBI, spring a trap on a clever criminal.

Gil obviously recognized Sanders's clipped manner of speech. "Is this Sanders? I need to talk to Sara. Her house has been broken into again."

"She can't come to the phone."

Gil chuckled. "Hope that doesn't mean you have her on another mission outside the U.S. Guess there's no need to ask because you won't give me a clear answer. Well, here's the situation. The damage is less than the last time when the drug dealers shot up her house."

"She'll be pleased."

Raps at the door.

Sanders noted the General was no longer on the phone and his discussion with Abid seemed to have grown quieter and more intense. Sanders peered through the peephole of his door. "Gil, I've a little problem here. Can you wait while I answer my door? Seems two Marine MPs are here." He turned to the General, "Are you expecting guests?"

The General said, "Yes, the Major sent two Marine MPs. We'll all leave."

"No General, I think you need to listen to my caller. It's urgent."

While Sanders updated Gil a bit, he watched Abid shrink as two Marine MPs shepherded him to a waiting van. As soon as the door closed, the General scowled. "May I remind you Sara is a minor character in this investigation. I've more pressing issues."

Sanders activated the speaker mode on his phone. "Sara's home was broken into."

Gil's voice boomed out. "Guess the double alarm system she installed was worth the money." Pause. "Hey, there's a slight echo now, you must have put her phone into speaker mode. Who's listening?"

The General glowered at Sanders and whispered, "I don't need to hear about a minor break in." In a louder voice, he said, "I'm a military type."

Sanders was surprised the General didn't indicate his rank. Modesty wasn't one of his virtues.

The General continued, "Sara's helping us decode a message. Tell me what you have."

"The guys who broke into her house are a weird pair. They have more master key sets than most locksmiths in Albuquerque. However, they cut the wires for the obvious alarm, but made no attempt to stop a second silent alarm to the Mercado Police Department. Pros don't make that mistake."

Sanders noted the General rolled his eyes in annoyance. "And?"

"We got to her home in three minutes." Gil guffawed. "We knew the way because we'd been there so many times. The only houses I visit more often are those of embattled couples who should be divorced."

The General was now pacing. Sanders even wanted to speed Gil's report. "Do you have the intruders?"

"Yep, two of them. They didn't put up a fight, but they're not talking. Won't even give their names, but I've sent their fingerprints to my FBI friend Ulysses Howe already. Not Hispanics. Might be from the Middle East. The damage is hard to assess."

"Explain."

"My computer expert says he doesn't think they attempted to hack the computer, but the debris in Sara's office is about six inches deep. They threw books off shelves and rifled through files. What should I look for?"

"I think they didn't look at the computer because they could hack it other ways" Sanders squinted. "I also think they want old things from twenty or even thirty years ago that aren't apt to be on the computer."

"I need more than that," said Gil.

"Let me think." Sanders continued after the General pushed a note toward him. "Black, bound thesis by Sara's past students."

"We'll look. Can you be more specific?"

Sanders read the General's note and shook his head. "Look for a thesis by a student with an Arab-sounding name."

The General interrupted, "This is beyond the scope of a local police dept. I'll order the FBI section head in Albuquerque to help."

Sanders shook his head again. "General, Gil doesn't…"

Gil must have heard the General. He laughed, "You mean my friend Ulysses Howe. When I sent him the fingerprints, he said he'd send agents to Sara's house to help me, once what he called the 'Washington big shots' sorted out their turf war."

The General reddened.

Sanders repressed a smile as he turned off the conference app. "Gil's no country hick. The drawl is his cover. I've worked with him and Ulysses Howe to track a drug czar and bring him from Bolivia to justice. He and Ulysses are a lot better detectives than your Major. Please cooperate with him." He turned the conference app back on.

The General growled. "I have to make a call first."

Sanders frowned. "Okay, Gil and I will finish up the basics."

The General whispered into his phone as he walked to the kitchen.

Sanders spoke to Gil. "I'm sure the FBI will reimburse you for necessary repairs to secure the house. Don't contact an insurance agent."

Gil guffawed. "Figured as much. Ulysses already said he has a man who can get the security system back in operation. I haven't put up any crime scene yellow tape."

"Thanks." Sanders glanced at the General whose face was now purplish red. He assumed the General would now cooperate with Gil and FBI agents in Albuquerque.

"Hey wait." Gil's voice was a half-octave higher. "Ulysses texted me. He identified one man." Pause, "Sanders, what is Sara into this time? Ulysses has already dispatched agents to pick up and hold the two men." Pause, "Are you sure Sara is okay?"

Sanders turned ashen as Gil spoke. He replied softly. "I hope so."

In the kitchen, the General cursed. "My counterpart at the FBI ordered me to make full disclosure immediately because Gil evidently caught a man on an international terrorist list. Tell him I'll call him on a secure line in two minutes. Hang up now."

Throughout all the turmoil, Bug with his flat nose pointed toward the front door lay on the wine-colored carpet. This was his typical position whenever Sara left him alone with Sanders. When

Sanders sat down at the dining room table, Bug trotted over and laid down at Sanders feet with his nose pointed toward the door. As Sanders scratched Bug's ears, he tried to listen to the General's phone conversation, but the General was being secretive and spoke softly. He thought about Sara. Had he dragged her into his world? No, but perhaps, her attachment to him made her more visible to foreign operatives.

He attempted to scoop Bug up, but the dog squirmed and insisted on staying on the floor staring at the door. Sometimes he worried that Sara secretly expected such absolute loyalty and attention from him. Was that her idea of love? He doubted it. Sara was too independent, but she was cloyingly attached to Bug. It was time to be honest. He and Sara had never talked about the future of their relationship. Now as he waited, he wondered if they had a future together.

J. L. Greger

CHAPTER 8: Thirty-three hours and counting

Mary received a call within seconds of the plane stopping its engines at the gate at O'Hare. She tensed and leaned over Sara to Susan. "Forget Plan A. We're doing Plan B."

Susan stiffened and tinkered with her earpiece and the device now in her jacket pocket. Sara heard only occasional words from both hushed conversations. "Someone on the plane?" "Who's at the gate?" "What color?"

Susan stopped her conversation long enough to hiss at Sara, "Keep your head down." She leaned forward and pretended to sort through her purse as she eyed departing passengers and muttered occasional comments about them to someone apparently at the gate.

Mary poked her. "Give me your fake ID. Someone else will need it."

When Sara fumbled in her purse, Mary grabbed the ID from Sara's purse and shoved it into a pocket of her pink jacket. Sara looked back and forth between her two supposed daughters. The worry lines on both faces made the women look older than two hours before. Sara prayed for strength to face the challenge, which hadn't been explained to her yet.

As the last passenger departed, Susan grabbed the wheel chair from the coat closet in first class, while Mary pulled out the bags and hustled Sara down the aisle. As they approached the exit, Mary whispered, "Act frail."

Sara didn't have to act. He knees were shaking. At the exit to the jet bridge, Susan rammed the chair under her so fast that Sara lost her balance and tumbled onto the seat. Mary slung a case onto Sara's lap and took the lead. The United posters to exotic locations on the jet bridge seemed to fly by. They stopped at the doorway to the airport only long enough for Mary to shove a small packet at the gate attendant. It could have been Sara's imagination, but a man in a navy suit seemed to trot beside her. A woman with a tan jacket appeared to follow Susan.

Again, Susan proved she wanted to be a race car driver, but to Sara's surprise they headed toward the airport exit, not the high-number gates in Terminal B of O'Hare, where the Madison flights generally departed.

The sidewalks were cleared of snow, but the street along the curb was a gray, slushy mess. Typical for Chicago in March. A gray sedan was waiting. The man in the navy suit pulled the suitcase from Sara's lap while Susan pushed Sara into the back seat and slammed the door. Mary slung the cases in the trunk and jumped into the back seat next to Sara behind the driver. The man in the navy suit stepped out to stop traffic in one lane, so the gray sedan could pull out quickly. Then he jumped into a second gray sedan.

Sara turned to look out the back window. "Will we drive to Madison with the guy in the navy suit in a caravan?"

Susan turned sideways in the front seat but kept texting. "Don't look back, and slump down a bit."

Sara did as instructed. She noticed an aluminum case between Mary and her on the seat. It might be a gun case. She also noted the pockets in both back doors contained emergency tools. The pocket on her side contained a glass hammer with a seatbelt cutter, a penknife, and a flashlight. This vehicle was too prepared for emergencies, and her companions were too nervous.

Susan asked the driver. "What kind of roads can we expect?"

"Good winter driving conditions on the highways. Side roads are snow packed, and glare ice could be a problem in spots. The traffic should be light at this hour, especially after I-94 splits off and we're on I-90 in rural Illinois."

Susan nodded and turned again toward Sara. This time she wasn't texting and seemed friendlier. "The guy in the navy suit is a diversion. I doubt you noticed the guy with longish hair in a blue parka at the gate. He'll be in the white van that accompanies us to Madison."

Mary's blonde ponytail bobbed up and down as she peered out the back window until their car left the airport. "The other gray car is on our tail as planned. The white van is several cars back." She texted frantically.

Susan must have noticed Sara's worried expression. "Confused? We've created two distractions for anyone tailing us. The gray sedan with the guy in the navy suit will veer off on I-94. We hope anyone shadowing us will follow him. We've also maintained the illusion we're flying to Madison. Three women, dressed like us, have taken our places on the flight to Madison."

Before Susan could turn away, Sara asked, "Why the change in plan?"

Susan mumbled, "Agents caught a stray internet comment on lines they're following. 'Beirut going to UW.' We assume you're Beirut."

Sara tried to stay calm. "Why the nickname?"

Susan turned. "We hope you'll figure that out when you talk to Doc's widow."

"I've been thinking. Are you sure Doc's widow is capable of answering questions? Are you sure she's safe?"

Susan hesitated. "No to both questions." She busied herself unpacking a large aluminum case in the front seat and assembling what looked like a rifle.

After several quiet minutes, Mary stopped texting. "Our plan failed. The lookout at the curb and the driver of the gray sedan think a black Chevy Blazer is tailing us." She tapped the driver's shoulder. "Lose him."

The driver nodded. "How many in the Blazer?"

"Don't know. Windows tinted. Obviously, a driver and a dark-haired, male passenger with no luggage, except a possible rifle case. They checked airport security photos. No evidence he was ever in the secure part of the airport, only the area around the exit."

The driver upped his speed and moved smoothly from lane to lane. After the other gray sedan sped off onto I-94, Mary thought they'd lost the Blazer but continued to look out the back window occasionally.

The driver and the two women guards seemed to relax. Sara thought this was a good time to talk. "I appreciate all your protection, but this situation doesn't make sense. What haven't you told me?"

Dead silence. Susan fingered her earpiece, and Mary hummed as she texted.

"Let me put this another way. Elvira Steinhaus is probably in her late seventies and not apt to remember much from thirty or forty years ago. She may have never known Doc's secrets. With a name like Elvira, I can't help but think she might be difficult, even if she's not senile. Doc sometimes groaned a bit about his nagging wife."

Silence.

"I can't get answers from her if you don't cooperate. What do you want to learn?"

Dead silence. Mary extracted a large handgun from the case between them and loaded it.

"It's time to end the charade. For example, are you concerned about operative F's safety? Or is she bringing something, such as a document, out of Iran? Something she can't transmit electronically."

Susan groaned. Sara hoped she'd get an answer, instead Susan said, "The General wants us to call this number. Mary, use your phone so I can keep my line open. Put it in speaker mode so Sara can hear."

"Hello."

Sara recognized Sanders's voice. She felt someone would listen to her now.

"Sara, stay calm. Your local police chief Gil Andrews arrested an international terrorist and his associate in your home in Albuquerque. One's an Iranian, the other a Palestinian. They were searching for something in your books and files, not the computer. Do you have any idea what they wanted?"

Sara winced at the news and leaned forward with her head in her hands to think. "Since one was a Palestinian, look for the thesis of my Palestinian grad student, Hanna Kafity."

"That's what I said. Gil found it and already gave it to the FBI."

Sara bit her lip. "Trouble is it was a meta-analysis of the importance of vitamin D intake, vitamin D status, and sunlight exposure on the incidence of osteoporosis among American women in fifty clinical trials. Nothing to do with the Middle East." Pause, "Well, Hanna might have cited in the literature review a couple articles about the high incidence of bone disease among Arab women wearing burqas. I guess the authors or the locations of those studies could be some sort of hint, but I doubt it."

"I'll tell Ulysses Howe anyway."

"Better yet, tell him Hanna is employed now at a cancer center in Montreal. She serves as their epidemiologist. Her address would be in my address book in the teak cabinet in my office." She gulped. "Wait. Maybe, that's what they wanted. It's with my Christmas cards and Christmas decorations."

Not only Sanders, but another male, gasped. "Don't you have your address book computerized?"

"Never got around to it. I hope they missed it because I don't have a backup.

The General spoke. "I already have Ulysses on the line. His agents will look for it."

"General, my next comment may sound a bit silly at first but be patient. It always bothered me how Doc handled certain grad students. His decisions and guidance for Mike and most students were logical. He rewarded hard work and accepted no nonsense, but he was different with Farideh, Souri, and especially Danny. As a prof, I always avoided playing favorites like he did."

The General yawned so loudly Sara could hear him. "That's your big insight?"

"During the flight, I remembered a comment Doc made to me before I left for grad school in North Carolina. He said a lot, but I remember this bit. 'It looks like you'll end up an academic. You'll have lots of chances to work with foreign students, like Farideh, and to consult in foreign locales. Don't get swept away by the excitement. It can be a dangerous game.' I thought at the time it was good advice. I still do, but he might also have been admitting more."

Sanders responded. "Profs who took assignments for USAID during the Cold War in the fifties through the seventies sometimes got too involved in local politics."

The General snorted, "Yeah, they were spies."

Sanders's voice was lower than usual. "Not that simple. They made cogent observations and developed friendships with locals, as Sara did in Bolivia. Then they made the mistake of trying to influence local politics and of distorting facts to please operatives from our government. Remember it was the Cold War. And... they were more easily controlled than Sara. I'll start a search of USAID records of the fifties, sixties and seventies for Doc."

Sara interrupted, "Also the agronomy professor for the grad student who was Souri's friend. General, I assume you've ascertained his and his prof's names by now."

"Mmm. My associates have."

"And?" She hid her annoyance at his unwillingness to share.

"Mark Olsen and Howard Baum."

"On the plane, I remembered I saw the agronomy prof and Doc at McDonald's on University Avenue, across from the Horticulture Building, lots of afternoons. They were an odd pair. Baum was a stick of a man, nearing retirement in Agronomy, and Doc, an associate professor in Stat, looked like the Pillsbury doughboy. Wouldn't think they had much in common."

The General grunted.

"Come on, General. My house was ransacked. I was stalked. I deserve your cooperation... your respect. Could the FBI or whomever you work with pull all the theses and dissertations written by students of Doc and Baum? I'd like to see those with data from the Middle East or written by foreign students."

"What are you looking for?"

"Not sure." Pause, "Trends. Seemingly insignificant details that keep reappearing. You know the type of stuff epidemiologists look for."

"We'll see."

Again, she ignored his half-hearted cooperation. "I don't suppose I'd be lucky enough to get to talk to Baum and Olsen."

"We're not incompetents. FBI agents with the help of Madison Police have both men in protective custody. But don't expect much. Baum is in his nineties and lives in a nursing home. I guess I'm supposed to call it an assisted living facility, called Oakwood Village in Madison. Olsen is now a professor in the Department of Agronomy at the University of Wisconsin-Madison. We figured you would talk to them after Elvira. She wouldn't let us move her to the same protected site, i.e. a locked psych ward at the UW Hospital, but we have guards at her house."

Sara heard tires squeal. She looked out of the sedan's back window and saw the white van's headlights sweep sideways as it careened between two lanes about four hundred feet behind them.

Susan focused a flashlight beam on the troubled vehicle. She screamed, "SOS! Van driver thinks someone shot his rear tires. We need immediate assistance. Get a helicopter here. I assume you have us on GPS but we're in the middle of snow-covered fields on I-90 about twenty or thirty miles from Rockford."

The driver of the sedan sped up. Mary handed her phone to Sara and grabbed the gun in the open case.

Susan opened her window, released her seatbelt, and leaned out of her window with a rifle. "No clear shot yet. Van's in the way."

A burst of shots. The white van tipped on its side and hurtled along the pavement until it skidded into the snow covered center strip of I-90. Sara saw the headlights of another car move rapidly forward. She wasn't sure in the light of a quarter moon, but she thought the vehicle was dark and looked like some type of SUV. Could be the Blazer that Mary thought they lost.

Susan fired. The Blazer swerved and then torpedoed forward.

Mary opened her window, released her seatbelt so she could turn to face the Blazer, too and aimed. She fired.

Susan yelled, "I can't get any more shots until he's even with us. It's up to you Mary." The driver rolled down his window as Susan positioned herself for the next shot.

Mary's ponytail bobbed as she continued to shoot. Now shots ripped into the gray sedan.

Sara slunk down and repeated over and over into the phone, "Under fire by black Blazer." In the excitement, she couldn't hear a response.

The Blazer was almost even with their rear bumper, when Mary sprayed the Blazer's windshield with bullets. Mary was reloading her gun when the Blazer plowed into them and then ricocheted toward the median. The shooting from the Blazer stopped. For a second, Sara thought the worst was over. The gray sedan flipped over and rotated on it roof.

Sara heard Sanders's voice. "Sara, are you all right?"

CHAPTER 9: Peril at thirty-one hours

Sara knew she had to escape the car before the gas tank exploded. She could hardly breathe because the straps of the seatbelt held her suspended. She clicked the seatbelt release repeatedly. Finally, she fell on top of Mary, who didn't move. She suppressed a scream because the passengers in the other car might hear.

The only noises from the front seat were groans from the driver. Susan wasn't in sight. Sara feared Susan had been thrown through an open window.

She had to get out. She groped the roof of the car in the darkness, and felt Mary's gun. The car had spun during the collision, and Sara's side faced the side of the road. This would be the safest exit because she wouldn't be visible to occupants in the Blazer.

She tried to unlatch the door. It didn't budge. She tried to lower the window. Nothing. She summoned all her strength and kicked the door. Again nothing.

She wondered whether the door would open if she shot the door hinge. The bullet might ricochet. A gunshot might also alert the occupants of the other car. She put the gun down.

She'd seen a glass hammer in the side pocket on her door of the car. Maybe that would work, but the shards of glass could kill her when she crawled through the broken window. She shoved the hammer into her jacket pocket with the phone.

That left Mary's open window. But then she'd be in full view of any survivor in the Blazer.

She heard Sanders's voice again and grabbed the phone in her pocket. How could she have forgotten her best source of help? "Mary and Susan probably dead," she sobbed. She forced herself to concentrate. No time to cry. "Driver and I are in the rolled over car with the Blazer nearby. No idea whether they're dead or coming for us. I can't get the door open."

"Help is on the way. What's the condition of the Blazer?"

J. L. Greger

She peeked out of Mary's open window. "The Blazer rolled and slid on the glare ice to the opposite side of the highway."

She heard a cough. Then another. It wasn't Mary or her driver. It came from the Blazer.

"I think someone in the other car is alive. I have Mary's gun. She loaded it before our car flipped."

Sanders response was low and smooth. "Do you remember your lessons at the shooting range? Wait until they get close enough that you can see them clearly."

She saw and heard nothing at first. Then she heard the crunch of gravel. In the light of the quarter moon, she saw someone stagger toward her. She placed the gun on the edge of window frame, which was the top in the rolled over car. Her hand shook too much to raise the gun. She stretched out over Mary, so she could aim the gun better. Eerie, but no time to think about anything but the man from the Blazer.

He didn't appear to have a gun, but he fumbled in his pockets. She saw a flick of light. Not a flashlight. Maybe a lighter. It went out. The next glimmer of light quivered as he played with the device. The flame was steady. How had he found a way to make the lighter stay lit? She aimed at his chest, let him take two more steps, and fired. He staggered, but lifted his arm. He was going to throw the lit lighter at the sedan. She fired again and again. The gun clicked the last time. She was out of bullets.

The man fell backward into a heap at the edge of the highway. The lighter landed only ten feet from the sedan.

Any gas or oil on the road could ignite. She had to get out of the car. She clambered over Mary out of the window. She heard the man gasping, but she moved forward anyway. She picked up the lighter and using her best underhand pitch threw it at the Blazer. She wished she'd learned to do an overhand pitch in gym class in high school.

Determined to get the driver out, she rushed back to the sedan. The two cars were only about forty feet apart. She leaned through the open window but couldn't reach the seatbelt buckle because the air bag was in the way. She pulled the emergency hammer out of her pocket and slashed the air bag and seatbelt.

A flash of heat went along her back as the Blazer exploded. She felt her hair. No, she wasn't on fire. The flames shot higher and higher. At least the scene was well lit.

The driver moaned as he fell. She pulled at him. He only moved an inch or two. She yanked again and again. The driver sensed the urgency and crawled as she dragged him.

She collapsed on top of the whimpering driver about thirty feet from the sedan. In the scramble, she'd lost the gun, the phone, and the emergency hammer. She was defenseless. She began to recite a prayer.

She heard hisses. Even with the light from the burning Blazer, she couldn't see gasoline or fluids on the road, but assumed the worst. She summoned all her energy and pulled the driver further down the road. He no longer could crawl. They'd only moved about twenty more feet when the gray sedan exploded. She kept pulling the driver and praying.

J. L. Greger

CHAPTER 10: Arrival in Madison at twenty-nine hours

Sirens converged from behind and ahead of her. Above her, the buzz of a helicopter turned into a roar as it neared the ground. She was too tired to even watch the helicopter's descent as she plopped down on the gravel on the side of the road by the moaning driver.

"Sara, Sara." A man and a woman with a stretcher ran from the helicopter toward her.

She never thought her name sounded so good. The next few minutes were hazy. The helicopter crew told her they would evacuate the driver and her to the University of Wisconsin Hospital in Madison.

Before the helicopter took off, a state policewoman handed her an envelope. "You were impressive back there. Good luck."

The female paramedic gave her a bottle of water and a shot to "relax" her, when she asked the helicopter crew questions. The pilot told her to read the message in the envelope. Sara watched for a couple of minutes as the paramedics adjusted an i.v. drip into the driver's arm, checked his arms and legs, and transmitted test results to physicians in the hospital. She gulped when they noted one of his shoulders was dislocated. She must have injured him when she lugged him from the car, but the alternative was worse. At least he was able to wiggle his fingers and toes, which suggested he had no spinal injuries apt to cause permanent damage.

She read the transcribed message from Sanders slowly.

Sara,
Relax. The General increased security.
Howard Baum and, to a lesser extent, Doc were important sources of data on Iran for the U.S. in the 1960s and 1970s. USAID records don't mention the types of data they provided to other agencies. FBI agents will meet you at the hospital and debrief you before you meet Elvira.
I want you to get back to me.
Love, S

Her eyes focused on the last line. Sanders was seldom affectionate in public. She must have scared him.

She tried to concentrate on Doc. It wasn't easy. Her seat in the helicopter vibrated. The rotor roared and stress emanated from of the crew as they stabilized the sedan driver. Visions of Susan or Mary kept invading her thoughts of Doc. Like most undergraduates, she'd never considered him as a person with a private life, only an employer and mentor. Thus, she remembered him as an obese, middle-aged man, who wheezed as he shuffled across campus. Now, she realized he was only in his late thirties and recently tenured, when she was an undergrad in his research group.

Sara ran various scenarios in her head. None made sense. The average prof doesn't know whom to contact if he or she observes something strange in the field. She certainly didn't, until she met Sanders and his crew. How did Doc develop contacts, assuming he did? And when?

She asked the paramedic for paper, wrote a request, and handed it to the pilot.

***

As the helicopter settled onto the roof of the hospital, an extremely thin, young man in a navy suit stood slightly apart from the four in tired green scrubs and tried to comb his hair tousled by the helicopter's giant rotor. While those in scrubs raced to get the sedan driver, the suited man steadied Sara as she stooped to step from the helicopter.

He studied her a bit too long before he said "Hi, lucky lady. I'm FBI agent Norm Budzinski."

She must have grimaced, because he added, "Sorry we only let you have muscle relaxants. No painkillers stronger than aspirin, because you need to be sharp when you talk to Elvira and Baum. The agents and police so far have extracted mainly crap, but we think she's not as senile as she pretends. Her daughter reports her mother's memory of past events is pretty good, but calls her a diva. Baum is almost comatose." He sighed. "I can't get a handle on Olsen. Cooperative, but spacey."

Sara looked back to the helicopter as the paramedics raced past with the loaded stretcher. "What about the rest of the crew with me?"

"The Marine lieutenant and FBI agent whom you knew as Susan and Mary are dead. I didn't know Susan, but Mary was a crackerjack woman." He looked away. "The driver and the agent in the white van, which was your backup, are in serious condition, but they survived because they kept their seatbelts buckled. They're being stabilized in a Rockford hospital. Police are still analyzing the wreckage. Appears three were in the Blazer."

"The driver with me?"

"Listed in serious condition."

"I hope the info we get is worth the sacrifice." Sara brushed tears from her eyes. "I can't let myself think about the crash scene now. Awful." She felt like every muscle in her body was complaining. She didn't want to contemplate what she'd feel like without the muscle relaxants as she stepped forward gingerly. She grabbed his arm and hobbled toward the elevator inside the building.

As they waited for the elevator, Norm stared at Sara. "Lucky lady, nothing in your record indicated you were a crack shot. Who trained you?"

Sara limped into the elevator and smiled. "Sanders. Will he be notified I'm safe in Madison?"

"The State Department official with the General? You betcha. By the way, the accident record won't mention the lighter or that you riddled the one guy with bullets."

"I was scared. It was him or the driver and me."

"You betcha." Norm grasped her arm firmly and guided her from the elevator and out a back door of the hospital to a small parking lot. A heavy woman with her gray hair in a bob was waiting in a black sedan along with the driver. As the car departed, Sara noticed a Madison Police Department squad car followed them.

A box of black, bound books, two small reading lights, and two cans of Diet Coke sat on the back seat between Sara and the woman. She said, "I'm Inge Ohm. Call me Inge. Sanders told us you'd think better if we gave you pop." She motioned to the books "These are the theses and dissertations you requested. All twenty-four of them. We think only the eight on top are of interest. The rest have no apparent tie to the Middle East."

Norm positioned the lights so Sara could work. She swallowed a big slug of soda before she began to page through the top thesis. "Please, give me slips of paper. I want to mark important pages."

Inge tore pages from a notebook, Sara stuck two strips in the first thesis. The wrinkles on Norm's forehead increased. "Can I help?"

Sara kept paging through theses. "No. Why don't you brief me?"

"That's my department," said Inge as she thumbed through a file. "Otto Steinhaus, the man you call Doc, was a grad student in Iran in sixty-eight. Bit unusual. He already had earned a master's in statistics when he worked at the medical school in Pahlavi University, now called Shiraz University, collecting data from Iranian military records. Seems he worked for someone sorta famous — Dr. James Halstead, husband of Anna Roosevelt. Yes, the daughter of FDR. Appears Halstead developed an interest in the causes of dwarfism and lack of sexual development among Iranian villagers when he and his wife were in residence in Iran in fifty-eight and fifty-nine. Unusual topic. Probably of interest, because the Iranian army couldn't draft about three percent of the rural villagers because of this syndrome. Halstead even got funding from National Institutes of Health in the U.S."

She closed the file and pulled another one. Sara paged through the theses and marked occasional ones with slips of paper, while Norm looked back and forth between them. "Betcha, you're surprised."

"No, Doc told me he went to University of Michigan to work with a prof with extensive international contacts. At the time, he was warning me not to pick a graduate school based on one person. Seems the prof left Michigan before Doc finished his dissertation. The prof must have been Halstead."

"Fits." Inge nodded. "Halstead went to Michigan and then Kentucky after Iran. He stayed only a short time at both places." She shoved a stack of pages at Sara. "Our guys located your Doc's dissertation at Michigan about twenty minutes before the helicopter landed. It's a statistical analysis of geophagy — I guess that's intentionally eating dirt or clay — among peasants in the Middle East. I was printing out the first twenty pages they faxed me when you landed."

Sara immediately started to scan the new document. "I see in his dedication Doc thanked Halstead for serving on his committee and helping him obtain the raw data from Iran and Egypt."

"Saw that too." Inge hesitated. "General Purcell told FBI staff not to go on a wild goose chase for this dissertation, but Ulysses Howe, the head FBI guy in Albuquerque, insisted we listen to your hunches. Why did you want to see it?"

Sara rubbed her eyes and then regretted it because she guessed she had smeared the last traces of her eyeliner. "On the plane, I wondered how Doc got involved in Iranian politics so early in his career? I knew he collected data for his dissertation outside the U.S."

"Like I said before, you're a lucky lady," said Norm.

"More like, she's good at deduction." Inge smoothed the collar of her violet suit.

Sara figured she was going to work well with Inge. "But we're nowhere on interpreting the message from the so-called F.

"Maybe not." Inge appeared to listen to her earpiece. "We've got several people looking at this new angle. As far as we can tell, neither Halstead nor his wife Anna Roosevelt were engaged in espionage. Of course, Anna had all sorts of contacts. She'd even been with her father at Yalta in forty-five."

Sara stopped paging through the loose pages. "As far as I can see, Doc worked with people from the medical schools at the Universities of Shiraz and Tehran. I can't find a mention of Tabriz."

Norm said, "What difference does that make?"

Sara shrugged. "F mentioned me in her email. Since my only connections with Iran are through Doc, Farideh, and Souri, I assumed F wanted me to look in their records for further clues. I guessed the location of Tabriz was important because the email message came form Tabriz. But I can't find any indication that Doc gathered data in Tabriz. On the other hand, Baum's students worked in northern Iran near Tabriz. Hope I'm not looking for the proverbial needle in a haystack — in the wrong haystack."

"I'll ask our analysts to look for Tabriz in all the documents." Inge adjusted her sparkly amethyst earrings. "Darn things hurt. Besides, the analysts can do it electronically better than we can here in a poorly lit car."

Norm turned off Sara's reading light. "You need to hear a few details about Howard Baum from Inge. He seems to have been a real Indy Jones in his day."

Inge clucked. "Norm likes hyperbole. Baum worked on one of the first agricultural projects sponsored by USAID in Iran in the late fifties. Then he led a project, an off-shoot of the green revolution, to develop drought resistant crops for the cooler climate of northern Iran in the sixties. When USAID declared Iran no longer needed their help, he garnered funds from various private foundations and agrochemical companies to continue his research during the seventies."

Sara for a moment had a flashback of the crash scene. She shivered. "Did Baum meet Doc in Iran? Was he Doc's controller or whatever you call a spy's boss?"

"First question first. Our analysts don't think so, but Baum routinely trained Peace Corp volunteers on the needs of Iranian peasants. Now, it gets interesting. He also spoke on the same topic at several schools for police and military in Iran."

The faces of Mary and Susan flashed before her eyes. She shook her head. "Sorry. I'm having flashbacks of the accident."

"Understandable." Inge handed her a cookie. "I find a little food helps sometimes. Can you go on?"

"I have to." After Sara took a couple of bites, she said, "One of the guys arrested in Washington near Sanders's home was from SAVAK. Did he meet Baum?"

"Good point." Silence as Inge texted. "Sent the question to our analysts in D.C. Now your second question. The FBI is pressuring our colleagues to uncover Baum's and Doc's Washington and Iranian contacts. Your friend Sanders gave us everything from USAID records already. No evidence that Baum and Doc worked together overseas." She peered at Sara. "Smart man, and he is concerned about you."

Sara ignored Inge's unspoken question about Sanders because she thought she might cry if she allowed herself to think about how much she wished he was here with her. "How does the terrorist at my house and the ones in the Bronco relate to all of this?"

"My guess is they're cheap hired help. If those trying to stop F thought Dr. Baum and Elvira were a threat, they would have hired terrorists to attack them, not you. Somehow you hold a key. Of course, we've kept Baum, Olsen, and Elvira in more secluded and guarded spots."

"Lucky me."

CHAPTER 11: Confusion reigns

Sara's anxiety increased as the black sedan passed two uniformed officers in a Madison Police patrol car idling one-half block before Elvira's house. Two men sat in a blue car positioned across the street from the house. She saw an unmarked car idling one-half block ahead. The driver of the black sedan pulled in front of the house.

┆ Before he leapt out of the car, Norm said, "Remember, we're in a hurry." He ran until he hit a patch of ice on the poorly shoveled cement sidewalk. He skidded to a stop after almost losing his balance, turned, and waited for Sara and Inge.

Sara hesitated in the car and stared at the hulking, gray craftsman style house on Adams Street on the west side of Madison. This house, like most built in the first decade of the twentieth century, looked like a fortress. Especially ominous in the dim light of street lamps. Everyone expected her to storm this stronghold and extract useful data from Elvira in time to meet the deadline. She gave herself a ten percent chance of success.

As she climbed the cement steps and crossed the wide screened porch, which seemed to be a storage place for outdoor furniture and yard tools, she noted white paint around the door was peeling. The house reminded her of Doc — large and slightly untidy. She remembered his shirts were often stained with bits of catsup from lunch or ink from a pen stuck carelessly into a pocket.

She'd attended two Christmas parties at this house, but she remembered little about it, other than it was big. She recalled about as much about the hostess. She looked tiny next to Doc.

When they reached the door, Inge whispered, "Forget Norm's advice. Take your time and get Elvira to like and trust you. Then the rest should flow." She said more softly, "God willing."

Sara stood for a second and surveyed the interior scene. The house was somber with dark wood around windows and doors, almost black wood rafters, and stained oak floors. The walls were a deep teal blue shade. Sara suspected Elvira had changed little in this house since Doc died about fifteen years ago.

An attractive older woman with dyed, copper-colored hair was coiled in a fetal position on a leather sofa under a crocheted turquoise and purple afghan. She appeared to be napping. Not the white-haired hag Sara had expected.

A man in a gray suit paced under the arch to the dining room and whispered into a mouthpiece suspended in front of his face. He pointed to an oak dining room chair placed near the sofa. Sara figured he was directing her, because Inge settled into a leather Queen Anne chair near the fireplace and turned on a reading lamp. Inge had told Sara she would record the conversation and take notes, but she didn't want to be in Elvira's line of sight because police officers and FBI agents seemed to irritate her. Norm disappeared into a room beyond the dining room.

As Sara sat down, Elvira opened one eye and groaned. She pointed and flexed her feet before she sat upright. Her movements were as fluid and graceful as those of a cat, but her eyes were another story. Her gaze seemed to dart about the room. "Why are you bothering an old lady at this ungodly hour?" Her voice was screechy like a Siamese cat in heat.

Sara leaned forward and forced a smile. "Mrs. Steinhaus, I doubt you'll remember me. I attended two Christmas parties here when I worked in Doc's statistics group as an undergrad assistant in seventy-eight and seventy-nine." Sara knew she should be polite and say 'you look the same' or 'the food was great,' but she remembered nothing about the event, except it was boring. She also recognized she wasn't glib enough to fake remembrances. "I hadn't remembered your house had so much historic character, but then an eighteen or nineteen-year-old isn't observant of decors."

Elvira scowled. "I see... What do you remember? Exactly."

Sara shrugged. "The house was big and had dark woodwork."

Elvira nodded. "Mmm. At least, you're honest. Why do you want to see me? This young man..." She pointed to the agent who no longer paced under the arches but stood with Norm. "He told me a cock and bull story. Insisted my husband was a spy in Iran and one of his past students needed to get out with a message. Doc, that's what I called him, was a hard working professor."

"They told me that story too." Sara thought a little white lie was okay. "I believed them after someone attempted to kill me as I drove from Chicago to Madison."

The eyes that bore into Sara were green. Sara suspected Elvira had been a beauty when she was young. Sara was jolted from her thoughts by Elvira's squawk. "So what? Nothing to do with my husband or me. It's your problem." Elvira pointed a finger, with a nail polished in a copper tone to match her hair, at Sara's chest.

"Please, be patient with me. I've never been to Iran. None of my grad students were from Iran. Though I've consulted in Lebanon and the United Arab Emirates and visited the standard tourist sites in Egypt and Turkey."

"Oh." Elvira gazed around the room, turning her head frequently and almost spastically. "When were you in Lebanon?"

Sara gave an expansive answer and hoped it would encourage Elvira to do the same. She ended with, "Mainly Beirut. Although I visited an outlying farm owned by the American University of Beirut in ninety-nine."

Elvira continued her eerie eye movements as she bit her lips until they bled. Sara figured fear induced Elvira's behavior. But fear of what?

Suddenly Elvira leaned back on the sofa. "What did you do in the Emirates? And when were you there?"

Sara decided a calm answer might soothe Elvira. "A sheik, actually the cousin of one the head sheiks in the Emirates, was an Oxford-educated economist and the education minister. In ninety, he wanted an evaluation of their educational system, specifically their main university at Al Ain."

Elvira knitted her brows. "Odd. You being a woman."

"Professionally, I use my initials instead of my first name. I doubt they realized I was a woman until I sent them my passport to get my visa."

"Mmm. What were the Emirates like?"

Sara perceived time was passing quickly but recognized she hadn't gained Elvira's trust. "I suspect we saw only the best of the Emirates. Modern supermarkets, better than most in the U.S., but no traditional markets. Superhighways but not many rutted paths. Miles of empty wasteland along the sixty miles of highway from Dubai to Al Ain, but with irrigation lines strung in the median strip. So, palm trees and plants abounded between two strips of concrete in a plain of shifting sand. The laboratory for one sheik's racing camels contained more and newer equipment than any lab we saw at the university. Funny, in the middle of the lab was a large ornate chair for the sheik."

"What was the university like?" Elvira stood and glared at the men in her kitchen.

"Basic, with limited laboratories. Men and women were taught separately."

Elvira waved her hand toward her kitchen. "I wish those men wouldn't roam through my home. They have no right."

Sara recognized she had lost Elvira's attention. She stood and pushed Elvira gently back onto the sofa. "Our most interesting observations were in the differences between men and women students. We found female students actively participated in class discussions, while most of the male students didn't take notes during class and made no attempt to answer the professors' questions."

Elvira remained seated but thumped the pillow on the sofa in apparent frustration.

Sara figured she'd better pep up her spiel. "Do you know why?" She touched Elvira's arm.

Elvira shifted on the sofa, but looked at Sara. "No, why?"

"The males understood they would move to supervisory positions after graduation and be given a home when they married, regardless of their grades. The females reported if they flunked out, they would be married within a month and were then their husband's property. The young women weren't eager to lose the relative freedom they enjoyed in college any sooner than necessary. They studied more than the men. The net result was the best Emirate-born computer technician was a woman. Her husband had reluctantly agreed to let her work outside their home."

"How and where did you interview the women?"

Sara noted Elvira continued to frown, but now her voice betrayed interest, and her eyes focused on Sara's face. "The review team interviewed women in the courtyard of their dorm. The dorm looked as most Westerners envision a harem. The walls around the building were tall, maybe fifteen feet, and topped with glass shards and coiled barbwire. The women shed the burqas they wore to class and were dressed in turquoise, purple, red, and hot pink dresses, which were generally long, loose-fitting, and looked like they were made from silk — slightly lustrous and lightweight."

"I would have expected them to be in jeans."

"Me too. Maybe, they wore their best clothes in honor the review team, but it seemed at the time as though Scheherazade had stepped out of the *Arabian Nights*."

Sara noticed Elvira's frown had softened. "I suspect you and Doc saw a different situation in Iran in the seventies."

"Who said I ever went to Iran?"

Sara arched her eyebrows. According to U.S. Immigration Services, Elvira had flown in and out of Tehran twice. "Really?"

"Oh, once."

Sara coughed.

"Or twice."

"Where did you go?"

"Mmm. All over."

Sara thought Elvira enjoyed the game. "Tabriz?"

"No. Doc worked with staff at the main universities in Tehran and Shiraz. Always south of Tehran."

"What was your favorite place?"

"Mmm. Along the Persian Gulf. The water was turquoise, and you could forget the desert."

"So, you went to the Strait of Hormuz?" Sara noticed Inge flashed a thumbs-up.

"No... the port closer to Shiraz."

Sara was stumped. Inge rushed forward with a map of Iran on her tablet screen.

Elvira pointed to Bandar Bushehr. "Quiet, historic. Good wine. At that time, few women wore chadors in Tehran or Shiraz. They dressed like women on American TV shows. Bushehr was depressed, and many women wore chadors. Doc and I played a little game. I would wear a chador on weekends in Bushehr."

Sara wanted to say, "I want political secrets not sexual ones." She managed to keep a straight face. "Why?"

Elvira picked up the pace. Her voice was harsh, but less strident. "I could carry... a camera undetected." She paused and waited for Sara to respond.

"A camera?"

Elvira sighed. "Iran, with help from Russia, was building a nuclear reactor. Guards at the site confiscated or destroyed cameras if they caught you taking photos anywhere near the construction site."

Sara debated what to do. Inge rushed back to her seat and typed frantically. "Elvira, let's stop playing games. You knew Doc was spying for the U.S. because you helped him."

Elvira looked at her lap.

"Where else did you take pictures?"

Elvira's lips quivered. "Such a long time ago. Doc also collected details about the Tehran Nuclear Center. The U.S. helped build it in the sixties, but got nervous about its uses. While Doc collected data and performed statistical analyses on villagers who failed their draft physicals because of stunted growth, I carried a little portable Geiger counter in my bright purple purse and followed garbage trucks and other vehicles that left the nuclear site. I also wandered around the chemistry and physics buildings at the university with my purple purse." She sniffed. "Didn't learn much."

"And who told you to go to Bushehr or any site?"

Elvira looked around the room warily and rubbed her hands like she was washing them. "It's a secret."

"Not anymore."

Elvira's eyes were wide open as she stared at Sara. "The veiled lady won't like it. I don't want her to visit me again."

Inge rolled her eyes. "Just our luck. We were finally making progress."

Sara placed her hands on Elvira's to stop the hand washing routine, which made Sara nervous. "You're safe now with Inge and the other FBI agents to protect you."

Elvira jerked her hands away and held one finger in front of her lips. "Shhh. She'll hear you. She might shoot at me again."

Sara leaned forward. She wanted to ask about the woman who shot or at least tried to shoot Elvira, but thought the question would only lead Elvira further into her fantasies or nightmares. She decided to switch back to the original topic before Elvira spooked. "I bet it was fun gathering data, but what did Doc and you do with the data?"

Elvira squinted and pointed to the sky. "Upstairs in heaven."

"Mmm." Sara feared this interview was about over. "Did Doc share what you learned with anyone?"

Elvira wrinkled her brow and focused on her lap. "He gave it to a man in the embassy."

Inge gave Sara a high sign with her fingers.

"Tell me about him."

"I never met him." Elvira smiled for the first time. "If you doubt me, there's the proof." She pointed to a large purple leather tote bag on the mantle of the fireplace. "Please bring the tote and the Geiger counter back to me after you do your analyses or whatever. It reminds me of the first time Doc and I worked together."

During the resulting flurry of activity, Sara asked, "How and why did you convince your daughter and these agents that you were forgetful?"

A tear slid down Elvira's cheek. "After Doc died, my daughter wasn't interested in my adventures when I hinted of them. She thought I was hallucinating. So, I answered most of her questions with 'I forget' or acted dumb. When the police banged on my door today, they frightened me." She shook her head. "No, they were rude and annoying, and I didn't care about some agent, called F, in Iran." She pulled on Sara's sleeve and lowered her voice. "F might be the veiled lady. She wanted to kill me because she wanted Doc."

Sara ignored the ludicrous comments on F desiring the obese Doc. "Where?"

Elvira resumed her hand washing routine. "Doc tried to hide from me the fact she had his baby."

This interview was going down the tubes. "Where did F try to kill you?"

In a low, slurred voice, "In Beirut." Elvira suddenly stood and seemed to take command. "It's all in heaven — my attic."

As soon as Elvira said "attic," a Madison police officer and the FBI agent in gray raced up the stairs near the front door. Sara followed Elvira because she expected the old woman to trudge slowly up the two flights of stairs to the third floor attic. However, Sara had to work to keep up and decided that she needed more muscle relaxant.

The reason for Elvira's agility was obvious when they reached the third floor landing. The whole attic was an exercise studio with yoga mats, a treadmill, a few weights, and a TV/stereo system. Unlike the rest of the house, the walls were painted a pale yellow and the furniture was sparse and painted white.

Elvira must have noticed Sara's surprise. "I keep fit without others knowing my business. My daughter never comes up here. This is my heaven." She fished a key from the top drawer of a white painted chest and opened the door on a wall covered with dozens of framed examples of Arabic calligraphy. Behind the locked door, rows of boxes set on shelves, which extended the width of the house on both sides of the eight-foot deep room.

"Doc and I began storing items in the attic after our first trip together. During the eighties, we constructed the closet to prevent our daughter from stumbling into our secrets. As you can see all the boxes are labeled to look like they're field data from his research with the university, but there's more in them."

The FBI agents gasped. There were at least a hundred boxes

Sara didn't want to push Elvira back into her fantasy, but time was short. She uttered a prayer and charged ahead. "Where should they begin?" She said more softly, "F said contact Almquist and sent the message from Tabriz. Those are our only clues, and time is limited."

"I know. The agent," she pointed to the man in gray, "told me a dozen times. I've done a bit of thinking. Nothing from Tabriz. Nothing on you per se. Mmm." Elvira walked into her closet and ran her hands over the boxes until she came to one marked *1973*.

Norm grabbed the box and put it on table in the main room, where he and Inge began to page through files.

"Doc started at the UW in the fall of seventy-two. He'd gotten a little money from the Graduate School here and a little money from Dr. Halstead's NIH grant to collect data to extend his doctoral research in Iran during the summer of seventy-three. He was such a smart man. Everyone liked him."

Sara wanted Elvira to focus. She guided Elvira to a chair where Elvira couldn't watch Norm and Inge rifling through the file. "And what did Doc study in Iran?"

"Mmm. Although Doc's thesis focused on clay eating by poor rural Iranians, new data from Egypt suggested zinc deficiency was the primary cause of the dwarfism."

"Cut to the action." Norm continued with a series of expletives.

Sara interrupted, "You don't need to explain. I'm familiar with this research."

"Well, yes. Doc designed a sampling grid to assess the relative importance of the clay eating and zinc intake on the health of Iranian peasants. It was ingenious. He was so clever." Her eyes fluttered. "We had an excuse to travel all over southern Iran. The man at the embassy was thrilled."

"What man at the embassy?"

Elvira seemed to ignore Sara's question. "Doc figured our trip in seventy-three might be his last. USAID had suspended operation in

Iran. Dissidents were everywhere. The SAVAK guards were surly with Americans who seemed too nosy. Doc and the man in the embassy came up with a plan to recruit an Iranian to be a grad student in Doc's lab."

Sara wanted to say, "finally," but didn't want to distract Elvira.

"The man suggested Farideh because her husband had been accepted in the nuclear engineering program at UW, and she was good in math and wanted to get a student visa, too. Most importantly, he knew she and her husband were covert dissidents who wanted to get out from under the Shah's thumb in Iran. I don't know the details and doubt the man would have put anything in writing."

Norm whistled. "OMG, found the file on Farideh. Her application to grad school. Lots of notes. Gold mine of background on her and her husband."

He was running down the stairs when Inge shrieked, "Wait." She held up a single page of handwritten notes. "Appears to be notes on a man — an attaché in the Tehran embassy. Note the 'Just in case' written in a different color of ink at the top." Norm flew up the stairs.

Elvira stood, gasped at the material strewn on the table, and snatched the page from Inge. "Doc's handwriting." She turned pale as she scanned the page. "Never saw this." She gulped. "That's why Doc never let me meet him." She pointed near the bottom of the page. "Look."

Inge read the handwriting with difficulty. "B too tight with SAVAK. Convinced B that E knows nothing. She's my cover." She looked at Elvira. "I assume you're E. Is Dr. Baum B?"

Elvira's eyes flashed fire. "No. Doc wasn't afraid of him. He was afraid of the man in the embassy." Elvira's eyes started to scan the room.

Sara put her hand on Elvira's shoulder in an attempt to calm her. "So, Doc referred to the man in the embassy as B?

Elvira trembled violently and pushed Sara's hand from her shoulder. "Doc never identified the man. Called him... He... never used even an initial." Her voice trailed off. "B, B,... Don't remember meeting anyone with a last name or first name beginning with B in Iran. I thought Doc told me everything." She mumbled names.

Inge ignored Elvira's mutterings. "Have the analysts find B pronto." She gave the file to Norm, who galloped down the stairs. She rose and grabbed Elvira's hands. "We believe hundreds, perhaps more, lives could depend on getting F and her package out of Iran. Anything else important?"

For a moment, Elvira looked like a queen on a throne, with her posture perfect and her smile triumphant. "Doc heard from Farideh in eighty-one. At least, he thought so. It was a picture postcard with only "Remember" written on the back. She paused. "I don't recall the picture on the card, but Doc and I were both convinced Farideh or her husband sent it.... Can't recollect why. Oh dear."

"She may have survived prison? Show me where to look." Inge rushed to the closet.

Elvira stood. Her focus flitted erratically around the room. Sara feared another relapse into fantasy. She pushed Elvira back in the chair. "Do you remember Souri Fekri?"

Elvira seemed to settle into the chair and closed her eyes. "Would do anything for money. Doc thought she was disgusting. But she came later."

"Would she know the man in the embassy?"

Elvira shrugged.

"Who might know about the man in the embassy?"

"Baum. Sly old fox. There was a rumor. An old ag professor from Michigan State, a friend of Baum, was in northern Iran about the time of the hostage takeover. He was..."

Sara interrupted, "Why is he important?"

Elvira's eyes widened. "He got out into Turkey. Took him several months. Never mentioned in the press despite all hype on the hostages."

"Get another analyst here now." Inge mouthed curses as she listened for a few seconds. "No excuses. Send one to see Baum. Ask about a professor in agriculture at Michigan State who was in Iran at time of the takeover and escaped through Turkey." She listened a bit more.

She pointed to Sara. "Baum is in bad shape, but his former grad student isn't. Push them for answers. The analyst will play bad cop, while you take a softer approach. Go." She put an arm around Elvira and winked at Sara. "Elvira and I are friends now. We'll find all Doc's secrets."

As Sara turned to run down the stairs, Elvira looked up at Inge. "I read Farsi and Arabic. Doc didn't have time to learn. That's why I decorated the house with Arabic calligraphy. Cheaper than rugs. More interesting. Notice the gold frames. I learned how to take cheap frames and paint them to look like they were covered in gold leaf. Don't you think they look lovely after all these years?"

Sara was happy to escape Elvira's chaotic world. She pitied Inge. Elvira would make her earn every clue. She hoped Baum would be easier to interview than Elvira.

CHAPTER 12: Twenty-seven hours until the deadline

Sara couldn't believe her eyes. The old man, lying in a hospital bed, was almost as white as his sheets. Even his blue eyes were a faded pale blue.

Norm, who had accompanied her from Elvira's home to the best guarded section — the locked psych ward — of the hospital, whistled. "You gotta to be kidding. Let's skip Baum and talk to Mark Olsen, his former graduate student."

The woman holding Baum's right hand looked up. "Dad wants to help. Look at the way he's gripping my hand. He keeps saying... I think, Mickel or Mickelson."

Norm nodded. "Our analysts figured out Mickelson was the name of the ag professor who escaped Iran during the hostage crisis in December of seventy-nine. He's dead. Our agents are talking to his son now. Anything else?" He pulled the sleeve of a woman FBI agent standing by the door. "Where's Olsen?"

Sara watched the old man. Tears trickled from his eyes. She ran her fingers down his left arm and squeezed his hand. "Dr. Baum, I'm Sara Almquist. I'm going to ask you questions. If the answer is yes, squeeze my hand. If the answer is no, squeeze your daughter's hand. "Did Doc call you B? Did anyone call you B?"

Two squeezes. "No to both," said the daughter.

"Did you report to B in the Iran embassy?"

The daughter said, "He squeezed my hand."

Sara wondered whether Baum was capable of squeezing her hand. "Did Mark Olsen meet B in the Iran?"

She felt slight pressure on her hand.

The woman agent whispered into Sara's ear details that she'd extracted from Baum. "He doesn't know who F is, but he recognized Farideh's name. He thinks Farideh survived prison. Not sure why. Thinks F was in Beirut in ninety-five. But I can't follow his reasoning. The daughter was ignorant until today how deep her father's contacts in Iran were. She can add nothing."

J. L. Greger

Norm stopped his frantic texting and whispered in Sara's other ear. "Souri was in Beirut in ninety-nine and several times since then. I'm out of here. When you get tired of charades, talk to Olsen, next door." He slammed the door behind him.

Sara slowly ascertained that Baum thought Souri and Farideh knew B, and that B was in Washington, D.C. now. When she told him she'd been in Beirut in ninety-nine, he squeezed her hand repeatedly, but he couldn't answer her follow-up questions. Or perhaps, she thought she hadn't asked the questions right.

As she exited to talk to Olsen, the daughter hugged Sara. "Thanks for making Dad feel useful. Push Olsen. I remember Dad grumbled, 'darn grad student has to lay every Iranian female he meets.' Olsen is... well you'll see." She blushed.

Sara strode into the next room and before she took a seat at the table stared at a buff, man with his hair-streaked blond. He didn't look much like the gawky grad student of over thirty-five years ago. She bet he thought he was God's gift to women now. She'd seen many aging profs like him. They all loved to counsel women students. "You had an affair with Souri Fekri. Did you have sex with Farideh Hossein, too?"

Norm and the other agent gaped.

Olsen blanched and the pockmarks from his acne were more obvious. "I... I didn't think old man Baum knew about Souri and me. Though he often lectured me about separating work and pleasure."

"Farideh?"

He tugged at his collar. "No way. She would have killed me."

Sara wanted to maintain a rapid pace. She barked the next question as she sat down at the far end of the table. "Were you ever in the embassy in Tehran?"

Olsen looked puzzled. "No, Baum forbid me. Said... 'the wolf would eat me alive' or something like that."

"Did you ever meet anyone with B as a first or last initial in Iran? Maybe an American."

"No... I don't think so." Beads of sweat appeared on his forehead.

"Sure?" Sara noted Norm continued to gape at her, but the other man was texting.

Olsen trembled and closed his eyes. "A guy came to visit me as I was completing my field trials. Weird guy. Told me to call him Bob, and not to tell Baum about his visit. As I remember, asked questions about the locations of all my fields. Made me take him to two remote sites. Poked around two old stone sheds on the sites."

Sara waited for thirty seconds. "Anything else about him?"

"Average height, dark hair." He closed his eyes. "Hair might have been dyed."

"Why do you say that? Did his roots show?"

"No... I don't know. It looked funny. Not natural."

Sara thought that was an ironic comment from Olsen with his obviously bleached hair. She suppressed a chuckle. "Think hard, his voice, his posture."

"Average looks."

Wait. Maybe, Olsen didn't want her or anyone to identify B. "Your best protection against B is for the FBI to find him fast."

Olsen slouched and closed his eyes. "Ramrod straight posture. Boston accent. Weird."

"How was he weird?"

"Traipsing through fields in northern Iran and wanting the names of field hands isn't typical. The guy was looking for something, but secretive. Flipped me his embassy ID, but held his thumb over his name. I think... I think I saw Robert. In the picture, he wore a military uniform."

"Rank? Which service?"

"How would I know? Main reason I applied to grad school was to avoid the military. Viet Nam. When the war ended, I figured I might as well finish grad school." Olsen wiped sweat from his forehead and upper lip.

Norm pulled Sara's sleeve and ushered her out of the room. "Liked your bad cop routine. Go for the kill now. We know he's never returned to Iran since his dissertation, but he led field trials in eastern Turkey for the Ford Foundation in the early eighties."

Sara nodded and headed back into the room. "Whom did you report to when you ran the field trials in Turkey?"

Blank stare. In a shaky voice, "I tested drought resistant wheat for the Ford Foundation. It was a logical extension of my dissertation research, and I was beginning the publish or perish treadmill."

"Cut the crap? No matter what you were told about secrecy, it doesn't apply. This is the FBI." She motioned to Norm and the other agent. "And they are working with the military. I'm no spy, but I've been dragged into this mess, created by Doc, Baum, and this so-called Bob. Let's crawl out of their mess before we're killed."

Olsen looked at the ceiling and sighed. "Bob again. Men and women, escaping from Iran in eighty-one and -two, trickled into my fields. I think most were SAVAK and their families. I never asked as I gave them new clothes. Actually, old rags from the farm workers, a little cash, and burned their clothes. Bob gave me a little money under the table to supplement my income in return for my services. The only one who talked was old man Mickelson, an ag prof from Michigan State."

"What did Mickelson say?" Sara noted both agents leaned forward.

"Nonsense." Sweat poured down Olsen's flushed face.

"Like what?"

"Bragged Kurds met him at an old stone shed on what sounded like one of my old field trial site — the most distant one, which Bob visited in Iran. They transferred him from one herding group to another. Mickelson gave names. I kept saying, 'Man, shut up,' but he thought it was a game."

Norm said, "Did you see Bob again?"

Olsen leaned forward with his head cradled by his hands. "Yeah, when I was completing my field trials in Turkey."

"And?"

Olsen sighed. "I finally got up my guts and told him I never wanted to see him again." He shook his head. "Can't believe I'm admitting this. Never told anyone, not even one of my three wives, about Bob in almost thirty years. Never wrote another application for funds to work abroad."

Sara touched his arm. "Why?"

"When I said weird, I was being kind. Bob would kick at dead birds and cats, laugh, and say, "That's what happens when you talk.""

Norm had already left the room before Sara asked, "Anything else?"

"Check how Mickelson and Doc died. Always wondered. Both were on overseas assignments. As usual Doc traveled with Elvira." He pulled his fingers through his hair. "Funny, I never was sure who was the brains in that pair."

CHAPTER 13: Sanders makes slow progress

The pounding in his head had triggered throbbing in his chest. Sanders attempted to lower his blood pressure by closing his eyes and slowly counting to ten, then twenty. He was used to being in charge or at least managing crises. Tonight he watched and listened as events spun out of control. He couldn't decide which was more nerve-racking — listening as Sara fired a round of shots, the silence after the phone clattered to the pavement, or watching the General dither though the investigation.

He opened his eyes. The silence was the worst. Although the General's lethargic approach to the crises was a close second.

In retrospect, he wasn't surprised by Sara's action during the crisis on the highway. After she admitted the only two sports she had excelled at in high school and college were archery and fencing, he'd taken her along to the FBI shooting range when he went for a refresher course. She wasn't an ace marksman, but she was competent. The FBI agents and military types, listening on the phone with him, doubted Sara would be able to focus enough during the emergency. Granted, Sara had the annoying habit of throwing all sorts of extraneous details and facts in when she spoke. It drove him crazy, but it fascinated him, because the details were often relevant. However, those who didn't know her thought she was ditzy. He knew she could focus. He'd never met anyone who could shut off her surroundings more than Sara when faced with a problem. Again, at times an annoying trait.

At first, he and everyone else were surprised when Sara threw the lit lighter into the Blazer. After a couple of seconds, he recognized Sara had proven why she won so many arguments in academia. She took no prisoners and believed in being thorough.

Her heroic efforts to save the driver had flabbergasted others. He'd never doubted she'd try. He blinked. He'd have acted exactly as Sara did. He wondered whether they were too alike to maintain a long-term relationship. He was uncertain whether he loved her, but he respected and liked her. More than any woman... or man. Was that enough?

He was jolted back to the present when the General poured himself a cup of coffee as he continued to talk on the phone. Sanders thought Sara was up to her assignment in Madison, if she had proper backup. He doubted she'd receive adequate support. The General had done a poor to mediocre job of leading the rescue of F. His subordinate, the Major, was an arrogant, uncooperative bumbler. Mary and Susan were nice women but not the crack guards he would have selected to protect a valuable witness like Sara.

His suspicions about the General's commitment to save F were aroused almost as soon as the General arrived at his home for dinner. He was too reserved, like he was at Princeton when he supplied booze, for a tidy profit, to local high school kids. What was the General hiding this time?

Accordingly, while the General had stood in his kitchen and argued over the phone with Gil about how to handle the terrorists who broke into Sara's house, Sanders called his boss, an Assistant Secretary of State. She quickly agreed he should continue to monitor the developing situation for the State Department. She added, "General Purcell knows more about the Middle East, particularly Iran, Syria and Lebanon, than almost anyone, but I don't trust him. He's cut too many questionable deals." She didn't elaborate.

Five minutes later, Sanders watched the General's complexion turn scarlet as he said "Yes, Commandant," in response to a call, which interrupted his extended phone conversation with Gil. Evidently, Gil hadn't trusted the General either, because less than five minutes after that conversation ended, the General received another call. Again, his face reddened as he said, "Yes, Commandant." This time he reluctantly added, "Yes... I'll share everything with Gil, FBI agents, and Sanders."

The General gazed past Sanders as he strode from the house. "You're supposed to come along to the briefing at the Marine Barracks. The limo is here."

The General received a call from two FBI agents in New Jersey before the limo pulled from the curb at Sanders's home. Sanders insisted the General put his phone in speaker mode.

A woman agent began. "When we got to her residence in Montclair, Souri's husband told us she was in Egypt on business. He admitted he hadn't talked to her since she landed at Cairo International Airport and checked into the Cairo Marriott two days ago because she was working in an area with poor cell phone reception for three days."

Now a male FBI agent spoke. "We also checked with the biotech firm that employs Souri. A secretary informed us Souri sometimes took three or four days of vacation before she began assignments in the Middle East. The only thing odd this time was she added the days at the last minute because her aunt was sick. Her husband claims Souri has no relatives left in the Middle East."

The woman agent spoke again. "Meanwhile, guards from the U.S. embassy in Cairo were dispatched to the Cairo Marriott. They confirmed that Souri had checked in two days ago, but no one remembered seeing her since then. The guards found her luggage in her room, but toiletries and a bulky item had been removed from her luggage. The embassy staff concluded she hadn't been kidnapped, and she had planned to be gone overnight."

Sanders now understood why Sara mistrusted Souri. However, the General's dazed expression and lack of questions was puzzling.

The male agent continued the tale. "The embassy staff checked flights departing Cairo. No one with a first name of Souri or last name of Fekri flew out of Cairo in the last two days. They reviewed camera footage at the Cairo airport during that time, but women in burqas are almost impossible to identify. Her husband, now a frightened man, confirmed Souri always carries a burqa with her when she travels to the Middle East."

As the limo pulled up to the Marine Barracks, the General muttered, "The Major could be right. She could be F. Doubt it, but she knows something. Too many coincidences." He straightened and gave the order. "Top priority. Find her, but try not to arouse her suspicion. She may be meeting F."

Sanders was satisfied. He would have given the same order.

Sanders followed the General down semi-dark hallways into a brightly lit conference room for a briefing at two in the morning. Officers in uniforms and agents in dark suits were aligned on two sides of the table like armies prepared for battle. All looked ready for action despite the time.

A suited representative reported on Hanna Kafity, Sara's Palestinian graduate student. Hanna had aroused the suspicions of the military community when she refused to go to the U.S. consulate in Montreal with U.S. military attachés dispatched to her home. However, FBI analysts trusted the report of constables in the Royal Canadian Mounted Police, who interviewed her for an hour. They concluded she harbored no ill will against Americans, even though she distrusted

Israelis after being bombed out of homes in Beirut and Jerusalem as a child. They also noted she knew members of Palestinian families with known jihadists and she had visited family members in Jerusalem in ninety-eight and in Beirut in ninety-nine.

Although Sanders remained silent during the report on Souri, he spoke during Hanna's review. "She's not apt to be a jihadist because she's a Christian. Sara received an Easter card from a couple of days ago."

The General snorted and suggested consulate staff continue to monitor Hanna. FBI agents thought it was a waste of limited resources. Sanders agreed with them, but liked the General's surprising thoroughness.

When the General asked for the update from Albuquerque, the muffled whispers and sounds of rustling paper from the speakerphone stopped. Ulysses Howe in a low bass said, "Despite pleas, bribes, and threats, the so-called terrorist has remained in a trance-like state since we captured him. His record suggests he's an unstable pyromaniac with a death wish. Doubtful he's capable of doing more than respond to orders."

Gil interrupted, "So we focused on his accomplice, a local Palestinian guy with a long rap sheet for petty theft. Talked like a blue jay after an imam at the New Mexico Islamic Center counseled him. Seems a nameless friend of a friend recruited our local guy to burglarize Sara's home for the terrorist. The local guy became worried when he saw all the fireworks, his word not mine, the terrorist brought to the site. So, the local guy tripped the backup alarm to my station because he feared the terrorist would blow up the house with both of them in it." He chuckled. "I think this is the first time I apprehended a man who was relieved to be arrested."

Ulysses coughed. "Our local guy wants to make a deal, but he has limited info. Here's his best piece. The terrorist told him to look for an address book and letters or cards in Arabic script."

Gil chuckled. "Obviously, the terrorist or whoever hired him was sloppy about homework. Sara can't read anything but English."

Ulysses continued, "The local guy says the terrorist muttered over and over, 'Must not know it's there.' I'm curious what my compatriots in Washington think the terrorist meant."

Several men and women around the table nodded. One spoke. "In the past, F identified the opening of fuel enrichment plants and leaked data on upgrades of the nuclear power plant at Bushehr. We think F will bring out plans for a new plant or a major upgrade of the facility in Bushehr. F has never broken cover before. This is big."

In the background, Gil said, "Yazd."

Ulysses voice boomed from speaker. "Gil reminded me. The local guy thought the terrorist said something like Yazd over and over again. When I said the word to the terrorist, his blood pressure went up."

"OMG." A woman at the table stood. "There are uranium mines, we thought poor quality, in Yazd province in Iran." She ran from the room, while several others typed frantically on their tablets.

The General smirked. "Let's complete our review of all leads. Graduate students of Doc next."

A new male voice issued from the speakerphone. "We scanned the backgrounds of Dr. Baum's and Doc's students. I'll let Agent Norm Budzinski and Sara Almquist assess Mark Olsen. They're still with him." Pages rustled. "Now the rest, except two, are of no interest. No travel to the Middle East. Little overlap with Farideh or Souri, except Mike Volkov, a successful statistics professor at Yeshiva University. He collaborates with researchers in Israel, has traveled there, and admits he knew Farideh, but says he avoided her. He told a colorful tale of a knife fight between Farideh and a guy name Danny. His report is on your screens now."

The General scanned the notes. "Not new. Merely confirms what Sara told me." Pause, "He should be monitored closely for the next twenty-four hours."

Sanders thought the General was wasting scarce resources and time. "F is a creative agent, but using an apparently unwilling Jewish contact is doubtful."

The voice from the speakerphone said, "We agree. Mike's a dead end, but Danny Blair is another story. He seemingly went to Beirut and disappeared less than one year after leaving Doc's group at UW-Madison. We dug deeper. His records for application to UW appear to be fictitious too. The CIA is being difficult."

A woman at the table squirmed.

The man on the speakerphone continued, "We think he's one of us, but he's deep undercover."

The General peered at the woman who had stopped squirming. "Anything to add?"

"He could be F. More likely one of F's contacts or handler."

Sanders was disappointed the General asked no more questions about Danny Blair.

A debate began when Abid, the clerk in the antique shop who contacted Sara, was mentioned. The General described Abid as "no-consequence low-life who should be released immediately." Sanders insisted Abid knew too many details and must be held in protective custody for the next twenty-four hours, or until F was rescued and Sara returned from her trip to Wisconsin.

The lead FBI analyst wanted to question Abid intensively because he believed the Major had not interviewed him well. When the General claimed rank, the FBI agent called his boss. In less than two minutes, the General's phone rang. The General said, "Yes, Commandant," several times.

The General's eyes bulged when the lead FBI analyst announced, "I'll begin the process immediately, as you and your Major continue to interview the SAVAK guard. Of course, we need to reconvene when all the details come in from Madison."

The General fussed a bit with his tablet as the rest filed out of the room before he motioned for Sanders to follow him to a dingy complex of rooms in the basement of the Marine Barracks. The Major had questioned the SAVAK guard for several hours, but had learned little. Sanders after five minutes decided the Major, besides being an uncreative interviewer, had alienated the SAVAK guard, who purportedly wanted F to succeed, with ethnic slurs and snide comments. Sanders expected the General to stop the charade, instead the General watched silently through a one-way mirror for twenty minutes. The whole time, he clenched his fists so tightly his knuckles were white.

Sanders recognized he couldn't discern his college roommate's motivations or thoughts. The General had always been an enigma. He could be tired or ill, but he looked hale and healthy. He could dislike F and not want to rescue her. Sanders discarded the notion because an experienced officer, like the General, wouldn't let his personal feelings alter his judgment. Furthermore, he had never hinted he knew F. He could have a secret. Sanders pondered Abid's comments. The General had been posted in Beirut in the early eighties. He might have been the lieutenant who approved Abid's visa to the U.S. from Beirut. A mistake, but not worth lying about more than thirty years later. If he was worried about what Abid would say, why did he monitor the interrogation of the SAVAK guard instead of Abid's?

He assumed the General was stumped and was too proud to admit he didn't know what to do. His excellent memory, bravado, and ability to ingratiate himself with superiors, not his analytical skills, had propelled him through Princeton and, Sanders suspected, the Marines. He shrugged. Although his own perspectives had changed during the last thirty years, he thought the General had retained his outdated, patrician attitudes after watching him interact with Sara and Abid. Enough time wasted.

Sanders wondered whether Sara had wheedled answers from Elvira in Madison. No need to text her. Sara wasn't that modern. She wouldn't monitor her emails or texts while she conducted interviews. He liked that feature about Sara. When she spoke to you, you knew she was concentrating only on you. He emailed her anyway.

A minute later, someone named Norm called. "I'm Sara's gofer here. She's questioning Baum now. So, this is my chance to be the boss. Find out whether the SAVAK guard met Kurds at an agricultural field research station north of Tabriz when he escaped Iran. See whether your SAVAK guard met a younger, thinner, and dark-haired version of this man in Turkey?" Images of Olsen now and as a student more than thirty years ago appeared.

When Sanders flashed the screen at the General, he was surprised by the General's response. The General seemed to breathe more slowly and unclenched his hands before he knocked on the window.

The Major, glowering, rushed into the observation room. "What's wrong?"

"Be direct." The General nodded toward Sanders's computer screen.

The Major followed the order and was ruder than normal as he shoved computer screen images of Olsen in front of the SAVAK guard. The guard denied ever meeting Olsen. The two men stared at each other in an apparent stalemate.

Sanders decided it was time to overstep his authority. "If you don't take over this interview, I will."

The General sighed, ambled into the interrogation room, and put his hand on the guard's shoulder without ever looking directly at the Major or the guard. "We know you escaped through northern Iran into Turkey. Save us all a lot of unpleasantness. Give us the details." He sauntered back into the viewing room without waiting to hear an answer.

Meanwhile, Sanders adjusted his phone so Norm could hear everything. The SAVAK guard spoke rapidly, almost as if he was relieved to get a meaty question. Norm said several times, "Good, fits with Olsen's narrative."

Sanders felt his dull headache lessening until the Major returned to his typical unproductive questions. Norm muttered, "Odd. Why does the Major ask such dumb questions?"

The General scowled at the speakerphone each time Norm spoke. After the fifth "odd," the General said, "Turn him off. I have to send a message to the crews in Turkey preparing to meet F."

Sanders continued to listen to Norm's comments through an ear jack. It was comforting to know he wasn't the only one appalled by the Major.

Norm sucked in his breath. "I forgot the most important question. Ask whether the SAVAK guard ever met an attaché, probably military, from the Tehran embassy in the seventies, who called himself Bob."

Sanders felt like a fool. The General's middle name was Robert. He couldn't remember the General ever using his middle name, but wait... The teens who bought beer from him in college always asked for Bob.

He fiddled a bit with his phone, aimed, and emailed the image to Norm. The General seemed not to notice.

CHAPTER 14: Sanders is running out of time

"While Norm finishes up with Olsen, I want to do a reality check." Sara paused. "And to hear your voice."

"Reality checks are a good thing." Sanders wished the General would do one.

"I'm so tired, I hardly know which end is up. We're facing a deadline, but no one has any idea what will occur then. I've assumed F will be killed then. But how could someone predict F will be dead in thirty-six hours if Iranian Police don't have F already incarcerated. Could F have set the timeline? Why? I'm confused."

Sanders felt a twinge go up his left arm, but he didn't mention it to Sara. "Don't lose confidence in yourself. You're doing fine."

Sara's response was at a higher pitch than normal. "Two more items. Why did F mention my name if she — let's call F a she — plans to exit Iran through northern border with Turkey? Why not mention Olsen instead? He confirmed Farideh laid out the statistical testing grid for his fieldwork in graduate school. Two, why would F publicize her intended route by sending an uncoded message from Tabriz? Iranian police must be looking for her along the intended route already."

Sanders felt better knowing Sara was in her business mode. Alert and wary, but he wished she'd be a little romantic. "What are you trying to say?"

"Tabriz is a red herring. It's the only way the facts make sense. And, I think one of the characters in Madison is hiding important details. Honey, am I being paranoid?"

He decided to forget the "honey" and focus on her anxiety. "Trust your gut. I think someone here is intentionally slowing this investigation and perhaps not for an obvious reason." He lowered his voice. "The General is off-kilter. The Major can't be as inept as he seems. And Abid's note did say, "Trust your memory, not those in authority.""

"I figured you were doubting the General when you sent his picture. Unfortunately, Olsen failed to recognize him, or he was lying. Equally likely."

A twinge of pain shot through Sanders's chest. "Drat."

"I said worse. Olsen mentioned Bob had a Boston accent. As I remember, Danny seemed to almost tack an "r" onto some words, like idea, at the end."

"Mmm."

Sara spoke before he had a chance to say more. "I asked for a photo of Danny. Inge found a blurry shot in his application to the UW Grad School. Olsen blinked before he said, "I've never seen that guy." I'd give you two to one odds that he lied, but I wouldn't have recognized Danny in the photo either."

"Elvira must have photos."

"Exactly what I thought, but she claims she has no photos of Farideh, Souri, or Danny. Strange. Doc took photos of the group at his Christmas parties. From the looks of the closet, she saved everything else. And Elivra is... She's not normal."

"Explain." Sanders massaged his fingers, which felt tingly.

"Moody. Either she likes to play games or has a weak hold on reality. But Inge found no psychological exams in her medical records, even though the daughter says she's a hypochondriac." Sara sighed. "Then there's Olsen. He's probably angry, because the steroids, which he popped to build up his muscles, made him impotent."

Sanders coughed. "You don't like him."

"I'm only stating the obvious. I trust Baum, but he can't talk."

"I've got an idea. I'll check on Danny and Elvira with a couple of old friends."

"What?"

"Too early to say."

"Okay... Did you see Elvira's comments about Bushehr in Inge's notes? Sort of the forerunner of F's spying on nuclear facilities. Perhaps we're missing the obvious. F will go south through Doc's old stamping ground in Shiraz to the Persian Gulf coast to escape. Then it makes sense that my name was mentioned instead of Olsen's."

Sanders had scanned Inge's report, but nothing had clicked until now. "The port of Bushehr is about one hundred and fifty miles almost due east of Kuwait City across the Persian Gulf. Not an impossible trip. Sailboat could do it in eight hours with the right wind. Propelled boats could dart across in much less."

"Yes, but the port at Bushehr is probably well guarded because it's the site of Iran's biggest nuclear power reactor."

"True. I bet naval personnel at Al Udeid Air Base in Qatar could identify several accessible ports in Iran along the Persian Gulf."

"Why Al Udeid?"

"It's the hub of all American activities in the Persian Gulf." He coughed. "All I have to do is get the General to request their help. Hell, I'll... go over his head. The Commandant must know the General isn't performing well."

"Good luck. I'll study Doc's thesis and notes for any mention of towns along the coast. I bet Elvira knows the answer either consciously or subconsciously." Pause, "Sanders, I miss you. Somehow I feel safer when we talk."

He wished her feeling was reality.

***

Thirty minutes later, Sanders called Sara with a new piece in the puzzle. No answer. He called Norm.

"Oh, about fifteen minutes ago, she talked to Inge. Odd, she giggled a bit and rushed over to Elvira's house."

Sanders felt like a horse had kicked his chest, but he managed to yell, "Stop her. She's in danger."

CHAPTER 15: Sara makes a mistake

Sara almost tripped on all the black fabric surrounding her as she climbed the steep steps to the attic. FBI agents had been unable to quickly find a chador in Madison and had given her a more restrictive burqa, which covered all her face except her eyes. At least the burqa the FBI agents gave her was short.

The worst part about the burqa was how little she could see through the eyeholes. No, on second thought, the worst part was how claustrophobic and hot she felt. Neither she nor Inge was sure the "veiled lady" was the best method to pry secrets from Elvira, but Elvira had evaded all of Inge's questions. The other agents had yet to find any photos. They figured they didn't have anything to lose.

Near the top of the stairs, Sara stood motionless while Inge recited the rehearsed lines. "Elvira, look. Is that the veiled lady?"

Elvira turned white and trembled.

Sara disguised her alto voice with a high falsetto. "I won't leave until you give me pictures." She bounced a bit on the stair to make it creak.

Inge grabbed Elvira's arm. "Do you know which pictures she wants?"

Elvira let out a low moan. She pulled her arm from Inge's grip.

"I'll leave and never come back, when I get the pictures." Sara realized the routine was hokey and was sure her lack of experience as an actor was apparent. The snickers of two Madison Police officers on the stairs below confirmed her thoughts. She climbed another step.

Elvira shrieked and ran toward the white chest, not the closet. "Beirut." She took out a key from the drawer and unlocked the cabinet below. She tore the lid off one shoebox, and clawed through the contents of the box. "No, no," she screamed. She threw the box on the floor. Snapshots, mostly in color, scattered on the floor.

An FBI agent, who had been searching through boxes in the closet, lunged for the box and its contents. Inge looked ready to grab the next box.

Consistent with her role, Sara lifted her arms to shoulder height to extend the burqa to its fullest extent. "Get me the ones I want." Sara had no idea what was special about the photos from Beirut, but she figured Elvira had conjured a reason in her cloudy mind.

Elvira threw the lid off a second box onto the floor. She gave a little squeak and reached in.

Sara couldn't believe her eyes. Elvira was pointing a handgun straight at her. Instinct took over. She fell to her knees and slid down the stairs, but she couldn't go far because police officers were in the way. They pushed her forward until they saw the gun.

Elvira fired. Sara felt a searing hot pain in her left arm. She tumbled back and bounced on one stair, another, and one more before a police officer's body stopped her. Sara wasn't sure who fired the next shots. She was busy clawing her way out of the black fabric cocoon. Instead, she seemed to be more and more entwined in its folds. Getting hotter and hotter. Sweat poured out. Besides being hot and scared, she was damp.

All she saw was black. Gunshots, screams, and moans confused her further. As she pulled at fabric with her right hand, her fingers became sticky.

Finally, she saw light and heaved the heavy black fabric down the stairs. In the process, she bounced down two steps and looked up. The policeman, who had been immediately behind her, panted and held his shoulder as blood trickled between his fingers. Another officer knelt several steps above her and aimed his gun toward Elvira's previous location. Noises from the spot indicated the scuffle continued, but she couldn't see past the police officers. The high pitch screams suggested Elvira was alive.

Her first impulse was to be smart — forget about F and Elvira, crawl down the stairs, limp out the front door, hail a cab to the airport, and get back to Sanders and Bug. If the bullet had been several inches to the right, she'd be dead. Almost dead two times in a day. If misfortunes came in threes, she feared the next episode.

She mentally slapped herself and returned to practical thinking. She shouldn't distract the police. Better tend to her own first aid. Her sleeve was torn and stained red. The bullet must have hit her triceps. Hell, she was no anatomist. The red came from the fleshy part of her upper arm. She gingerly felt the area. It stung. She lifted the arm. Hurt like hell, but she could move it. Most likely, the bone wasn't broken. She wiggled her fingers. Doubtful any major nerve damage. She couldn't make and apply a tourniquet on her arm. The red area didn't seem to be growing much. Probably didn't need a tourniquet immediately.

Sara thought for a second, found her phone in her pocket, dialed nine-one-one, and yelled. "Shooting. Police injured."

An annoyingly calm voice said, "Police on the way to the Adams Street address. Stay on the line."

Repeated bangs on the front door. Weird sounds evidently at the door. The sounds of a crash and feet in hard-soled shoes racing across old, wooden floors, and up the stairs. Men in dark suits and uniformed Madison police streamed toward and around her. All the while, the wails from Elvira continued.

One EMT knelt by Sara. "Let's get you out of here."

"No, the photos are critical if we're going to save F. I've got to see them."

"Okay." As he examined her arm, he talked soothingly, probably to distract her. "Inge turned her phone to speaker mode as you started your routine." He snickered. "Don't quit your day job. We'd been in sooner, as soon as Sanders called, but the house was locked like Fort Knox. It took an axe to break down the door." He tied a white cloth tightly around her blood-splattered sleeve above the wound. "Think the bullet's gone. Probably will find it in the wall. Are you sure you can stand?"

Sara gulped. "We'll see. Pull me up." She felt light-headed, but was determined not to fail when they were so close to answers.

A paramedic ran up. "Wrong way."

"I have to see the photos from Beirut."

As the EMT helped Sara up the stairs, the wails stopped. She prayed Elvira was alive and could point out what was important in the photos in Beirut.

The scene would have been funny if the situation hadn't been so serious. Elvira had managed to shoot almost everyone in the room, but all the bodies were squirming, including Elvira. An FBI agent lay spread eagle on top of Elvira. When he moved slightly, Elvira flailed and screamed. A police officer was crumpled near the chest.

Blood was trickling from Inge's right lower leg, but she clearly was in charge of the situation. She motioned to the lead paramedic and pointed to the two men on the floor and one on the stair. "Those three are hurt the worst. Get them out." She waved her hand, clutching a stack of snapshots, toward Elvira. "Can you put her in some sort of straight jacket and not sedate her? We have to ask her questions and we can't take a delay. I don't think she was shot, only slugged in the gut when the man tackled her, after she kicked him repeatedly."

The lead paramedic medic nodded. "We came prepared. Sanders in Washington apprised us of her mental history — her nervous breakdown in Beirut in ninety-five."

Inge blinked. "I guess we pushed too hard." When she saw Sara, standing but with an EMT adjusting a rag tied around her arm, she motioned her forward. "Are you up to examining Elvira's snapshots?"

Sara waited until EMTs had strapped the hysterical Elvira and the wounded FBI agent and two police officers onto gurneys. The agent, who had tackled Elvira, appeared to be in the most pain and vomited repeatedly. Sara carefully negotiated a path around the victims as paramedics connected them to i.v. lines and whisked them down the stairs.

Inge flipped the photos to Sara. "The first one is a shot of people in front of grenade-blasted buildings and remnants of concrete structures. I can't identify the location, let alone anyone in the crowd. Of course, the occasional woman in a burqa suggests the Middle East, and the dress styles of women in Western garb suggest the nineties."

A paramedic examined Inge's wound and advised her surgery would be necessary. She ignored him.

Sara pointed to an ugly, tall shell of a concrete building in the photo. "This could be the old Holiday Inn in Beirut. It was a pockmarked reminder of the Lebanese Civil War in ninety-nine when I was there." She drew the picture closer. "Look at the man with the red, streaked with gray, hair. His shirt's half-unbuttoned. I think he's the focus of this image." She handed the photo back to Inge.

Sara flinched as a paramedic took the tourniquet off, cut the left sleeve off her blouse, wiped her arm with a disinfectant, and applied bandaging. "Clean flesh wound. Might be good to get a couple of stitches."

The paramedic, working on Inge, was less calm. He warned her again that she needed surgery to remove the bullet.

Inge ignored him as she sent an image of the first photo with Sara's comments to the General, her bosses in Washington, and Norm.

Sara examined the second photo. The same man was in this snapshot, but he was closer. "The sneer looks familiar. I think I've seen this man. Where?"

She examined the third photo. The man leaned against a woman in a modified burqa, more of a long black robe and black headscarf. She

J. L. Greger

wondered if this was F. "Look how he's got the woman pinned against the concrete wall and has his arms on both sides of her so she can't move. Seems like a dumb move in a Moslem area or the actions of a cocky jerk. Sorta reminds me... That's it... Could be Danny, twenty pounds heavier and a lot older. But I'm not sure."

Inge grabbed the third photo and relayed the image. She called Norm to see whether Olsen could identify the "Danny-look-alike."

Sara stared at the fourth image. The woman in the black headscarf was approaching whoever held the camera. Her face was thin, haggard. She leaned on a cane in one hand and held a small object in her right hand. "What's in the woman's hand? Better blow this up."

Sara gasped at the fifth photo. The woman pointed a revolver toward the camera. "No wonder Elvira's afraid of the veiled lady. Did she shoot Elvira?"

Inge drummed out messages on her tablet. She pointed to a Madison Police officer. "Get the paramedic to ask Elvira if she's ever been shot. Check her arms and legs for scars." She looked at Sara. "Now we have more questions than before. Who is this veiled lady? Why would she attack Elvira or Doc? Was it under Danny's orders? Where is the bastard?

"I thought Elvira during her ramblings mentioned the man from the embassy was in Washington once."

"Yes, I've already alerted other analysts of the possibility."

Sara suddenly felt a spasm in her arm. "We'd better get to the hospital soon, but in all this, I forgot. Sanders suspects the General has a secret, but...."

An analyst, who had hidden in the closet during the shooting and had continued to sort through memorabilia as the wounded were removed, yelled, "I've found the Christmas party photos. The right ones. I think I recognize you Sara." He smirked. "You looked pretty good then." He raced forward.

Sara pointed to a man and a woman in the photos. "Finally, good shots of Danny and Farideh, granted more than thirty-five years ago. Look how he has his arm draped over Farideh's shoulder, and she's scowling."

As Sara spoke, the analyst relayed the images electronically because EMTs were lifting Inge and Sara onto stretchers.

The paramedic who had questioned Elvira whispered in Inge's ear. She sighed. "Okay, time to take all of us, including Elvira, to the hospital." At the sound of her name, Elvira who was laying on a gurney at the foot of the stairs, began to howl again.

J. L. Greger

CHAPTER 16: Questions for Sara

The ambulance ride was relaxing, at least as compared to the rest of her day. Sara and one EMT were the only passengers in the vehicle because Inge, Elvira and the paramedics had been rushed to the hospital in the first ambulance. The peaceful interlude ended when the doors of the vehicle slammed open, and Norm began to fire unpleasant details and questions at her.

"Olsen choked when he saw the first two photos from Beirut, vomited as he looked at the third, and cried as he examined the last two. Then he claimed he didn't recognize the man or the woman." Norm took a breath. "Odd, don't you think?"

"Sanders and I talked before Inge and I hatched our plan. Perhaps someone is deliberately trying to slow this investigation down — a covert way to kill F."

Norm stepped back to text as the crew rolled the gurney from the ambulance. As they adjusted the wheels, he said, "Olsen is convinced he'll be killed within twenty-four hours, if he identifies the man in the snapshots. Any idea who's jerking his chain?" He studied her face.

Sara shrugged. "If I had any ideas, I'd tell you."

"I left a pretty young police officer probing him. Are you sure the man is Danny Blair?" Again, he peered at her suspiciously. "What would Danny have on Olsen?"

"No, I'm not sure, but it's a good working hypothesis. As to your second question, death threats probably sealed Olsen's lips."

"From whom?"

Sara stared in amazement at Norm. "I'm a consultant not a seer."

He nodded and pulled a sheet over her head. "Don't want anyone to recognize you during your ride through the hospital."

As Sara was rolled through the noisy emergency room, Norm ran alongside the gurney. "They're prepping Inge for surgery. Elvira's already in the psych lock-down unit with Olsen and Baum. Boy, that bird belongs there. And it's the safest place for you, too. No one thinks you're in danger, at least from Elvira's bullet. If you don't get a few stitches, you may have a bigger scar on your arm. No big deal."

Sara resisted making a comment until the gurney had bumped over a rough patch and she heard elevator doors close. "Hope you were gentler with Elvira than me."

"You betcha. I assigned a psychiatrist, who has queried terrorists, from the Wisconsin National Guard to handle her. Do you think Elvira is intentionally slowing the investigation? And we're all wasting our time?"

Sara thought Norm's unanswerable questions suggested he had lost faith in himself. "Think it's pretty obvious neither Inge nor I understand Elvira. I have no idea of her intent."

The elevator doors banged open. The gurney jiggled again as the crew raced along. They stopped and waited as doors swished open. The new area sounded busy with lots of different soft noises. More doors swished open. Silence. A nurse pulled the sheet off Sara's face and helped her move to a chair at a table in a patient room that had been converted to a makeshift office. Norm was already seated and studying his tablet.

"News update." Norm looked up from his screen. "Baum recognized the man in the photos. He hit the side rail on his bed repeatedly after his daughter showed him the photos from Beirut. She thought the pounding meant Danny was 'bad,' whatever that means."

"So, have they apprehended Danny in Washington?"

"No, but Sanders." He smirked. "He's your boyfriend, isn't he?" He peered at Sara for several seconds before he returned to tapping on his tablet.

She purposely didn't allow a change in her facial expression.

"Well anyway, details aren't clear, but Sanders requested embassy staff in Beirut check medical records at the American University of Beirut's hospital during the time of Doc's and Elvira's visit there in ninety-five. About the time you began your act for Elvira, he emailed me this psych report."

She perused four xeroxed pages of dense print that he shoved toward her. She shook slightly. "Inge and I wouldn't have pushed Elvira so hard if we'd known."

"Just as well. The psychiatrist says Elvira is singing like a bird now. Back to my point, how did Sanders know to look there?"

"I was a consultant at American University of Beirut, in ninety-nine. We both thought it was the best medical school in the Middle East — where you wanted to be treated if you became ill or injured anywhere in the Middle East."

"How did that come up in conversation?"

She wondered what he really wanted. "I don't know. Probably, when he queried me about why I was foolhardy enough to consult in Beirut and the United Arab Emirates. Or when we compared notes on Beirut. He was there before the civil war. You know the way couples talk."

Norm chuckled. "Not like that. Back to my question, how did he know to ask about hospital records at American University of Beirut?"

"The Major at the start thought Beirut was important. Elvira hinted interest in Beirut, too." Pause. "Like I said, its hospital is the best one in the Lebanon."

"That's all?"

She shrugged. "Logical guess."

Norm frowned. "Look at line thirty on page two. It's starred in the margin."

Sara read aloud, "American patient referred by Lieutenant Robert Daniels after emotional trauma of being threatened by someone with a gun." She shook her head. "Where's the medical report on Doc?"

"Embassy staff discovered an American couple, under the name of Steinhaus, were logged into the emergency room, but all records were lost, except for this psych report."

"The American University of Beirut lost a lot of their records during the civil war."

Norm glared at her. "Civil war ended in ninety."

She shrugged. What could she say except that she was weary and hungry. She forced herself to concentrate. She looked at the date on the file. "Typical psychiatrist. He filed his report two weeks after the shooting. If the other files were intentionally expunged, the perpetrator forgot, or didn't know, the medical and psychological reports would be separate."

Another man entered the room and whispered in Norm's ear. Both men stared at her.

She blinked. "I can tell my responses are disappointing you. What am I missing? Remember I've been on my feet for over twenty-four hours and almost killed twice."

"Read the starred sentence again."

She stopped this time at the words: *Lieutenant Robert Daniels.* "A man in a military uniform with a first name of Robert on his badge threatened Olsen in Iran and Turkey. Bob is the nickname for Robert. A man with the last name of Daniels might have a nickname of Danny. It also makes the other facts fit. Danny Blair's ineptness at statistics, and Doc's patience with him. Even the fiery interactions between Danny and Farideh. Gee, I'm slow today. Did Olsen know Danny and Bob were the same person before today?"

"We're working on that. The question is when did you know?"

She tensed. "Just now."

"Not before?"

"Guys, maybe I should have guessed sooner but, like I said, this has been a long day. I'm lucky to be alive."

"That's part of our confusion. You're too lucky." More whispering. "When do you think Sanders knew?"

Sara blinked. "He might not know. I doubt the General has shared everything with him."

"Are you sure? He found the medical report."

She shrugged. To be honest, she never knew how much Sanders knew. There was no reason to admit that detail.

Norm smirked. "Lot you don't know about Sanders Has he told you much about his past women friends. He moves on when they're no longer useful. Your projects in Bolivia and Cuba are about done."

"What?" His comments were insulting. "Sanders and I may not be a traditional couple, but we trust each other."

The second man spoke for the first time. "Probably, you shouldn't."

She liked being the investigator more than being a suspect or a victim. She wanted to cry, but she was too angry to give them the satisfaction. They were fishing, but for what?

She decided the best response was to state a few facts and reveal as little emotion as possible. "Sanders has more experience in the Middle East than you realize. He was posted to the embassy in Afghanistan for a few months in seventy-nine, but he was recalled to the U.S. after the U.S. ambassador to Afghanistan was kidnapped and killed."

"We know he's also traveled extensively in the region. Why did he contact the General?"

Sara returned their blank stares. "Why not? The General was his college roommate at Princeton. It's no secret that the General is an expert in counterintelligence and has responsibilities in the Middle East."

Norm leaned forward. "What would you say if I told you the General claims Sanders and you have slowed the investigation?"

"Impossible. We've cooperated fully." For a second, Sara debated whether she should blurt out her suspicions. Why not. "We think the General has been secretive and inexplicably slow."

"Why?"

Sara bit her lip. She needed to give good examples. "Endless, pointless questions to Abid and the SAVAK guard, but none about their contacts." Pause. "His trust of the Major, who manages to insult everyone needlessly." Pause. "Most importantly, his refusal to initiate a discussion with U.S. military in the Persian Gulf. Sanders thinks it could take several hours to get rescue ships and crews, at least appropriate ones, to ports on Iran's coast."

"Why does Sanders insist F will escape through a port on the Persian Gulf?"

"Me. F would have mentioned Olsen, not me, if she planned to escape through Tabriz. Olsen knows lots of details about that route; I know nothing."

Norm shook his head. "I agree with General Purcell. I don't think I'd bother looking for F at random ports."

They were trying and succeeding at provoking her. She counted to ten. "Like I said, Sanders thought the General was hiding something. He didn't give details, except he suspected the General might have supervised Bob or whatever you want to call him at some time because they both worked out of the embassies in Tehran and Beirut." Pause, "Of course, that was before Elvira's photos were uncovered."

"So, he suspected Danny and Bob were the same person all along."

"I doubt it, but ask him."

"Anything to add?"

"I'd like a Diet Coke, a sandwich, and, oh, a chance to see the rest of the photos from Beirut in Elvira's attic."

Both men walked out the room. Sara tried the door. It was locked.

CHAPTER 17: Sanders feels time slipping away

Sanders had forgotten to take his Prilosec. He hoped heartburn was the reason for the twinges in his chest. He figured better late than never and swallowed the pill with a swig of coffee.

The General had refused to contact anyone at Al Udeid, the U.S. air base near Doha, Qatar, and stormed out of the viewing room. Sanders called his boss, explained his fears and requested she set up a virtual meeting with the Marine Corps Commandant, FBI brass, and pertinent military types at Al Udeid to discuss plans for extracting F from Iran. His boss wasn't enthused, but said she'd get back to him within fifteen minutes.

While he waited, he studied maps of the Persian Gulf and surfed the Web for data. The Major had stopped questioning the SAVAK officer, and now suited individuals, probably FBI agents, were talking to the SAVAK officer on the other side of the mirrored window. They had turned off the sound system.

The northernmost port on the gulf in Iran was Khorramshahr. The city was deserted in eighty after a battle in the city during the Iran-Iraq War, but the city was now a shipbuilding and repair facility for the Iranian Navy. Nearby was another port mainly of interest because it was at the terminus of the Trans-Iranian Railway, linking the Persian Gulf and the Caspian Sea. He doubted F would choose to go to these locations because they were a six- to an eight-hour drive from Shiraz, but he guessed U.S. military in Iraq could retrieve her easily from this area.

As far as he could see, there were no other major Iranian ports on the Persian Gulf coast as you moved south until you reached Bandar Bushehr, the site of a nuclear power plant and an international airport. It was about a three- to a four-hour hour drive from Shiraz and about one hundred, fifty miles due east of Kuwait City. He suspected this was where F was headed for two reasons. She obviously knew the area, judging from her previous leaks on the nuclear facilities on Bushehr. It was also a site Doc and Elvira had explored. But he had no idea where F

J. L. Greger

would go in Bushehr. He hoped Sara would extract some helpful tidbit from Doc's papers, but he guessed the task was impossible.

Kharg Island, an important oil export facility, was near Bushehr. It wasn't obvious how tourists would get from Bushehr to Kharg Island, but he guessed a dhow carrying fish could slip easily in and out of the port.

The next port of interest was Bandar Abbas, right across from Oman at the Strait of Hormuz. It was the headquarters for the Iranian navy and a railroad terminus with an international airport. Nearby in the strait were three islands. Larak Island was an oil export point and the site of a military base with few other residents. He doubted F would try to escape through Larak.

The other two islands nearby appeared to be the best exit points for F. Kish Island was a glitzy resort with free trade zone status. Qeshm Island had a flourishing ecotourism industry, especially among bird watchers, and was a UNESCO-recognized geopark. At least one biblical scholar had claimed Qeshm was the site of the Garden of the Eden. Sanders suspected that brought other tourists. Most of the hundred thousand residents were employed in fishing and dhow repair. He conjectured F and members of an extraction team could use a variety of excuses to travel around Qeshm. However, the island was rumored to have an underground military facility to house submarines on its southeast corner. The military presence on the island might be high.

Sanders scanned his maps until the Major entered the observation room. Sanders looked at his watch and suppressed his anger. He'd called his boss almost an hour before. It wasn't like her to not deliver as she promised. Time was running out to extract F and her package from Iran. He'd been wasting his time. Anyone familiar with the Persian Gulf ports in Iran could quickly supply all the data he'd extracted and a lot more in a couple of minutes.

The Major, smiling like a Cheshire cat, said, "They're ready for you now."

As he trailed the Major out of the bowels of Marine Barracks to the spacious conference room on the second floor, he guessed his boss had precipitated this meeting. He choked when he looked around the room. The General sat at the head of the table next to a tanned man with a buzz cut of his thin graying hair. Sanders recognized him as the Marine Corps Commandant and thought he had fairly recent experience in Afghanistan. Other uniformed officers sat across the table from the door. His boss sat with her back to him in a line of suited individuals.

The Major shoved him toward a seat next to his boss and left. Before he was seated, she said, "The General claims you have hampered the extraction of F from Iran. He claims your judgment has been clouded by your infatuation for Sara Almquist."

"Not true." Sanders remained standing.

"Sit down and listen. What we, as a group, must decide is whether your suggestions are valid. I'll deal with other issues later."

Several men at the table nodded, and the General smirked. However, Sanders noted the Commandant showed no emotions as he gazed intently at him.

The Commandant asked the General to present his argument for thinking F would follow the path from Tabriz used by several SAVAK agents in the early eighties. The General told of the email message, but omitted mention of the sentence, "Contact Almquist," until the Commandant reminded him of the detail. He never mentioned Sara's trip to Madison. Mainly, the General emphasized his expertise in Iranian affairs, and Sanders' lack of recent experience in the Middle East.

After two minutes, the Commandant asked, "Have you gained any data since your last written report thirty minutes ago?"

The General finally lost the grin of a used car salesman. "The SAVAK officer and Abid have been uncooperative, but in another hour…"

The Commandant turned to Sanders. "You captured Abid outside your home. Was he recalcitrant?"

Sanders realized his whole career was in jeopardy. More importantly, the U.S. was about to lose F, an important contact in Iran, if he was right. He hid his fear with a well-practiced cold stare. "No, he was afraid, but he mentioned that a young lieutenant had overlooked his background when he defected in Beirut in the early eighties. I believe the lieutenant in Beirut was General Purcell."

Sanders thought he heard several men at the table breathe more rapidly. The Commandant and his boss seemed unfazed.

The Commandant gazed at Sanders. "In two minutes, tell us why you think F will try to exit Iran via Shiraz on her way to the Iranian coast on the Persian Gulf. We have all your and Almquist's reports and emails of the last twenty-four hours."

"Then you know the only logical reason to mention Almquist was to direct attention to Doc Steinhaus, and that means sites like Bushehr and Beirut. There have been two attempts on Sara's life in the last twenty-four hours. A known terrorist ransacked her house. Obviously, someone thinks she's an important clue."

A man in a black suit spoke, "FBI agents in Madison and Ulysses Howe in our Albuquerque office have given us detailed reports. Skip those details."

"Okay. The problem with our theory is Sara and I can't figure out which port F will try to use. I suspect…

"Just a second." The Commandant pushed a button and spoke into the mouthpiece suspended in front of his face. Two officers in short sleeve shirts appeared on a large screen at the front of the room. One wore Navy white; one wore Marine khaki. The Commandant said, "We're joined by officers from Al Udeid. They have been monitoring F's messages and have seen all the data." He motioned to Sanders. "Continue with your comments."

Sanders thought for a second. "Sara Almquist and I think F sent messages from Tabriz as a diversion. She will try to escape through an Iranian port along the Persian Gulf, probably Bushehr, Kish or Qeshm." He motioned toward the tanned officers on the screen. "You can make better guesses than I can."

When he said "Qeshm," the officers on the screen became animated. One, with Meyers on his name tag, immediately said, "Not Bushehr, the Iranians are afraid we'll blow up their nuclear facility. Security is tight. If I wanted to get out of Iran, I'd go to Qeshm. Entrepreneurs in Oman have speedboats leaving Khasab in Oman for Qeshm dozens of times every day."

"Would Iranians, say university-types, know about this transport system?" When everyone gave Sanders a blank look, he added. "I think F is apt to be employed at a university because she, or he, seems to have access to data about nuclear facilities and often includes technical details in her reports."

Meyers replied, "We see wealthy Iranians shopping in the Emirates all the time. Generally, we don't see small ships sail from the major cities in the Emirates to Iran, instead we see trucks haul merchandise from Abu Dhabi and Dubai to the forlorn town of Khasab and full jet boats speed to Iran. We know the smugglers bribe the Iranian patrols along the Iranian coast. Yes, middle and upper class Iranians know about this crack in our embargo."

The naval officer said, "Yep, it's no secret to Iranians."

The Commandant pushed a button. The screen went blank.

A man in a black suit said, "Mr. Sanders, who is Lieutenant Robert Daniels?"

Everyone peered at him. The General flashed a smile from ear to ear. The same smile that he flaunted in his student days when he was about to lie.

"I don't know." Sanders felt sweat drip down his forehead. His career and future were on the line. "Wait… his name was on the psychiatrist report I received from the American University of Beirut."

Sanders' boss tapped his thigh as she spoke to the General. "Why don't you tell us about him. I believe he reported to you first in Iran and then in Beirut."

The General shook slightly, even as he smirked.

"I'm waiting." The Commandant pushed his chair back slightly so he could study the General.

Sanders looked around the table. He felt like sighing. For the first time in the last ten minutes, no one glared at him. Everyone eyed the General. He was sure his boss hadn't made a pass when she tapped his thigh. She was signaling he'd passed the test.

The General silently examined his watch.

The Commandant nodded to a woman Marine colonel. The colonel straightened a pile of papers. "We know Robert Daniels served under you in Tehran and Beirut. You granted him a nine-month leave of absence to attend the University of Wisconsin-Madison under the alias of Danny Blair in seventy-eight and early seventy-nine. As a private contractor, he made frequent trips to the Beirut, Ankara, and Cairo during the last thirty years. You authorized payment for several, including trips to Beirut in ninety-five and ninety-nine."

"Do you deny any of these facts?" The Commandant maintained a noncommittal look on his face.

The General shrugged and looked at his watch.

The colonel continued, "Robert Daniels seems to have disappeared about twenty hours ago." She peered at the General. "We've checked all your emails and calls."

The General remained relaxed.

"We found, with your secretary's help, a phone in her garbage. Interesting usage. Not a new phone, phone number, or email address. All had been used once, a year ago." The colonel's eyes seemed to bore into the General. "Until a lot of usage in the last two days."

The General stopped smiling.

"You received emails from Tabriz forty-six hours and twenty-six hours ago. The first email was also sent to the SAVAK guard, whom Major Jones questioned unsuccessfully for over six hours. Seems the Major never thought to ask to see the guard's phone. The FBI did."

The General looked at his watch. "Major Jones sometimes forgets details, but his heart is in the right place."

"I see." The colonel smiled slightly. "The second email was sent to several addresses and triggered the search for Almquist. You made a call on your discarded phone about twenty hours ago to an untraceable phone in Maryland."

Several men at the table cleared their throats.

"I never lied. I... I may not have mentioned certain details. Robert Daniels, using one of his many aliases, left Washington for Iran about thirteen hours ago. He's the only one who can extract F, but he works best alone. By now, he should be in the Middle East."

Sanders noticed the Commandant was unfazed by the revelation. Either he already knew Robert Daniels was in the Middle East or was a good poker player. "Will he go to Tabriz?"

"I doubt it. I don't try to prescribe actions to him, only outline the problem." The General seemed proud of his management style as he looked at individuals around the table.

"Where will he go?" The Commandant's voice remained soft.

"Don't know."

"Stop the semantics. Where do you guess he'll go?"

"The Emirates, either to Abu Dhabi or Dubai."

The Commandant's voice was slightly more strident. "And then where?"

"Khasab. He wanted to get there before American officers. Otherwise, the smugglers will balk, and we'll lose F."

The Commandant's voice was again soft, but the speed of the questions was quickening. "So, you think you saved F?"

The General grinned. "That's what you wanted."

"Look at these materials. We found them in a safe in Robert Daniels's Maryland condo." The colonel pushed compromising photos of several scantily clothed women toward the General. Many of the images were old Polaroid shots. Across a black-and-white one, which looked like it had been wadded up and then smoothed out, was written, "Bastard."

The General winced. "I don't ask how he gets foreign nationals to cooperate. In our business," he emphasized the our, "the most effective individuals have a few quirks."

A woman in a dark suit, probably an FBI agent, spoke. "All the reports from Madison indicate this Robert Daniels, aka Danny Blair, terrorized everyone. In fact, a Dr. Baum, who's on his deathbed, helped FBI agents find a copy of a letter from him to you. In seventy-nine, he demanded Robert Daniels be removed from the Madison campus or he'd leak the story to the Madison newspaper, the *Capitol Times*. Afterwards, he refused all assignments…"

The Commandant raised his voice. "Let's not worry about history now, but rather on extracting F out of Iran alive."

The woman pushed a faded, color Polaroid of a dark-haired, naked woman, reaching for a towel, toward the General. "Do you know who this woman is?"

"One of Daniels's many contacts. Photo looks old, from a vintage camera and film. Probably too old and cloudy to be of much use."

"Don't bet on it. We compared photos, which Sara Almquist and agents in Madison uncovered at great personal expense, to this and the rest of Robert Daniels's photos."

Sanders shivered at that comment, but recognized he couldn't ask any questions about Sara now.

"Amazing what computers can do." The woman tapped her manicured pink fingernails on the table. "We're seventy percent certain the woman in this blurry snapshot, dated August eighty-two, is Farideh Hossein."

Sanders gasped. "So Farideh survived torture in Iran after the Ayatollah Khomeini came to power, as Doc guessed."

The woman glared at him.

"Sorry to interrupt. But that's an important clue."

The agent waved her hand. "I'm glad you appreciate its significance." She and the colonel lined up more images of naked and scantily clad women in front of the General and made comments on each one.

Sanders thought the comments were vague, except the name Souri was mentioned once.

As he looked at each successive photo, the General seemed to shrink in his seat. On the last photo, someone had written, "Bitch, I'll kill your son if you fail again." The General puffed his chest. "These are

J. L. Greger

fakes. You're testing me. No one in their right mind would keep a photo with an incriminating comment."

The woman FBI agent picked up the last photo. "Also dated eighty-two. We think the same woman as in the earlier shot."

The Commandant said softly. "Do you think Robert Daniels is unbalanced and wants to kill F, not extract her?"

The General paled. His wide grin had been replaced by a nervous twitch of one eye.

Sanders remembered that as an undergrad the General developed the twitch when he'd been caught in a lie. It was also the only time he lost his glib tongue. Sanders knew he had only a few seconds to get an honest answer when he leaned toward the General. "Why did you send Sara to Madison?"

"Had to keep her out of Iran. Robert Daniels warned me she could identify him, Farideh, and others."

"Did you alert terrorists of her trip?"

Almost everyone at the table gasped. The General gave his usual grin and shook his head.

Sanders thought a few seconds. "Okay. Did you send uncoded emails about her trip to your staff and others?"

Several people around the table coughed and nodded. The General pretended to be puzzled.

"You knew terrorists and operatives were following your emails."

The General shrugged, but his eye twitched again. "Suppositions on your part. Why do you care? You'll be tired of Sara soon, just like all your other lady friends."

The Commandant stood and looked around the room. "Let's stop wasting time. I see no reason for our guests from the State Department to endure more of this discussion. Mr. Sanders, please accept my apology for this rough interrogation, but the Assistant Secretary and I thought neither you nor the General should know our new findings before the discussion." He nodded to her. "She was sure you were a straight arrow."

As they reached the door, the Commandant added, "You should listen to the tape of the FBI's interrogation of Sara Almquist when this situation is resolved. She never wavered in her defense of you. Personally, I think she was grilled harder than you. She's a keeper."

The door closed.

Sanders wiped sweat off his forehead. "What's next?"

His boss propelled him forward. "You join a discussion with the officers at Al Udeid."

"Is Sara all right?"

"She received a flesh wound. Others were hurt worse, but all survived."

J. L. Greger

CHAPTER 18: Time flying by for Sara

Sara's wound had continued to seep a bit, so a nurse stitched it. Less than ten minutes later, Norm bounced back into the locked room in the psych ward. "You passed. So, did I." He handed her a can of Diet Coke.

"What are you talking about?" Sara gulped the soda.

I'll tell you when we get out of here." He yanked her from the chair, threw her coat over her shoulders, and pushed her down the hallway and through locked doors. Two uniformed Madison Police officers stepped in front of them and two uniformed campus security officers behind them as they passed out of the ward.

Sara felt petulant, probably because she was hungry, tired, and confused by the earlier interrogation. "Where are you taking me? Tell me now."

"You know, patience is a virtue." Norm snickered as his own comment. "I always wanted to see what was under the steely shell of professors like you." He began to whistle "On Wisconsin" as the group trouped into an elevator.

Sara decided to play his game. At least she could keep him from whistling off key. "What's under my steel shell?"

"More steel." He resumed whistling. Two of the police officers snickered.

"Why did you want to know?"

"Why not?

"You tormented me for no reason?"

"Of course not." He pushed her off the elevator onto the main floor. "Don't talk."

The group fell into formation. They almost ran as the officers listened to directions through their earphones and made one word replies. Two unmarked police sedans were parked at a back entrance of the hospital. Norm shoved Sara into the back seat of one and jumped into the front seat as the car roared off. The Madison police officers bounded into the second car.

Déjà vu. Sara prayed this trip would be less eventful than the one that began at O'Hare. "Where are we going?"

No reply. Norm looked straight ahead and whispered into his mouthpiece. The driver carried on a separate, quiet conversation, too.

Sara wondered whether she was about to be arrested. For what? "I have rights. Where am I going?"

They raced east down University Avenue past campus buildings.

"Just a sec." He said more softly into his mouthpiece, "What can I tell her?" After thirty seconds, he said "Roger," and turned to Sara. "Sorry about the grilling. Seems the General claimed you and your boyfriend were purposely trying to prevent the extraction of F from Iran. They told me to reduce you to tears to get at your motives."

Sara couldn't resist. "Sanders was better at it in Bolivia. He concluded I was a nosy do-gooder, who saw too many action movies."

The driver choked a cough. Norm shook his head. "Talk about tough love. Wouldn't want to see one of your lovers' spats." Pause, "I... actually the FBI bigwigs, listening to our earlier discussion, decided you were our best chance to get F and her secrets out of Iran. 'Course, Inge and Ulysses Howe already told them to trust you over the General. They're putting Sanders through his paces now in order to trip up the General."

"Oh dear. Is Sanders in on the plan?"

"Nope, military brass and FBI bigwigs will give him the third degree too."

A tear streaked down Sara's cheek. "What a sorry mess."

"You finally cry. I might have gotten upgraded if I could have gotten you to cry in front of witnesses." He laughed.

Sara wiped away the tear. "Where are we going?"

"First to Washington. Somebody in the State Department pulled some strings and called a friend. We'll fly on a private corporate jet. First time for me. Told them we were hungry and wanted more than McDonald's hamburgers."

"Good. How about a pizza from Lombardino's?"

"You're behind the times. Lombardino's is closed, but I ordered us pizza from a new hot spot, Salvatore's Tomato Pies." He scanned his tablet. "The bigwigs say you should try to sleep on this flight because your next location might be less comfortable."

"First, update me on Inge, Elvira and the crew."

"Last I heard Inge was in surgery."

"Hope she doesn't end up with a permanent limp."

Norm nodded. "Elvira is talking up a storm, but saying nothing important. Mainly raving the veiled lady wanted to kill her, so she could have Doc. I saw the pictures of Doc. Don't think Elvira needed to worry."

"Poor Elvira. I assume the FBI considers her a dead end now. Are agents still analyzing the contents of her attic?"

"Yep to both. Real treasure trove." The cars pulled off University Avenue and were in sight of the Dane County Regional Airport.

"What about Baum? I wished I could have spent more time with him."

"His daughter and two analysts are playing charades with him. Seems he had a stash of papers too, but his were in one box and better organized than Elvira's." He shook his head. "Hard to believe now, but he was one of our best authorities on Iran in the seventies and eighties. I don't have the patience to interview old geezers like him."

Sara laughed. "You'll get old too."

***

An hour after take-off, the co-pilot handed Sara his headphones. "A man, calling himself the Marine Corps Commandant, wants to talk to you. We verified his code." He leaned over to Norm and said more softly. "She doesn't look important."

Norm smirked. "Agreed, but she is today."

Sara was laughing when a brisk voice said, "Dr. Almquist, I hope you'll accept this assignment. Robert Daniels appears to have gone rogue. We think he plans to kill F before we can extract her and the documents she's carrying. We will fly you from Joint Base Andrews in Maryland to Al Udeid Air Base near Doha, Qatar."

"Why me?"

"You're the only able-bodied, non-criminal, who has ever met what we believe to be the key characters."

"So, you've hit bottom. What about the General?"

The Commandant coughed. "He's finally cooperating, but cannot leave the barracks, and his subordinate Major is also under investigation."

"I don't want to be difficult, but this assignment is potentially too hard and dangerous to put up with any more secrets."

"Understood. Unfortunately, we're a little short-staffed." Paused. "Staff from the FBI, State Department, Marine Corps, and Navy will send details to Norm Budzinski if you agree to this assignment."

"Won't I get there too late?" She waited only a second. "And I doubt I'll be of much use. The last time I saw Robert Daniels and Farideh Hossein was over thirty-five years ago. I…"

"You have knowledge and… traits we need. Sanders will accompany you."

Sara gave a sigh of satisfaction and then gasped. "Who'll take care of Bug?" Sara was surprised that she'd blurted the question out, but it was important to her.

The Commandant coughed. "I'd been told the dog would be your greatest concern. Sanders's assistant will take him to the kennel, which he used when you went on a previous assignment for the State Department with Sanders. Will you take this assignment?"

Sara wanted to go to bed for eight hours with Bug curled up beside her, or better yet with Sanders and Bug. She didn't want to fly to Qatar. She'd had enough adventures for this week, or month, or year. "Yes, but I reserve the right to refuse to enter Iran. Remember I'm no military commando, just a nosy epidemiology professor turned helpful consultant."

More coughs. "My assistant has sent Agent Budzinski details in code, and he will answer all your questions."

The phone went dead. Sara handed the headphone to the co-pilot and looked at Norm. "Have you decoded anything yet?"

Norm looked up from his tablet. "Don't rush me." After a few seconds, "Like touch screens better for games than for documents. This one is a complicated. Darn. No." He continued to curse and yell "no" for several minutes.

Sara put her seat in a reclining position. Norm would wake her after he decoded her instructions. She was drifting off when he said, "I'm surprised you're not taking your dog along."

Sara rubbed her eyes. "You remind me of several of my students. Always with smart answers." Pause, "You particularly resemble one, but he kept his head shaved, had a floppy mustache, and wore two nose rings. I think he called himself Bud."

Norm eyed her. "About time. I was one of your students in introductory epidemiology at Michigan State about ten years ago. You were a hard ass." He rubbed his tablet keypad furiously. "But I learned a lot. Loved your tales on field work in epidemiology. That's one reason I figured you could do this from the start. Field work in epidemiology is pretty similar to a crime investigation."

CHAPTER 19: Sara leaves for Al Udeid twenty hours before the deadline

Sara could feel Norm's hand on her back, pushing her up the stairs of a private jet bound for Qatar. She didn't think she was that slow. She decided not to grouse because he meant to be helpful, not irritating. Well, maybe. At least, she'd soon be able to talk to Sanders. Together they'd figure out what to do.

Sara expected Sanders would greet her at the door. Instead, Sanders's boss stood in the galley. Sara had met her several times before. In the back, three men sat in what looked like gray leather recliners. One with his gray hair in a buzz cut seemed to ignore his colleagues and focused on the two women at the front of the plane, but he remained seated.

"There's two changes of clothes in the case." Sanders's boss pointed to a suitcase, which Sara recognized as the one she'd left unpacked in her room a day ago.

"Thanks. Where's Sanders?"

"He not going." His boss clasped her hands in front of her and looked more like a nervous church soloist than an Assistant Secretary of State. "He's too tired."

Sara suddenly felt heat rise up her neck. "What aren't you telling me? I won't go until I see him." She stepped back, but Norm pushed her forward.

The official raised her hands into a more prayer-like position. "His chest pains during last eight hours weren't indigestion, like he thought."

Sara fell sideways slightly to lean against the closet. She gasped for air. "Is... is he alive?" She felt sweat bead up on her upper lip.

"He's at NIH Clinical Center awaiting bypass surgery."

"He needs me." Sara turned to leave. Norm grabbed her good arm and turned her around.

Sanders's boss spoke rapidly now. "He thought you'd say that. Wouldn't let them anesthetize him until he talked to you. She picked up a phone from a nearby table, fumbled, and handed it to Sara.

Sanders's voice was low and dull. "Sara, complete this mission. I'm sorry, but I can't..."

"Honey, I won't desert you when you need me. Why didn't you tell me?"

He sighed. "Hoped I was imagining problems. You had enough of your own."

"I could be at the hospital in less than an hour. So, I could be there when you came out of surgery."

"No, go. My daughter is here. I love you."

Sara whispered, "Sanders fight to live. I'll get back to you as fast as I can. Love you."

The phone went dead.

She wanted to cry, but couldn't. There was really nothing useful she could do for Sanders. His daughter, a law student, as his closest relative would make any decisions anyway. A wave of heat went up her neck, and her temples seemed to vibrate. Worst of all, she felt nauseated. "I'm not sure I can do this." She stepped forward and dropped into a roomy seat, lowered her head and massaged her forehead. "This is an impossible trip alone. Everyone I trust is in a hospital, Sanders and Inge, or too far away, Ulysses Howe and Gil Andrews."

"I'll go along." Norm beamed.

"Way beyond your pay grade." Sanders's boss motioned for him to leave and sank into the recliner next to Sara. "We have a solution. The Commandant will accompany you. It's his way of apologizing for not removing General Purcell from this investigation sooner."

She waited for Sara to respond.

Sara emitted low groans.

"He thought we needed a fast plane that afforded more privacy than a standard military transport. Due to peculiarities in law, I can authorize the use of these more expensive jets if a Congressional delegation is on board. I found two of the more discreet senators from the defense appropriation committee. They wanted to see Al Udeid and, I suspect, have a chance to kibitz with the Commandant for several hours."

Sara remained bent over her lap. "Too little, too late."

The man with the buzz cut approached. Sara noted he wore the khaki shirt and tie and green trousers of the Marine Corp. "Hi, I'm Joe."

He grabbed Sara's hand with a firm shake. "We'll have plenty of time to rescue F. This baby is fast and I guarantee we'll get cleared immediately." He turned. "Madam Secretary, it's time for you to leave." He moved forward to talk to the pilots.

Sara stood and walked Sanders's boss to the door. "Keep me informed, no matter what. Worry and anticipation are worse than bad news."

She hugged Sara and almost bounded off the plane as the engines were revved. A Marine corporal slammed the door shut and announced, "Take a seat."

The Commandant slid into the seat next to Sara's. "As soon as we're off, officers at Al Udeid, led by Captain Meyers, will get you, actually both of us, up to speed. Shame Sanders isn't here. He's the one who talked the most to Meyers."

Sara's head ached. She could smell her own sweat. She understood she should try to be pleasant, but couldn't muster the energy. "Any chance I could clean up and change clothes."

"After our initial update."

Sara forced a weak smile.

"You can also chat with the senators. I warned them you might want to reserve your strength for the tasks ahead. They aren't cleared for all the details of our mission, but that's more a theoretical than a real problem. You don't have to be careful in conversation around them."

Sara nodded as the jet roared down the runway. The plane had hardly cleared the city when a screen dropped down in front of her. A naval officer in summer whites and a Marine captain in a short sleeve khaki shirt appeared.

"Sir, we received news five minutes ago." The Marine captain, probably around forty, fumbled with a computer in front of him. "F, or at least someone signing as F, sent another email from Tabriz. Different location. We think an open access computer in a library at the Tabriz University of Medical Sciences. 'I'll recognize Almquist.' is the message."

Sara gasped.

"Anything else?" said the Commandant.

"Yes, sir. We're perplexed. If F is in Tabriz, he or she must plan to take the northern route to Turkey and use Kurds as guides." He stared at Sara. "My apologies, Ma'am, in not acknowledging you. I'm Captain Tom Meyers, call me Meyers." He turned his focus to the Commandant. "Almquist isn't needed if F takes the northern route.

However, F apparently recognizes we have no way of identifying her at an Iranian port. I think F will go south."

Sara sighed. She had to stop thinking about Sanders and focus on this mission. "How is F so sure she'll recognize me?"

"Probably through internet images." Meyers paused. "You look like your picture on the website for the Department of Epidemiology at Michigan State."

"Mmm. F wouldn't know I looked the same. She must have seen me sometime in the last ten years or so? Both the General and Elvira mentioned Beirut. I was there in ninety-nine and again in two thousand-nine."

The officer, his mouth open, poked at a computer keyboard. The Commandant studied his tablet.

Sara figured they were communicating by emails to exclude her. This was not the time for paranoia. "No basis for that guess. Just trying to give you details that might be important."

The Commandant looked up. "Assume F based the comment on more than a photo. Proceed with our plans to greet F on the coast, but alert Incirlik Air Base in Turkey."

"Sir, they deployed vehicles to get to Van almost nine hours ago per General Purcell's orders. It's the closest city in Turkey to Tabriz. A distance of one hundred sixty miles. They report they'll be in Van in less than an hour. Kurds with several of our Marine advisors will be sent on to likely locations near the border. They should be in place in two hours. Do you want to change their orders?"

"No. Let's keep up the charade."

Sara strove to concentrate on the discussion but lapsed into thoughts about Sanders, Bug, and her home in New Mexico. She mentally shook herself because she knew this mission could fail if she didn't get control of herself. She forced herself to stare at the screen and promised herself to re-evaluate her activities after this mission was over. "I've been thinking. Maybe, F isn't one person but a team."

Both men stopped studying their computers. The stone-faced Commandant blinked twice.

"On the flight from Madison, I reviewed examples of data F relayed out of Iran over the last thirty years with a couple of FBI analysts. We thought F could be two or even several individuals. It's unlikely that Farideh Hossein as an epidemiologist would have access to engineering plans for nuclear facilities, unless her husband wasn't executed in seventy-nine or eighty, as believed."

Meyers spoke, "The analysts shared your thoughts with us. FBI agents grilled Farideh Hossein's sister, who never returned to Iran after her student days. The sister insisted Farideh's husband was executed, but admitted she occasionally gets unsigned postcards. She saved them. All but one were from Iran. That one, postmarked in ninety-nine, was from Beirut. The last card with a photo of a qanãt arrived about a month ago and was postmarked from Yazd."

Sara rubbed her temples. Were they trying to confuse her. She didn't know what a qanãt was? Where was Yazd? Why did Meyers mention them. She noted the lines on the Commandant's tanned faced rippled around his mouth as he tapped out a note. What secrets were they withholding now? Gee, she needed Sanders to explain what she was missing. She shook her head. It was probably best to ignore these details now.

"Okay, the other possibility is: F is a conglomerate of women, probably educated in the U.S., who survived torture or their husband's execution. The FBI analysts and I thought women and men, who weren't family members, were unlikely to collaborate because discussion between the genders would arouse suspicion."

Meyers nodded. "We liked that suggestion from you and the FBI analysts. Other agencies recombed their records on the trials and executions of American-educated scientists during the Iranian Revolution and its aftermath. We looked for information on women nuclear engineers and physicists released from prison. I'll supply you with photos of some of these women later."

Sara pursed her lips. "Another thought. Did you see the photo of what could be Farideh on which Robert Daniels wrote, 'Bitch, I'll kill your son' or something like that?"

"We did," said Meyers. The Commandant's lips twitched as he typed on his tablet.

"The photo was dated August in eighty-two. That son, if alive, would be in his thirties now. He could be F or part of the team." She paused. "Doc hid Elvira's participation in his spying activities from Robert Daniels. The incident in Beirut in ninety five suggests Daniels was angry when he found out. Anyway, it suggests Daniels isn't all-knowing and might not know fully who F is."

The naval officer on the screen spoke for the first time. "Glad you said that. We were wondering about that possibility, too. How well do you know Daniels?"

Sara sighed. "Not well, but I did identify him in the Beirut photos."

"Would he recognize you?"

"I don't know."

The Commandant didn't even look up. "Assume he would. Forget that idea. Back to F."

The naval officer faded back from the screen a bit.

Sara was uncomfortable about the undercurrent conversation, but decided to charge ahead. "I was thinking about Olsen's comments. Norm may not have forwarded this tidbit. Think he'd left the room. Olsen noted both Doc and Mickelson died overseas. He suspected Robert Daniels might have killed them."

The naval officer disappeared from the screen, and the Commandant leaned forward. Meyers gulped, "Are you suggesting we may be able to charge Robert Daniels with the murder of two Americans?"

"Remember Elvira claimed a veiled woman with Robert Daniels shot at her in ninety-five. Elvira said Doc died of a heart attack in Beirut in ninety-nine. Lots of ways to induce one. Probably drug residues would be missed in a fast, foreign autopsy."

The Commandant's lips twitched. "Meyers, I think we can allow Sara access to all records." He handed her his tablet. "We were concerned the stress of this extended investigation was too much for you, especially without Sanders. But he was convinced you'd bounce back within an hour. He was wrong." He looked at his watch. "You bounced back in less than a half-hour. Here's the next big question."

Sara read the title of the email, "Where is Robert Daniels?"

CHAPTER 20: Lt. Steve Nasi at Al Udeid in Qatar

Lieutenant Steve Nasi was the son of an oilman and had been raised in a series of oil towns in the Southwest — Artesia, Odessa, Carlsbad, and Farmington. When he was assigned to the Marine intelligence unit at Al Udeid Air Base, he figured it would be a cakewalk. Sure, it was hot, dry, and sandy, but he was used to desert landscapes and oil rigs. After six months at the base, a thirty-minute to two-hour drive to central Doha depending on traffic conditions, he still couldn't believe the Arabian Desert. He'd told his parents, "It's like the White Sands area of New Mexico, but dyed red, brown, and gray and extended endlessly."

He was less sure how he felt about the people because he'd dealt with so few native Qataris. First off, they constituted less than twenty percent of the population of Qatar. Second, they were above his grade level. Mainly, Captain Meyers handled them. However, he'd found the native Qatari men to be aloof, at least in public places. He didn't have a death wish. He'd spoken to only two Qatari women, and they were with their husbands.

The expats were another story. They couldn't be lumped into one category. The expat engineers, accountants, architects, bankers, and educators from Egypt, India, and Lebanon were circumspect, efficient, and seldom engaged in boisterous activities requiring police action. Of course, he wasn't savvy about what occurred in their "national" enclaves at the edge of Doha each night.

On the other hand, the expat professionals from Europe were lively and mingled with tourists at the restaurants of The Pearl, the artificial island in Doha's west lagoon. He'd been told the restaurants were livelier before the Qatar government banned the sale of alcohol. He didn't know. The prices at most places on The Pearl were stratospheric, and he'd visited only two.

Then there were the expat laborers, many from Nepal, India, Pakistan, and the Philippines. They were mostly men, who sent their wages back to their families, and lived in the old, non-renovated sections of Doha. The Qatari police thought them the source of most criminal activity in Doha. He'd found them to be his best sources of dirt on Qatar and really the whole area. Amazing what an unhappy houseboy could tell you. However, he recognized these neighborhoods were tinderboxes with thirty men for every woman. Female military personnel found it wise to avoid cafés and stores in areas frequented by the laborers. Although, the more adventurous women became adept at responding to all insults hurled at them by saying "dog" in Arabic.

Al Udeid. What could he say? A black hole. Rows of trailers, Quonset huts, and tents, with occasional low, stuccoed buildings and long runways. All in shades of gray and brown. The only glimpse he saw of the color green most days was in the camouflage uniforms worn by most enlisted personnel. Even most of their uniforms were in shades of tan and gray.

Nasi decided his thoughts on Qatar were unusually negative today. The last twelve hours had been tedious. He'd monitored electronic responses after an agent, known only as F, sent an uncoded email from Iran. No one knew whether F had thrown caution to the winds to create a diversion or was in dire straits. Most of the U.S. intelligence community thought the latter.

Before he went off duty at three a.m., he saw a useless alert from Major Jones. Everyone, but Captain Meyers, in U.S. Marine intelligence called Major Jones "the Major" and snickered when they mentioned him. Such a jerk, but Captain Meyers was too polite to say the truth.

The Major wanted commercial airlines to report anyone who booked a flight to Ankara, Kuwait City, Abu Dhabi, Dubai or Doha from Washington, D.C. or New York City less than four hours before flight time, but he didn't bother to contact corporations that flew private jets regularly to the Middle East. As the right hand man of the general in charge of Middle East intelligence, the Major should have known late bookings were commonplace on flights to these cities, especially on corporate jets. Nasi wondered whether the Major's action related to F's email. He was sure the alert would raise chatter among those he monitored.

As he wandered over to the rec hall for a beer, he boosted his mood by thinking of the sleek, new skyscrapers in Doha along the Corniche, the waterfront promenade. A number of these towers housed grand versions of American shopping malls. Several with central ice rinks.

The dark notes in these malls were the stores featuring the long black robes worn by most Moslem women. He noticed the black robes

J. L. Greger

varied. Women from Saudi Arabia wore burqas that hid everything but two small eyeholes. Many Moslem women wore robes and scarves that showed all or part of their face. He thought all the robes were ugly.

He shook his head. He needed to think positively. Even with all the restrictions, many young women found ways to flirt. They often wore colorful shoes in a variety of styles. He'd never been a "shoe man" before he came to Qatar, but he now frequently imagined the appearance of veiled women, based on their shoes.

The rec hall was quieter than customary. After only one beer, he returned to check coded electronic transmissions one more time. Everything important was being directed to Incirlik Air Base in Turkey. Apparently, the Major thought F would try to escape Iran through Tabriz and the Kurdish territories. Nasi thought the Iranians stopped the leaks through that route years ago. He relaxed for the first time all day. If the Major was right, he wouldn't have to participate in a high-risk rescue.

He reported to work at six in the afternoon the next day. Around nine, Captain Meyers ordered him to the debriefing room to answer questions via Skype from a State Department official. He assumed this was one more State Department official annoyed by the Major's rudeness and ineptness.

After two minutes of conversation, he decided this State Department official — Sanders — was different. His questions weren't based on idle curiosity, insults, or half-baked ideas.

The situation was simple at one level. F needed to be extracted from Iran. She, probably not a he, would be at one of the Iranian ports along the Persian Gulf with possibly engineering plans for an unknown nuclear facility. Sanders thought, and Meyers agreed, the whole bit about the northern route was a ruse to divert Iranian guards. Nasi figured the Iranians had already reached the same conclusion. They weren't apt to be as dumb as the Major.

On a practical level, the issues were complex. Plenty of guesses about F's exit port, but little knowledge. Meyers and a naval intelligence officer felt Qeshm was most likely. No one, except perhaps a rogue ex-agent, called Robert Daniels, could identify F. Most likely, he wanted to kill her to protect his secrets. Sanders mistrusted the General, but he was silent on his reasons. Then there was the joker, the Major. He'd put Robert or Bob Daniels on a no-fly list two hours ago, but that was too late because most direct flights to Middle Eastern destinations left

Washington between nine and ten p.m. Eastern Standard Time. These flights would arrive in the Middle East in the next two hours.

It wasn't nice to know your boss's boss was a screw up, but there is reason for hope. The Marine Commandant had allowed the FBI to take over from his compromised staff in Washington. Agents had searched Robert Daniels's condos in Washington and on the Maryland shore. They found two passports for a man resembling Robert Daniels, but with unknown aliases, in the safe at the condo on the Maryland shore.

Airport security reviewed footage of check-ins for all the direct flights from Washington to Dubai, Abu Dhabi, Kuwait City, and Doha. Connections wasted time, and they assumed Robert Daniels had no time to waste. The computer facial recognition software found no European or American white male, between twenty and seventy years of age, in Western clothes who matched photos that a woman named Sara had found of Robert Daniels. Then FBI agents re-examined the tapes and ran computer recognition software on all men in non-Western garb for commercial and, as much as they could, on private jets. They found a match — a man of about the right height and face shape with dark skin, wearing a traditional flowing white Arabian thawb with a black agal holding his white ghutrah in place on his head. In other words, he was in traditional Arab garb. He was on the flight to Dubai and in business class.

The pilot of the Dubai flight was told to monitor the passenger, but not try to detain him. U.S. Air Force personnel were assigned to greet the man believed to be Robert Daniels at the gate in less than an hour. He was traveling under the alias Nazir Malouf, a citizen of Lebanon.

Sanders briefed Nasi on Robert Daniels while Meyers and naval officers arranged for the transport of Robert Daniels to Al Udeid, where he could be questioned more effectively than in the Emirates. Sanders signed off before the plane arrived because he said he was "too exhausted to think."

The mood of quiet optimism was shattered when two Air Force lieutenants reported the suspect had escaped. They allowed him to enter a bathroom alone while they waited with his carry-on at the only entrance. That was a stupid move. When he didn't reappear after several minutes, they found a white thawb, stained at the neck and cuff with makeup, on the floor in one stall. Only light-skinned men in Western garb had departed the bathroom while they waited.

At that point, Nasi stood. "So, I'm off to see our friends in Khasab. I always smell like goats after one of these trips."

"Get off it. They don't get many goats in trade anymore," said Meyers as he poked at his computer. "I've authorized a Black Hawk to take you and wait. This is your lucky day. I've assigned Sarge and a corporal to accompany you. Assume Robert Daniels has known our friends in Khasab for years and pays well."

Nasi was pleased his back-up would be Sarge, that's what everyone called Sergeant Errol Garner. Sarge was smart, experienced, and big enough at six four to scare most locals.

The first hour of the flight was uneventful. Then Meyers relayed the bad news. Sanders was much worse off than he had admitted. He was undergoing cardiac by-pass surgery. The Commandant, noting the vacuum in those who understood the situation, had decided to fly to Al Udeid with the only known individual who might be able to recognize Robert Daniels and F — a middle-aged professor named Sara Almquist. Nasi figured she'd be a prima donna, but Meyers noted Sanders had spoken highly of her. To make matters worse, two senators would accompany them. Senators on site always made the whole Al Udeid base uneasy, especially Meyers, who was bucking for the Major's position. At least they wouldn't arrive for another eight hours.

Meyers's other updates were not unexpected, but disappointing. Airport officials in Dubai cooperated but didn't see Robert Daniels exit the airport. Qatari officials pursued their customary policy in response to queries. They would do nothing to upset Iran and interfere with their preparations for the FIFA World Cup tournament in Doha in two thousand-twenty-two, because they needed the cheap expertise of engineers from Iran.

Nasi figured he, flying from Doha, and Robert Daniels, driving from Dubai, would arrive in Khasab about the same time, if he was lucky, very lucky. He suspected Robert Daniels was like the honey badger in the Arabian Desert — a smart but mean predator who understood the area and its residents well.

CHAPTER 21: Lt. Steve Nasi searches Khasab, Oman

Nasi thought flying over the Persian Gulf at night was a waste. During the day, he could watch dolphins cavort in the turquoise water. At night, he saw only the somber lights on the large oil tankers, cargo ships, and naval escort vessels as they formed convoys to pass through the Strait of Hormuz. However, the scene was more varied than what he saw when he flew the seemingly endless seas of drifting gray and tan sand of the Arabian desert. This wasn't desert like you saw in New Mexico and Arizona, teeming with wildlife and scruffy plants. During all his flights in the last six months, he's seen caravans of camels twice and a galloping herd of gazelles once.

He spotted the craggy hills around the port of Khasab. Some idiot had described Khasab as the Norway of Arabia. One abounded in trees, and the other was treeless. But it was true, both had plenty of small deep harbors. Then he saw the so-called Khasab Castle, a crenulated tan structure that the Portuguese built by the shore not as much as a fortress but as a supply depot.

He had always thought he could adjust to any location that the Marines sent him, but he doubted he could last more than two years at Al Udeid. That would be too bad. In college he had endured thirty hours of Arabic studies, twelve of them studying Arabic and six studying Farsi, to prepare him for a military career in the Middle East.

Nasi and his companions waited until the rotors stopped and the sand settled before they went in different directions. He sauntered toward an Indian expat sitting in an aluminum-framed chair of woven red and white plastic mesh in front of a stone hut with a single light bulb dangling over the doorway.

The smell of goats was everywhere. Over a hundred were penned in a grove of olive trees. He was surprised the trees survived the goats. This smuggler had obviously been busy today because trucks arrived at least four times a day to cart goats to sites in the Emirates after they delivered merchandise, used to be cigarettes, now mainly electronics and high-end Western clothes from the malls of Dubai.

J. L. Greger

"Kumari, how goes the smuggling business?"

The scrawny, black haired man in a gray thawb, the standard robe on the Arabian peninsula, frowned and stood. "You again. I not smuggle. I buy and sell goods. Not my fault governments can't get along."

Nasi flashed a photo of Robert Daniels. "Seen him? Skin might be darker. Might be heavier."

Nasi thought the way Kumari seemed to shove him toward the olive grove before he answered was strange, but Kumari was strange. Besides the goat pen was better lit than the hut because Kumari had strung strands of Christmas lights on each tree.

"My friend Bobby."

"Have you seen him today?"

Silence. Kumari rubbed his fingers together.

Nasi handed him ten U.S. dollars. He thought he heard a child cry and turned toward the hut.

Kumari nudged him as he thrust out an upturned palm. "So little?"

He handed Kumari ten more dollars and focused on the man's face.

"Bobby in a hurry. Offer me a hundred dollars, but not tell me where he go."

"Okay, the pilot of the speed boat must have radioed you."

"I tell Bobby no. Last time, he throw cargo overboard and make my pilot take him to Qeshm. I lost..." Kumari waved his hands expansively to explain his losses.

"I'm in a hurry, too. What happened today?"

Kumari blinked and reached around a tree and pulled out a shotgun. "I call him crazy. He see gun and roar off on motorcycle."

Nasi dreaded going from smuggler to smuggler. This one spoke English. The others didn't, although he suspected several understood English. He understood and read Arabic, at least modern standard Arabic, but the smugglers spoke a smattering of colloquial dialects. He knew he'd better hurry. "How long ago?"

"Twenty minutes."

He turned to go and heard another cry from the shed. "When was the last incident?"

"My memory weak." Kumari moved to stand between Nasi and the shed.

Another twenty.

"I think. A week, no two weeks ago, not sure."

Nasi jogged to join the sergeant and corporal who were interviewing another smuggler further down the coast. Altogether, they spoke to five smugglers during the next hour. None admitted seeing Robert Daniels today, but one admitted he'd taken him to Qeshm several times in the past.

As they wandered along the shore and around Khasab, he noticed that a gray-haired man in a tan thawb followed at a distance. Nasi sent the sergeant and corporal on to the last known smuggler and stopped at a café near Lulu's Hypermarket. He selected a dimly lit outdoor table, drank Coca Cola, and waited. The man slid into a chair at the next table.

The man used a combination of Arabic and Farsi. "You want to find Bobby?"

"Yes, I pay." Nasi pulled out a pouch.

"Bobby bad man. Time Americans stop him. He waits for Kumari's boat."

"Where?"

"In stone shed."

Nasi gave him twenty and texted the sergeant and corporal. The trio, with guns drawn and night hunting lights on their helmets, heard the high-pitched wails of a child as they approached Kumari's hut. They saw no one. The sergeant and the corporal crouched on either side of the rough-hewn log door jambs. Nasi kicked the decrepit wood door.

A wailing toddler waddled out.

Nasi looked into the small windowless stone structure. A man, covered with debris apparently from the overturned shelves, lay there. "All clear."

While the corporal radioed Meyers, Sarge scanned the coast and area behind the shed. Nasi examined the body. It was Kumari. His right eye was already swollen shut. His hands were bound behind him.

Nasi pulled a dirty rag from Kumari's mouth. He immediately spit out a tooth and drooled a slimy mixture of blood and saliva. When he stopped coughing, he whimpered. "I quit business. Too dangerous."

"Kumari, where's Robert Daniels?"

"He swing my baby by feet. Say he throw her in water." He moaned prayers.

"Where is he now?"

"He hit me" Kumari spit more blood as Nasi helped him sit up. "Jet boat arrive. Pilot see Bobby and run." Kumari winced. "Bobby shoot at him, but my man run too fast. Bobby take boat."

"How long?"

"Twenty minutes ago." Kumari rubbed the welts already appearing on his wrists.

"Truth this time?"

"Sure. I want Bobby dead," pause, "and my boat."

Sarge picked up the screaming toddler and cradled her before he placed her by her father. She stopped sobbing when Kumari stroked her hair.

"Where will he go?"

"Same as before. Qeshm. Not main harbor. Small cove. Hard to find." Kumari rubbed his left eye, which was bloodshot but not swollen shut.

"How would you and your daughter like to take a ride in a helicopter? All you have to do is point out your boat. After we snag Bobby, you take the boat home. We take Bobby."

Kumari's hands fumbled on the overturned shelves, and he rose unsteadily. "What if boat damaged?

"We buy you a new one."

"We go. You carry baby."

***

Nasi waited to contact Meyers until the helicopter was churning over the Persian Gulf headed for the Iranian island of Qeshm. As expected, Meyers reamed Nasi a new one for not contacting him before he acted. His instructions to Nasi were clear but almost impossible. Bring Robert Daniels back alive, injured was okay, and don't go into Iranian territory.

Nasi didn't acknowledge the "I-told-you-so" look on Sarge's face and focused his eyes on the water below. The Black Hawk flew low and focused search lights on the water. He sucked in his breath as a smuggler jet boat barely missed being pulled into the wake of a tanker. "Is that one yours?"

Kumari squinted. "No, my pilots aren't stupid."

"Bobby might be."

Kumari sighed and looked again. "No."

The helicopter pilot reminded them they would be in Iranian air space within ten minutes. The corporal tapped out coded messages to Meyers while Sarge scanned maps of Qeshm and complained. As might be expected, the maps of Iran available on U.S. computer systems weren't up to date. Officially, U.S. troops hadn't been there since the eighties. The satellite images were good, but Iranians camouflaged key points well.

After a few minutes, the corporal whispered in Sarge's ear. Sarge typed a message and pushed his phone toward Nasi:

Meyers says Kumari will cut our throats to save Daniels.
Can't retrieve Daniels from Qeshm at night.

Nasi nodded as shoved the phone back towards Sarge, who pocketed his phone and whistled softly as he tinkered with the rifle at his side.

Nasi checked the lock on Kumari's seat harness. "See that boat?" He tried to control the tenor of voice to disguise his nervousness, but failed.

"Dhow fishing boat. Not my jet boat." Kumari's disgust was obvious.

"Wait, look up ahead."

"That's it." Kumari shoved the baby to Nasi as he leaned out of the helicopter for a better view. Nasi pushed her back into Kumari's lap and tightened the harness more.

Nasi tapped the pilot on the shoulder. The helicopter's low whup-whup-whup sound deepened as it buzzed lower. Nasi nodded to the sergeant. Using the speaker system on the helicopter, he delivered what he realized was a useless message. "U.S. Marines. Robert Daniels, give up peaceably."

The jet boat blasted forward.

Sarge fired rapidly. Water boiled up behind the jet boat.

"Robert Daniels, this is your last chance to surrender." Nasi liked how the sound system made his voice sound authoritative. He doubted Daniels was impressed.

The jet bloat changed direction slightly and zigzagged forward.

The pilot sped up the helicopter. Sarge and the corporal fired more shots. The water around the boat swirled with white foam.

Sarge grumbled, "He asked for it."

More shots. A geyser of splintered plastic and metal replaced the jet boat. Nasi scanned the area for a man. Only pieces of the boat were visible. At least, the water wasn't streaked red.

The rotor emitted a whumpa-whumpa-whumpa sound as the helicopter hovered over the wreck. The corporal tightened a harness about himself and was ready to be lowered on a tag line to the wreckage.

The sergeant loaded darts into a handgun and handed it to the corporal. "Don't be a hero, tranquilize him."

Nasi ignored Kumari's whimpers, "My boat, my boat," as he scanned the water.

"I see a hand on the biggest piece of blue plastic." He focused a search light on the hand and flicked on the sound system. "Robert Daniels, we know you're alive. Let us rescue you."

No changes below.

Nasi lowered the corporal, while the sergeant kept his rifle focused on the white hand on the six-foot piece of blue plastic in the dark water. The corporal swung in a circle twenty feet above the water. He waited for the man to surface for air.

The man's arm swung higher over the plastic. He took a stroke with his other arm.

"He's playing chicken with us." Sarge was now in a harness and ready to rappel to the water's surface.

The corporal lowered himself to swing less than three feet above the plastic debris and aimed his stun gun. Nasi saw the man slap at his shoulder. Timing was crucial. If they moved too fast, Daniels would put up a fight, and the crew could be injured. Too slow, Daniels would drown.

Sarge zipped down his line, and the corporal lowered himself two more feet and grabbed for Daniels's arm. Daniels splashed wildly in the water. Within seconds, Sarge swam toward him. When Sarge endeavored to place a belt over Daniels's shoulders, Daniels lobbed his hand at him. Sarge planted his fist, the size of a small ham, in Daniels's belly and completed his task. He cinched a mesh belt around Daniels's chest. Nasi perceived Sarge was angry and expected no cooperation from Daniels when he placed a mesh belt between Daniels's legs and hooked it to the chest strap along with hooks to the tag line that the corporal offered.

The corporal gave the signal and the helicopter rose slightly as the tag line swung erratically. Once the limp body swung in a smaller circle, the winch groaned as it pulled the corporal and Daniels up. Nasi was ready. He checked Daniels's vitals and tied him securely before the winch drew the sergeant up.

The pilot reported they would fly only a short distance to a dock loading ship nearby in Emirate waters, not all the way to Al Udeid. Sarge snickered. "Plenty of time to get answers, if we tighten the straps a bit."

CHAPTER 22: Lt. Steve Nasi at fourteen hours before the deadline

Robert Daniels, aka Bobby, Danny, Robert, Bob, Nazir Malouf, and God-knows how many other aliases, refused to acknowledge Nasi's questions. Daniels blanched when Sarge tightened the harness, including the mesh between his legs, but he continued to stare defiantly at Nasi.

"I don't like defiant pissants, especially traitors, who get other Americans killed." Sarge pulled a knife, waved the blade in front of Daniels's face, and then slit Daniels's khakis and tee shirt.

Nasi found a thousand U.S. dollars, lots of Iranian rials, a passport for Nazir Malouf, and a small gun in a blue waterproof pouch in the pocket of the khakis. This time in response to questions, Daniels spat at him.

Sarge put on a plastic glove and smirked as he reached into Daniels's boxer shorts. After he tore a red plastic pouch from the waistband, he continued to grope the man. Daniels bit his lips during the examination. The sergeant showed Nasi a smaller plastic bag. Kumari took one look at the second bag and retched onto Sarge.

Nasi stifled a snicker as he handed the swearing sergeant a grease rag from under the pilot's seat. After Sarge wiped most of the odorous debris off the packet and himself, he handed the packet to Nasi and pitched the stinky rag and glove into the gulf. Kumari hiccupped violently.

Nasi thought this might be a window of opportunity with Kumari. He fumbled through a duffle bag and pulled out a black bag and earmuffs that Sarge positioned on Daniels's head. He hoped they could augment Kumari's fear and induce Daniels to consider his options. Besides, he didn't want Daniels to see or hear his interactions with Kumari. He whispered into Kumari's ear. "You can avoid our enhanced questioning techniques if you tell us everything you know."

"Sure." Kumari trembled so much the baby began to wail.

The child's high-pitched screams made Nasi want to scream, too. He motioned for the corporal to hold the child, as he looked directly into Kumari's eyes. "I mean everything."

The corporal had no children of his own and handled the toddler awkwardly. Her shrill howls almost drowned the whup-whup-whup sound of the helicopter blades. Daniels must have heard the screams despite the earmuffs because he tensed his hands into fists.

Kumari was transfixed, with his mouth agape, and seemed unable to comprehend questions, even when reiterated several times. Occasionally he responded, "Sure. Sure."

Sarge leaned over and hoisted the girl onto his lap. At first, she wiggled against his damp clothes when he caressed her in his arms. She quieted when he crooned, "No one hurt baby," over and over.

Nasi resumed his questions. Kumari told them the exact location of the cove where Daniels always asked to be landed. He generally requested they return in three hours. About six months ago, a woman in a black chador and veil accompanied him to Qeshm. They returned the next day. "How do you know it was the same woman?"

"She smell the same."

Nasi wasn't prepared for that answer. "Was she dirty?"

"No, no. Good."

"Like cooking smells?"

Kumari cocked his head. "No. Sweet," pause, "Rich," pause, "Not native."

Nasi assumed the woman wore a Western commercial perfume to mask the odor of stale sweat under the chador. He guessed she seldom wore the garb and noticed the stench more than those accustomed to them. Kumari remembered nothing else about her.

The pilot announced they would land in ten minutes on the ship. Meyers and a crack team of interrogators were already there. Nasi realized this was his last chance to get intelligence from Kumari and win brownie points with Meyers. Experienced interrogators would take over.

"So, except for that one time, was Bobby always alone?"

Kumari frowned and hesitated. "No."

"I'm waiting, and I'm kinder than the next group of questioners."

"He take smelly woman another time."

"When?"

Kumari waved his hands wildly.

This was hopeless. It would be easier to pull hen's teeth than interview Kumari. "When was the last time you took a woman to Qeshm?" Nasi figured this would also be a way to gauge the illegal movement of Iranians by this route.

Kumari smiled revealing his missing tooth. "Smelly woman yesterday."

"Darn." He'd hoped to convince Meyers to not have the professional interrogators talk to Kumari, who thought of himself as a businessman and didn't consider smuggling intrinsically bad. But poor Kumari knew too much, not to be questioned thoroughly. However, he thought Robert Daniels deserved their attention.

***

Guards reached in and pulled Robert Daniels from his seat before the helicopter's rotor stopped turning. While the sergeant and corporal helped a trembling Kumari and his daughter disembark, Nasi rushed to update Meyers who was waiting on deck. He only said two sentences about his mission before Meyers unleashed a stream of "drats." Nasi thought Meyers's favorite curse word demonstrated his boss's controlled nature. Suddenly, Meyers lowered his voice. "Nasi, you damaged the chances of the trained investigators to obtain valuable data."

Bad sign. When Meyers spoke in that low, slow voice, he was plotting revenge or what he called discipline. Nasi thought either the heat or the job was getting to Meyers. Sure, he and Sarge asked the suspects more questions than usual during the helicopter ride, but they'd seen a window of opportunity and taken it. Made him think twice about trying to advance in the Marines. He gulped and explained his reasoning. Meyers pressed his lips together so tightly that they turned white.

Sarge interrupted the conversation. "Sir, may I speak to you in private. The medical team is ready to take Kumari and his daughter to sick bay." Sarge shoved Nasi inside a small compartment and whispered, "Let me calm him," before he let Meyers lead the way.

Nasi hadn't enlisted in the Navy per se for a reason. Rough water made him sick. The small compartments, like this one, made him dream of the big skies in rural New Mexico. Maybe the Captain was irritable because he disliked sailing, too.

When Meyers returned in thirty minutes, he wasn't smiling, but he seemed less tense. "Do you think we should keep Kumari here until the mission is over, so he can't spill secrets," He emphasized the next words, "or should we return him to Khasab with his new boat and see who else shows up at his marina."

Nasi understood Meyers's question was a compliment, but he suspected Meyers hadn't extracted an important detail from Kumari. "Where and when is Kumari going to retrieve the scented woman? She went yesterday. Could be F's guide out or could be F's assassin. 'Course, her trip could be a coincidence."

Meyers bit his lips and rushed out of the room. Nasi smiled. He thought he'd earned more brownie points because Meyers hadn't asked those questions.

Twenty minutes later, Meyers returned with Kumari. Nasi snickered. "Kumari, you smell of lemons in your clean clothes." Secretly, he suspected the staff in sick bay showered Kumari to prevent the spread of fleas or whatever else infested his greasy hair and dirty clothes.

Kumari shook his wet hair like a dog after a bath. "Americans worry too much about smell."

Meyers, belching drats, pushed Kumari into a chair, and stepped outside the compartment to whisper to someone.

Nasi assumed Kumari hadn't answered Meyers's question because Meyers always said drat when he didn't get what he wanted. He figured he'd just gotten another window of opportunity. "Talking of smell. Kumari, you know that woman in black — the one who smelled good — when does she want you to pick her up on Qeshm?"

Kumari shook his head.

Nasi winked at Kumari. "I want to see whether Bobby had told us the truth, but I guess you don't want any more money."

Kumari's mouth flew open. "Bobby talked?"

Boy, the window of opportunity was wide open. Nasi shrugged. "When and where?"

Kumari lowered his head and held out his hand, confirming that the woman gave him instructions, but he needed an inducement.

Nasi placed ten dollars on Kumari's palm. "Did Captain Meyers tell you he'd give you a bigger, better boat? Might let you use it today."

Meyers opened the door. Sarge stepped in with the toddler. Now she was dressed in a pink, ruffled mass of lace and ribbons. Pink sandals were on her feet. She cooed when Sarge slid her onto Kumari's lap.

Nasi wondered how Meyers thought to bring that outfit from Al Udeid? Guess Meyers deserved to be the boss.

Kumari's face glowed as he bounced his daughter on his knee.

Nasi was surprised by his own thoughts. He wanted to feel like that someday, not immediately, but soon. Of course, he'd have to convince his girlfriend to say yes first, and she wasn't exactly enthused about Al Udeid and Doha when she visited two months ago. "So, Kumari, when and where will you pick up the scented lady in your new boat?"

"Same place. Today. Time, how you say it, not sure. An hour before sunrise. If not then, in three hours. Dangerous."

Meyers looked at his watch and bit his lip again.

Nasi mused that one of these times, Meyers was going to bite it off.

Meyers ran out of the compartment and returned in five minutes. "Kumari, you and Lieutenant Nasi are going to retrieve the scented lady from Qeshm in your new, bigger, faster boat."

Kumari scurried for the door. Meyers stepped out of his way.

Nasi stood slowly, thinking. "Kumari, what else did she tell you."

Kumari was ready to run through the door, but Sarge shoved his thick arm across the doorway. "What else did she say?"

Kumari's shoulders dropped. He tightened the grip on his daughter. "She bring a friend."

CHAPTER 23: Sara at twelve hours and counting

Sara awoke with a start. The roomy leather seats on the plane reclined into comfortable beds but someone had nudged her. She saw the corporal who was serving as a flight attendant and felt the cold as he thrust a can of diet cola into her hand. She slurped a long draught and motioned for him to bring her a second can.

The Commandant alternately scrutinized the screen in front of him and glanced at her. "She's awake now and will answer your questions."

She must have looked confused.

"After you cleaned up and ate, you slept for five hours. A lot has happened."

She stretched her hands above her head and rubbed her eyes. "How's Sanders? Can I speak to him?"

"The surgeons expect him to recover completely from his triple bypass surgery. Too soon for you to call the ICU. Now an Al Udeid update." He turned on a second screen and turned it towards Sara. Captain Meyers with a strong five o'clock shadow appeared.

"Commandant, as you know, an interrogation team is questioning Robert Daniels. Surprisingly, Lieutenant Nasi extracted data from the smuggler from Khasab." Almost as an aside. "Seems he and a sergeant were more effective than our interrogation team."

"Often, men on the ground are the best. Give them my congratulations."

Meyers sucked in his breath.

The Commandant looked impatient. "What did you learn?"

"We have a before sunrise deadline."

The Commandant looked at his watch. "Enough time?"

Meyers pointed out specks on a map. "The jet boat only has to cross a short stretch of the Persian Gulf to Qeshm from the dock loading ship. We'll launch other jet boats in different directions as a diversionary tactic."

"The mission?"

"Pick up a woman in a full black robe and veil. Her only identification is the smuggler claims she smells of an expensive Western perfume."

"And I don't suppose you brought a hunting dog along?" The Commandant chuckled.

Meyers frowned. "No sir, but I flew bottles of perfume from the commissary to our ship. Kumari identified Shalimar. Ma'am I know this is weird, but do you remember whether any of the potential women smelled of Shalimar?"

Sara closed her eyes and thought. "I don't identify other women by their scent. I'd do better tracking the aroma of an aftershave."

The Commandant chuckled. Meyers didn't.

"But I know the scent of Shalimar. It makes cells on the inside of my nose, at the bridge, twitch when I smell it, and I sneeze. As an undergrad, I sneezed a lot in church on Sunday. Shalimar was popular among the church ladies. Farideh didn't wear perfume. And I don't remember sneezing a lot around Souri."

The Commandant shook his head. "Not much of a clue. Anything else?"

"The scented woman, that's what we're calling her, told Kumari she'd bring a friend with her. Could be F. She told him if she wasn't at the secret cove on Qeshm at sunrise, to come back in three hours."

"Iranians are apt to get suspicious when a jet boat goes to the backside of the island repeatedly. Send Kumari alone with plenty of money for bribes. Don't want our men caught on Iranian territory."

Meyers looked skeptical. "Okay, but I'll keep his daughter with us. Should cement his loyalty."

The Commandant's deep wrinkles around his eyes twitched. "A child doesn't belong on a mission or as a pawn. Now, let's discuss Robert Daniels until you get new updates. Did he carry any documents?"

"Again, Nasi and the sergeant were efficient. We gained passport pages with two new aliases."

"Good, have you checked the past use of these aliases?"

"In the works, one is obviously an alias for Robert Daniels. This time he's an Egyptian businessman. The other is a Lebanese woman with a scar on her right cheek. Both look older, more wrinkled, than their early sixties."

Sara was now fully awake. "Farideh would be about sixty-five. The woman with a gun in the photos from Beirut in ninety-five appeared to have a scar on her right cheek. Can you check whether these passports were used to enter or leave Beirut in ninety-five?"

Meyers smiled. "My thoughts, too. Analysts are already working on it. Note, we don't have a full passport. Only the first two pages. Robert Daniels limited the material he transported in that orifice."

The Commandant coughed. "Your crew was thorough. Not an easy search to do on an uncooperative man on a helicopter."

Sara thought for thirty seconds before she understood the Commandant's comment and Meyers's snickers. "Guess it proves they're important. Has Robert Daniels said anything?"

"He keeps repeating, 'I report only to the General.' Commandant, will you allow it?"

"Of course, immediately. The General knows his career is over, but wants to avoid a court martial. He'll cooperate."

"I forgot. Two other items were in the plastic bag with the incomplete passports — a cyanide capsule and a list of numbers. We, of course, are keeping Daniels under constant surveillance."

"Tell the interrogators to stop their customary techniques. Takes too long to break an experienced agent. Send in a chaplain whom you've briefed. Emphasize F is a person, not a commodity. Have him try to get at Daniels's motives."

Sara had divided views of the man who sat beside her. His actions and words, so far, conveyed integrity and determination. He would have been a much better roommate for Sanders at Princeton than the General. They appeared to have similar worldviews and the confidence to act on their convictions. However, the Commandant must have noticed the General's deterioration as an administrator over the last few years. Why hadn't he moved the General from the sensitive spot of head of Marine intelligence in the Middle East? She wasn't sure she could trust the Commandant.

The Commandant was a conundrum, but she had a more personal riddle to address — Sanders. What a fool she'd been. Bug even sensed Sanders's importance to her. Bug had refused to eat when Sanders had spent the first two nights in her bed in Albuquerque. After a couple of days, which included long walks for the three of them in the bosque by her home, Bug had let Sanders take him on his bathroom walks and sat by Sanders's chair at dinner. In Washington, Bug preferred to stay the night at Sanders's home than in the room that she rented. Well, at least he seemed less restless. Of course, Sanders bribed Bug with tasty leftovers.

She appreciated Sanders's kindness to Bug. Maybe, that was the problem. She described Sanders as smart and kind. She enjoyed the sex. She appreciated and respected him, but she hadn't admitted to her self how much she liked the man and being with him. She was sure she hadn't told him. Although she had admitted to his daughter that he was a special man. Of course, he hadn't said he loved her, but he had ended calls and emails during the last day with the word "love."

Maybe, the problem was she perceived there was a dark side to his diplomatic activities. She'd met several of his undercover contacts in Bolivia and Cuba. She'd learned the hard way that she didn't want to know more about them, and he never spoke of them or the techniques they used to extract information.

Then too, she enjoyed — no, needed was a better word — the open areas of rural New Mexico and time alone with Bug to think and be creative. Sanders was inextricably linked to Washington or at least its bureaucracy. She doubted they could blend their worlds.

She emptied the second can of diet cola. Then, it hit her. "Have the agents in Madison asked Olsen who wore Shalimar. Maybe let him smell some. I'm pretty sure that hound dog will know."

The Commandant sucked in his breath and looked up from his tablet. "I thought you were thinking of Sanders."

"What made you say that?"

Your face... the worry lines on your forehead disappear whenever you say his name. I assumed you were thinking of him. Then out of the blue, you mention Olsen." In an aside, he muttered, "Don't understand her as well as I imagined."

"Should I call Norm or does this request have to go through complicated military channels? Norm will have trouble pulling an answer from Olsen, but he'll ferret more from Olsen than a military type."

"You don't like Olsen much, and don't have much faith in military intelligence. I'll call my counterpart at the FBI."

As Sara waited for the Commandant to finish his call, she debated how to address him. He'd introduced himself as Joe, and her father had instilled in her a dislike of formal military titles. "Joe, you're the second man today, or at least in the last twenty-four hours, who has observed my reaction to Olsen. Maybe I've seen too many wolves in academia, and..."

"I'll put a call through to the ICU. I'm sure Sanders would like to hear your voice."

CHAPTER 24: Sara with eleven hours to go

"At this point in a field study, I like to check all the details."

The Commandant's lips quivered. "What stage is that?"

Sara guessed he was biting his tongue, and trying to be polite. He, unlike Sanders, wasn't used to her thought processes. "When we're about to enter the key phase of the study and everyone needs to understand the protocol." She paused. "And frankly, I don't."

He sighed. "We'll arrive at Al Udeid in a little less than three hours. A helicopter will take us to the command center for this operation, a dock loading ship in the international shipping lanes of the Persian Gulf near the Emirates. Someone will then have to go into Iran for F."

Sara threw caution to the wind. "So, we'll arrive at the command center only seven hours before deadline. Isn't that too late in the game to make a difference? Unless…" She decided to be cautious and not finish her sentence.

He scowled.

"Well, anyway, why don't I try to sort out details with my FBI contacts. Make sure we have all the details when we arrive at Al Udeid."

"The Major should have taken care of those details."

"What? I thought he was under house arrest, or whatever you call it in the military, with the General."

The Commandant straightened in his seat. "We decided the Major wasn't part of the General's schemes, and was too inept to recognize them. Accordingly, the Major has no long-term future in the Marine Corps, but he knows this situation and we're short-staffed. He's acting as our liaison with the FBI now."

Sara frowned, while he squinted at his tablet. He slid further and further into his seat as he read messages. "Sara, go ahead and talk to your contacts at the FBI. The Major has insulted someone again." He hunkered down and swiveled his seat. They each were in their own private space.

First, she called Ulysses Howe in Albuquerque. She needed to talk to someone she trusted. Funny, trust was big with her today. Probably because she had so little trust for those around her. "Hi. This is a long shot. Do you remember the pseudo-theory of six degrees of separation?"

"Yeah," Ulysses replied, "you can connect any individual to any other by no more than five intermediaries."

"The theory is hooey, but we're desperate. I'll email two photos of Robert Daniels in his Arab disguises to you. Can you see whether the terrorist who broke into my house recognizes either?"

Ulysses laughed. "I've always liked your style, but don't get your hopes up. Our terrorist hasn't spoken since Gil arrested him. He wouldn't even talk to the imam from the Islamic Center in Albuquerque. Remember we can't apply the techniques they use at Al Udeid."

"I don't want you to be unethical, but could you apply a blood pressure cuff or some sort of lie detector to him? See whether he involuntarily responds to these photos when mixed in with lots of others. Same when you mention lots of names along with Daniels's aliases."

"I'll push it." She heard background noise and Ulysses cursing, "Machine is so slow." The swoosh of papers. "The guy knows a lot about disguise. I wouldn't recognize the men in these new photos were the same man as in the earlier snapshot. I'll get back as soon as I have an answer."

"Thanks. I want you and Gil to know how much I appreciate you two."

"That sounds like a good-bye. Relax. Sanders won't let the military brass put you in danger."

"Sanders had triple by-pass surgery a few hours ago."

"Now I understand your angst. Don't let the military bigwigs push you beyond your limit. You've always known your limits in the past."

"But I had good back up." She wondered why she'd said that? Was it part of her realization of how important Sanders had become to her. Or did it reflect her distrust of the Commandant. He seemed honorable... but, he was facing a scandal, which could ruin his career and tarnish the Marine Corps because of the General and Robert Daniels. He was desperate.

"Mmm. Trust your instincts. God bless."

She wished Ulysses had told her that she was being silly, not basically confirming her worries.

She contacted Norm in Madison. "Is Inge out of surgery?"

"Another lucky lady. Been out for hours. She's chomping at the bit to talk to you. Says she can sleep after this crisis has passed. The Major is being a dick. So, is Olsen. Both don't play well in the sandbox with others."

At this point, Norm's breezy style was what she needed. "Tell me something I don't know.

"Olsen smelled the Shalimar and tensed up. He claims he's known many women who wear it, but no one connected to Iran or Robert Daniels."

"You think he lied?"

"Is Bill Gates rich? Inge told me to assure Olsen the Marines now had Robert Daniels in custody. He didn't believe me. And the stupid Major won't send me a picture of Daniels in custody."

"Let me see what I can do."

"Where are you now? I thought planes over the Atlantic could receive messages bounced from satellites, but I was told you were unreachable. Is the military brass yanking your chain?"

Sara chuckled at Norm's brashness. Probably why she had taught at universities for so long. She liked the energetic, uncensored comments of smart young men and women. "Long story. Let's talk about a project for you and Inge. Basically, I want you to play epidemiologist."

"She'll like this better than I will."

"You'll enter the dates when all the characters who've been mentioned in this investigation, including me, Robert Daniels, the General, and the Major, were in Lebanon, Egypt, Oman, and the Emirates during the last thirty years in a computer file. Have the analysts also add dates when female Iranian physicists and nuclear engineers were in these locations, too. Look for overlaps. Compare these overlaps to when F's past leaks were received in Washington."

"Sounds like a lot of work, but it makes sense. Just like contact is necessary to spread most diseases, contact is necessary to transmit military secrets, especially documents, at least before emails and texting."

"I expect Inge or another analyst has already started the project. Have them add one other factor. Male Iranian physicists or nuclear engineers who are now thirty-one to thirty-seven."

"You lost me."

"Robert Daniels threatened to kill the son of one of the women in the compromising pictures. I'm guessing the woman is Farideh. She didn't look pregnant when she left the U.S. early in seventy-nine. So, the child was probably born in late seventy-nine, at the earliest. Her husband was executed, most likely in eighty, but she could have been raped in prison. Hence, my guesstimate of the son's age. I'm guessing the son might have been trained in physics or engineering. It's one way to explain how F has acquired nuclear secrets."

"Inge will love this. I'm emailing her now, but I'll walk over and talk to her."

"I'll have a photo of Robert Daniels in custody relayed to you. Not sure how, but…"

"Gotcha."

"Joe." She tapped the Commandant on the shoulder. "Olsen knows who the scented lady is, but won't talk until he sees proof that Robert Daniels is in custody. The Major stonewalled FBI agent Norm Budzinski." She noted his eyebrows were arched. "I understand, info on Daniels's capture is top secret because it could set off a cascade of unexpected events and prevent the extraction of F and her package, but…"

"You talk more when you're on weak ground." He tapped keys on his tablet. "Olsen is in Madison. Budzinski doesn't have clearance to receive this level of classified data."

"The senior analyst, Inge Ohm must have clearance. She's functional after her surgery."

"I see." He typed several messages. "The image will be delivered to her within thirty minutes."

"Thanks."

"Now I've a similar type request for you to work on. The General says he can get Robert Daniels to talk if he gets an answer to his question: How did Michelson and Doc die? He's seen the autopsy reports, but says they can be fixed in Beirut. He wants more. Any ideas?"

"Let me think a bit about my contacts at American University of Beirut."

The Commandant swiveled his chair away, and after a minute turned back. "The General insists your Palestinian grad student, the one in Montreal with relatives in Beirut, knows something."

"Hanna Kafity? Sanders said the Royal Mounties were satisfied with her answers."

He looked down to avoid her gaze. "The General's comments aren't logical, but old hunting dogs seldom lose their sense of smell totally. Please, contact her, casually."

"How am I supposed to do that?"

"Think about it." He swirled away.

Sara was brooding over her next move, when the Commandant handed her his phone. "Norm Budzinski is persistent. I'd like to shoot whoever gave him my number."

"Update." Norm's voice sounded peppier than before. "You and Inge think alike. Analysts were already working on the project. One of them, poor guy, probed Elvira with questions. Guess he knows now where to look in her junk. Inge will email a report to you in the next half-hour."

"Good."

"Oh, one sad note. Old man Baum died. First time a relative thanked me for questioning a dying relative. His daughter said, 'He died happy because he had one last chance to be useful.' Is that how you, as an old prof, want to go... with your boots on?"

Sara thought not.

After ten seconds, Norm said, "Sorry. I was trying to be funny. I know you're under pressure. Don't trust the military types too much." He hung up.

***

Sara scanned the email. "Inge, are you sure?"

"Hanna Kafity, Nazir Malouf aka Robert Daniels, Mickelson, and two female Iranian scientists were in Beirut on two of the same days in ninety-five. Mickelson was found dead in his hotel room on the second of these days. Nazir appears to have flown from Beirut to Paris on the morning of the second day. The Iranian women scientists and Hanna's travels never overlap with any of the characters in this puzzle again, but all three appear to have visited with faculty members at the American University of Beirut."

"So, the General might be right. Hanna could subconsciously know an important detail."

"Or she could be more deeply involved. I contacted the Royal Canadian Mounties. They'll have her at their station any moment. Will you question her?"

"Not exactly a friendly, relaxed chat, but I'll try."

Inge sighed. "Nothing's perfect in this case. We also suggested she be detained until your mission is over."

"Is that necessary?"

"I doubt it, but it protects you and her. One more point. About two months later, we see another overlap. Robert Daniels, not using an alias, is in Beirut at the same time as Doc and Elvira. On the third day of their visit Doc has a heart attack, and Robert Daniels flies to Ankara, Turkey the same day. Then it gets cute. We looked for Iranian women on the flight. None. We looked for women with citizenship in Turkey or Lebanon who never flew internationally before or after."

"You assumed the use of a forged passport, which was discarded after one use."

"Yes, again nothing. We loosened our parameters. One Lebanese woman surfaced. She flew from Ankara to Beirut a day earlier on the same flight as Robert Daniels and left on the same flight with Daniels. The Major reluctantly found records that indicate Robert Daniels was a consultant for the Marines in Turkey and Beirut at that time."

"So, you assume Daniels imported the veiled lady in Elvira's pictures from Iran, probably through Tabriz and into Kurdish territory."

"It fits, and shows Daniels had the balls to do it openly."

"Also means Farideh, or at least the veiled lady, knows the northern route out of Iran. Maybe the General has been right, and I've been wrong."

"Girl, don't lose confidence in yourself. We don't have the whole story on the General, yet."

Sara heard a phone ring and Inge mutter undecipherable phrases to herself. "The Royal Canadian Mounties are ready to join us. If you don't mind, I'd like to listen in. Don't acknowledge me to Hanna. Good luck."

After a series of phone clicks. Sara swallowed hard. "Hanna are you on the line?"

A meek, "Yes."

"Hanna, this isn't fair to you, but it appears we both may have been around several nasty characters and have seen more than we should. Think hard. When you were in Beirut in ninety-five, did you see or hear anything odd?"

"This is silly." A long sigh. "Let's see. I gave a seminar in the medical school at American University of Beirut. This was my first big international opportunity after grad school with you. My boss in Montreal wanted to enroll patients from American University of Beirut's hospital in a clinical trial for stomach cancer. He thought their patients would be a good extension of his work with the Middle Eastern immigrant pool here in eastern Canada. He hoped I, as someone who attended American University of Beirut as an undergrad, would be more likely to garner cooperation of physicians there than anyone else on our team. And twenty years later, I can affirm he was right."

"Sounds interesting, but let's forget the science for now. Sometimes I get weird questions or odd suggestions at my seminars or afterwards as I talk to faculty members and staff. Anything like that for you?"

"No." Her voice sounded defiant.

"Maybe, chatter over cocktails or dinner?"

"No."

The ensuing silence worried Sara, but she couldn't think of a useful transition.

"OMG." Hanna gasped. "A pathologist told a weird tale over dinner. He prefaced by saying the labs weren't always up to par in Beirut. Actually, the labs at American University of Beirut are good, but they were recovering from the civil war in ninety-five."

"No excuses are needed. I agree. It is a strong point in the academic world of the Middle East."

"Mmm, let's see if I can get this right. A U.S. citizen was found dead in his hotel room. They brought the elderly man to the hospital morgue for autopsy along with an open jar of canned homemade lamb stew found in his hotel room. The pathologist found evidence of respiratory and cardiac failure, not due to coronary heart disease, but due to muscle tetany induced by botulinum poisoning. It also appeared the man had fallen because he had a contusion on his head. I don't remember any more details but the pathologist sent the canned lamb stew out for analyses. The lab found high levels of botulinum toxin, but here's the mystery. They found no rod-shaped *Clostridium botulinum* bacteria or *Clostridium botulinum* endospores in the food. The pathologist thought it strange the toxin was present, without a means to produce it, i.e. the bacteria in some form."

"So, what happened?"

"He cursed the lab for their ineptness, and I assume reported the man died of *Clostridium botulinum* food poisoning."

"Wow." Sara swallowed a slug of diet soda and thought. "Nowadays, it wouldn't be hard to get a large amount of botulinum toxin, because of all the cosmetic uses of Botox, the commercial form of the botulinum toxin." Sara took another gulp. "I don't think it would have been easy to get the toxin then."

"So, the autopsy was okay. Are we through now?" Hanna's voice reeked annoyance.

"Not so fast. I remember one or two labs in the Food Research Institute investigated botulism when I was an undergrad in Madison. As I remember, Farideh claimed one of the labs synthesized the toxin under a secret contract for the military. She wanted to picket the lab. It was another brouhaha among her, Danny, and Doc."

Sara heard several gasps. Hanna must have too. "Who's listening in?"

"Hanna, stay calm. You may have spotted a murder, and several of us know the murderer."

"OMG. Who was this guy? Never mind, the less I know the better."

"Anything else? No matter how minor."

"No." This time the answer was soft, not defiant. "Oh, this is dreadful. I'd no idea. What type of mess are you in? Can I…"

Inge interrupted, "Better tell her the bad news."

"Hanna, we know you aren't guilty of anything, but we're afraid others might want the info you gave me. So, you have to spend a few hours as guests of the Mounties. If I were you, I'd order out for your favorite foods. Something expensive. Maybe a rack of lamb from a local restaurant. I don't know how this is done, but I'm sure the FBI in the U.S. will cover the tab."

She heard several coughs. Both high pitched and low.

"I'll email you when this is over and explain the details, as I know them. I've got to go. Thanks for your help."

"God protect you."

A series of clicks. Inge was on the line. "What do you think?"

"I'm no microbiologist, but my guess is Mickelson was knocked out, injected with a large dose of botulinum toxin, and left to die. The extra toxin was put in the food to confuse the pathologist. Impossible to reconstruct. Clever. I never thought Robert Daniels, or Danny as I knew him, was that smart." Pause, "But Farideh was."

"Good point."

"Now who else was on the line? I heard a man cough"

"The General and the Major. The Commandant insisted to my bosses."

Sara looked over at the back of the Commandant's swivel chair. "I'll see how long it takes him to admit it." She looked at her emails. "I've got to respond to Ulysses in Albuquerque."

"Okay, but my epidemiology assignment turned up several confluences in ninety-nine. Get back to me. Wait. I forgot to tell you the so-called Lebanese woman was accompanied by a minor on both flights."

Sara sat there in a funk. She couldn't decide what irked her most. That the Commandant caved in to the General's demands again or, more likely, that she'd been drawn into this charade. No wonder F, presumably Farideh, was vigilant. She recognized Robert Daniels's skills and the General's duplicity.

The Commandant turned. "Thank you. You pulled out of one difficult woman what the rest of us couldn't, because she trusted you. The General will now confront Robert Daniels." He swiveled his chair, so he was again in his own private space.

She tapped him on the shoulder. She wanted to say Hanna wasn't difficult, but bit her tongue. "Joe, we need to talk? The General only wanted me to talk to Hanna to discover whether anyone else knew what Daniels had done. He's playing games. How can you trust him?

The Commandant's mouth tightened. "He has a long history of success in the Middle East."

"Are you sure? I think his real expertise is hiding his mistakes. Abid Jahanbani."

"Who?" He blinked. "Oh, the Iranian who lied to get a visa thirty years ago."

"Why did the General pretend not to know him? Don't forget Baum warned the General about Robert Daniels. I bet Inge will find written evidence yet that Doc complained about Daniels, too. I know he threw him out of grad school."

The Commandant's lips tightened. "This discussion can wait."

Being dismissed only raised Sara's ire. "I'd lock the General in a cell until he admitted what Daniels had on him. Maybe then we could decipher this mess. And, I'm beginning to wonder whether the Major's stupidity is a ruse to hide his complicity in the General's schemes."

"You don't understand." He swiveled away.

She realized she'd said too much.

CHAPTER 25: A long four hours for Lt. Steve Nasi

The scented lady wasn't at the cove before sunrise. When Kumari reported in at the dock loading ship afterwards, he was hysterical because he thought an Iranian patrol boat had spotted him.

Nasi left Kumari and his daughter with Sarge, while he reported to Meyers. "I want to give Kumari a different jet boat for the run in three hours and launch it from another ship. We'll launch the boat that Kumari used on this first trip from this dock loading ship five minutes before we launch the boat with Kumari. Of course, we'll also launch other jet boats as we did the last time to confuse the Iranian patrols."

Meyers reached for his antacids. Nasi had noted that lately Meyers popped them like candy. That was understandable. Meyers had to deal with the Major daily, granted only by phone or email. Rumor had it that the Major, besides being a screw-up, burned his underlings for his frequent misjudgments. Nasi didn't bet on missions. Too much like athletes betting on games. But he figured Kumari, if they followed the same routine, had an eighty percent chance of being stopped by Iranians, and a ten percent chance of being hauled to Iran and held for several days. The latter odds doubled if they found an Iranian woman on board. Yes, Captain Meyers could take his time. Nasi wanted a Solomonic decision from Meyers.

"Where did Kumari notice the tail?"

"Almost twenty miles from the incoming shipping lane, as he cleared the west side of the island."

"Obviously in Iranian waters. He must have been stopped by Iranian patrols before and paid the bribes."

"Yes, but always as he headed straight north from Khasab to the main port of Qeshm. Claims it's the semi-approved route for smugglers."

"Your plan is okay. I have two Omani trainees on stand-by. They'll take Kumari's original jet boat to the north side of Qeshm Island, but not as far east as the secret cove. I'll offer them double the standard hazardous duty rate and tell them to have fun." He dismissed Nasi without allowing further questions.

∗∗∗

The jet boat loaded with four goats bobbed in the aqua water at the shore. Kumari was too hysterical to yammer as he looked for movement among the mangroves. Nasi found the silence a relief as he peered across the water, dreading the sight of other ships. The stage was almost set for the appearance of the scented lady and her friend. One more prop needed to be put in place.

Kumari howled complaints as he dragged two cases of cigarettes over the sand and piled them on the roots of the mangroves. If Iranian patrols were watching, Nasi hoped they looked like standard smugglers. Of course, he'd have trouble explaining why they'd brought goats to Iran. On the other hand, the goats would look like a potential payment for goods, if they were stopped on the return trip, the most likely time to be stopped.

He and Sarge had talked. Neither trusted Kumari. Reluctantly, Nasi smeared grease on his face and donned a white robe. The sergeant scrounged and found a traditional embroidered cap to cover Nasi's short, brown hair. He didn't look like a native, but at five foot ten he was more passable as an Iranian than the sergeant, a black man of six foot four. He hadn't told the captain of this embellishment to the plan.

At nine forty Iranian time, which was eight ten in the morning in Al Udeid, Kumari returned to the boat. Nasi cursed the Iranian government. Why had Iranians put their time a half-hour out of sync with the rest of the world? He guessed it was one more way to assert their independence.

He ignored Kumari's pleas to leave immediately because he hated to strand a woman, probably an American, in Iran. However, he and Sarge had decided fifteen minutes was the maximum he should stay in the cove. He had a primitive radio system, upgraded slightly above the ones Kumari normally used on his boats. If Iranian border patrol stopped them, he hoped they wouldn't notice the upgrade.

Meyers had arranged for Kumari to have "papers" for the women. Amazing how quickly Meyers got passports for two Moslem women from Muscat in Oman. One even looked like photos of Souri Fekri. Meyers also provided two small Iranian handmade rugs to suggest a reason for the women's trip. Now it was a matter of luck. Sloppy guards would "fine" them and let them go. Observant guards would arrest them, take them to Tehran, and create an international incident.

A patrol boat sped by in the distance. Kumari whimpered with his head almost down to his lap. Nasi figured Kamari could win an award for worst lookout ever. Then he thought he saw movement at the edge of the grove of trees. He focused on the speck.

The speck became a person in black, but only one. He waved. He looked back at the water. A fishing boat was headed toward them. He hoped the person, presumably a woman, would hurry. He wanted to avoid questions from inquisitive fisherman. His Farsi wasn't that good. He couldn't leave the jet boat to speed up the woman's journey toward the shore because Kumari might take the boat and disappear. He jerked Kumari's head up. "Why don't you help her? We need to leave pronto."

Kumari sighed, crawled out of the boat, and lumbered up the shore. He met the woman halfway between the water and the mangroves. They appeared to argue. Both trudged toward the boat. Too slowly. The fishing boat glided into the cove and the fishermen beckoned to him. He waved back.

He hauled the woman onto the boat as Kumari bounded in. He said in Farsi, "Where's your friend?"

The woman replied in English, "Not coming."

He glanced over toward the fishing boat. Men were jumping off and in seconds would be asking questions. He'd smelled a whiff of Shalimar. No need to waste time asking Kumari whether she was the scented lady.

The engine roared as he maneuvered the boat out of the cove. He saw ships ahead. "Who are you?"

The woman bent over the side of the boat and vomited.

He repeated, "Who are you?"

She wiped her mouth with her black robe. "Doesn't matter."

"Yes, it does. See that boat ahead. Before Iranian patrols stop us, I need to know whether you're an American."

Between repeated retchings into the water, she said, "Left... my papers... in Cairo."

"Good." He pulled out papers for the woman. "You are now from Muscat in Oman. You visited a sick friend in Iran and bought these rugs." He kicked at them.

All the while, Kumari stared at the ships ahead. His soft mutterings became howls of terror.

"Shut up, Kumari. Don't draw attention to us. Try to act like a cool dude, who happens to be a smuggler."

"I am a cool dude." He lifted his chin and stuck out his chest.

"The first boat is a fishing boat. Act calm. Wave to them."

Kumari was pale, but he waved, granted it looked like an imitation of Queen Elizabeth's standard royal wave. The woman, with her head so far forward she was almost resting it in her lap, sobbed. At least she was no longer gagging. "She didn't trust me. Said I was leading her to him."

Nasi knew he wasn't good at dual tasking. Hell, he wasn't supposed to be; he wasn't a woman. He also wasn't an experienced jet boat pilot. "So, are you working for Robert Daniels?"

The woman gave him a terrified glance, stood, and looked ready to jump into the water. Kumari pulled on her black chador. The boat careened right. Nasi pulled in the opposite direction to stabilize it. He heard the sound of fabric tearing. "Kumari, sit on her."

He focused on stabilizing the boat as it continued to teeter while the woman and Kumari wrestled and the goats bawled. The overall panting, moaning, and bleating increased. Gradually the pants were louder than the soprano wails. A light shower of water sprayed him and the goats as he piloted the jet boat normally. During the tussle, he and the goats were soaked as the boat shimmied. When the torrent returned to splashes, the goats stopped their complaints.

He debated what to say. "Be quiet. We think Robert Daniels is bad too. No one will hurt you."

She stopped sobbing.

"What's your name?"

"Souri."

"Souri Fekri?"

She let out an, "Eek. How do you know?"

"Doesn't matter. Look at the passport I gave you. That's your name until I get you to safety."

He noticed the cramps in his gut lessened, or at least he noticed them less, when he questioned her. "Who were you trying to get out of Iran?"

"Farideh Hossein, but I never saw her, only her son."

Maybe this was another window of opportunity. "Describe him."

"Black hair, thin, medium height."

Maybe not. "How old?"

"Early thirties."

"What does he do?"

"Why?"

"Souri, give me a break. What's his profession?"

"Technician. Works with nuclear reactors."

Souri's face twisted into a sneer. "But he's odd."

"What's odd about him?"

"Everything."

Nasi stifled his annoyance. "Try to be more specific."

"Jumpy. Nervous."

Nasi jerked on the wheel to avoid dolphins swimming close by. "Give an example of his jumpiness."

"He never looks at me when he talks. His eyes dart all over. He moves his head like a wild horse." She paused. "Oh, his eyes are blue."

He watched as she shivered in the soaked black mass of fabric. She'd be more comfortable out of it, but removal of the chador would ruin their subterfuge. She wouldn't die from a chill, if he got her back to the ship. Now was the tricky time. They were approaching the shipping lines, about where Kumari had seen Iranian patrol boats.

"Look, look." Kumari pointed at his new jet boat, the one he'd used on the previous trip to Qeshm, lashed to an Iranian patrol boat.

"Shut up and be a cool dude." Nasi murmured, "Those poor Omanis. They'll earn their pay today." He resisted the urge to speed up. He headed the boat toward Khasab. Meyers had instructed if he had a close encounter with a patrol boat, he should head to Khasab, not the dock loading ship. They'd pick him up when it was safe.

Kumari chanted "cool dude" over and over. Thankfully, Souri remained quiet.

Nasi looked over his shoulder. No one was following him. He speeded up. "We're out of Iranian waters now."

The chants stopped.

"Souri, why did you go to Iran?"

"Robert Daniels made me."

"How?"

She pulled the wet black chador off. She looked like her photos. Short hair, with a wart on her lip. Her ivory silk top clung to her full figure.

"Did he blackmail you with photos?"

She looked up defiantly. "How did you know?"

"U.S. Marines, intelligence division, at your service."

She scowled. "Robert Daniels is a Marine."

"Not any more. He went rogue. Let me be the first to apologize to you. Now let's get back to business. Why wouldn't Farideh see you?"

"I don't know." She wrung water out of the chador and smoothed it on top of the cage that held the goats.

"I wouldn't do that Ma'am. They'll eat it."

She folded the chador into a bundle. "She thought if she came with me, we'd both be killed." She patted the packet and closed her eyes.

He figured the woman had more useful information, but this game of twenty questions wasn't easy. Maybe he wasn't cut out to work intelligence.

"Let's try again. Why didn't Farideh come with you?"

"She's waiting for someone else."

He sighed. "Who's that?"

"Sara Almquist."

"Where does she expect to see Sara?"

Souri looked confused. "I don't know. I'd guess where I went."

"Where's that?"

"I'll tell Sara, no one else."

Nasi suddenly thought the Commandant and Sara's trip might not be a waste, but would this Sara agree. "Why Sara?"

She combed her fingers through her hair. "I don't know."

He figured he might as well ask the big question. "Souri, are Farideh and F the same person?"

She shrugged. "Daniels thought so the first time he dragged me to Iran about five years ago. I don't think he's sure anymore. That's why he dragged me along to Iran a few weeks ago. He kept saying, 'I don't like my girls to keep secrets from me.' Bastard." She blinked. "I'm tired now." She lay down with her head on the bundle.

He watched water ooze out of the black wad onto the seat and heard Souri snore before he radioed the ship.

CHAPTER 26: Sara at eight hours out

Time was running out. In less than an hour, they'd land at Al Udeid.

Sara wanted to tie the disjointed events in Albuquerque, Washington, Madison, and Iran together and construct a logical scenario to explain the actions of the cast of characters. She hoped that would complete her involvement in the extraction of F from Iran, but she feared she was wrong.

Rather than pace the aisle aimlessly, she wandered back to talk to the two senators. If the worst-case scenario in her mind was correct, she'd need them to extract her from harm. Both were lawyers by training. One was a patrician Southern gentleman and the other a scion of a liberal New England family. They often delivered opposing messages on news clips on TV. However, they chatted amicably, as least as far as she could tell from a distance, throughout the flight.

Evidently, they had been apprised of her past activities, but both claimed unconvincingly to be mystified by her presence on the flight.

She responded honestly to their questions. "Frankly, I don't know why I'm involved. I could be the red herring, which F threw into the net to confuse the Iranians and U.S. agents she didn't trust, namely Robert Daniels. F may have counted on me to identify Robert Daniels, but he's already been captured. Or I may have another role, which scares me, because I'm no special agent."

Their noncommittal masks slipped when the northern senator said, "I'm sure you have another role in the extraction. The Commandant wouldn't have flown here with you if he didn't think it necessary. He's quite capable of asserting his decision without being on site." The southern senator laughed coyly.

She was being manipulated in a chess game, but no one had bothered to tell her the rules. She jumped in surprise when the steward tapped her on the shoulder. "Ulysses Howe wants to talk to you."

She relaxed when she heard his familiar deep bass. "Sara, we showed my boy, the terrorist, a dozen snapshots with two of Robert Daniels in his disguises mixed in. His blood pressure spiked when he

J. L. Greger

saw Daniels as Nazir Malouf, but he didn't respond to the name. Not much, but my guess is Daniels hired my boy while disguised as an Arab terrorist himself. Otherwise, my boy's a dead end."

"Thanks, have you had a chance to look at other data in this case?'

"Sara…, I don't want to alarm you, but someone has limited my access to any info on this case. Watch your step." The line went dead.

She tapped the Commandant on the shoulder. "Joe, what happened when the General confronted Daniels with evidence that he murdered Mickelson with botulinum toxin?"

"Who said he did?" He hardly moved his lips.

"I know the General and the Major listened to my conversation with Hanna Kafity. I heard their gasps and coughs. You said he'd talk to Daniels after I got the info."

"There was a change in plans." He paused, apparently thinking. "Meyers's team have used your data effectively with Daniels."

"And?"

"You were wrong on one point. Daniels administered the toxin in eye drops, not by injection."

Sara glared at him. She wondered if he was trying to be funny or to be insulting. "Not exactly an important detail."

The Commandant's lips curled slightly upward. "Agreed. But it shows why the General considered Daniels his most effective agent." He thumbed through notes. "Ingenious. By the way, Budzinski notified me Olsen remembered Souri Fekri wore Shalimar. I transmitted the data to Meyers. Budzinski wants you to call Inge." He shook his head. "I believe I've done more secretarial services for you than for anyone in a long while."

"Sorry. I'm trying to be helpful, and the systems on this plane are so complex. I probably…"

The Southern senator clapped a hand on her shoulder as he ambled from the galley to his seat. "And you're doing a great job. Joe, here, isn't good with compliments until a mission is over." The Commandant followed the senator to the back of the plane.

When she called Norm, she heard Inge's voice. "Ouch. Norm, I can't move as fast as you expect." Clattering noises, no other sounds from Inge filled the next thirty seconds. "Sara, glad you called. I hope I'm around the day Norm gets shot. He has no idea of how uncomfortable you can be."

Sara instinctively touched her bandaged arm. She'd been lucky. Her arm now ached only slightly more than an immunization. "Norm reminds me of a two-year-old hunting dog. Too much enthusiasm. What do you have?"

"I assume the Commandant told you Olsen suddenly remembered Souri's name after he was told Robert Daniels would be incarcerated for the rest of his life for Mickelson's murder."

Sara coughed. "I'm not sure our evidence that Mickelson was intentionally poisoned with *Clostridium* toxin would hold up with a jury."

"I'm not either, but a Captain Meyers hinted Robert Daniels would face a court martial, not a civilian jury. Okay... Let me pull the details I haven't shared yet."

Sara heard mild expletives and clicks. "First, Doc Steinhaus's death. Far as we can tell, the unfortunate result of obesity and stress."

"No foul play discernible?"

"Right, but when a shrewd character like Daniels is involved, anything is possible."

"Did you share the info on Doc's and Mickelson's deaths with Elvira?"

"Norm did. He said she was quieter afterwards. Now, the confluence of suspects in Beirut in ninety-nine. Do you remember I mentioned earlier a Lebanese woman and her child who were in Beirut in ninety-five at the time the veiled woman tried to shoot Elivra?"

Sara tensed. "Yes."

"She and her child, by then a teen-ager, were in Beirut in ninety-nine, too. According to flight records, for three of the seven days you were there."

"So, she might have seen me. I don't remember seeing anyone familiar during that trip. I reviewed biology programs in the med and the ag schools at the American University of Beirut. The university owned a farm, about forty acres, in the Beqaa's Valley, in an area controlled by Hezbollah during the Lebanese Civil War. The president of the university wanted advice on how the farm should be integrated into future research and teaching. Funny thing, the farm is now used as demonstration plots for drought resistant crops. You could say an outgrowth of work by Baum and Olsen."

"Okay."

"Since we were nearby, two faculty members took the evaluation team to the Roman ruins of Baalbek."

"So, lots of people knew you were in Beirut."

Sara could tell by Inge's tone that she was ready to change the topic. "Wait, I recalled a detail. I stayed at Marquand House, the official home of the president of the American University of Beirut. Quite an adventure. It's scary to find a panic room next to your bedroom. They installed it because one president of the university, Malcolm Kerr, had been killed in eighty-four during the Lebanese Civil War. Anyway, one day when I was walking on campus alone, a young man came up to me and said, 'You're the woman staying in the President's house.' I was surprised and asked him whether he lived in the cottage behind Marquand House, which was occupied by the president's housekeeper and her family. He seemed confused. I didn't think much about it until the head of campus security talked to me later in the day. The young man wasn't the housekeeper's son. I never walked around campus alone again."

"Odd. One more point, you stayed in Beirut for three days in two thousand-nine. Why?"

"The food is good, I think the best in the Middle East. I remember sitting in a café with the Mediterranean Sea lapping at its limestone base eight feet below and eating *hummus*, *baba ghanouj*, and my favorite *kibbeh*. Romantic. The history is mind-boggling. The Phoenician ruins, sarcophaguses, and relics date back over four thousand years. The place thrived the same time as ancient Egypt. So, when I spotted a three-day guided tour, I tacked it on to a vacation in Greece. Wanted to see how Beirut had changed in ten years."

"An odd choice for a vacation."

"Not really. You'd love it."

"Okay, back to what we've accomplished. None of the names we can trace appear to have been in Beirut in two thousand-nine, but most of the names we have are aliases. We used an improved facial recognition program to re-analyze all Robert Daniels's photos of naked women to see whether we could identify, even tentatively, any besides Farideh and Souri. Seems he focused on features other than their faces." She coughed. "No new matches with current passports. In other words, I'm stymied. Norm and I wish we could be more helpful."

"You've ferreted out more than the General and his entourage."

"I've got a few more odd facts. I've been around Norm too much, I use 'odd' now all the time. We learned the ex-SAVAK guard captured near Sanders's house was once a graduate student in physics at the University of Wisconsin-Madison. He denied knowing Farideh, but we assume he's lying. Anyway, he demanded to be transferred from the

General's domain to the FBI's jurisdiction. The story is too long to tell, but he claims Abid Jahanbani has been a lackey of the General's for thirty years, and *everyone*, whatever that means, knows it. He also hinted the General has a big secret."

"And the General didn't acknowledge he knew Abid. The General seems to have lots of secrets."

"Yes, er... er... FBI auditors tracked money in Robert Daniels's accounts... Could be millions in off shore accounts. When they started checking the General's accounts, they were ordered to cease their investigation. Seems DOD auditors took control."

"Are you saying it smells?"

"Be careful. Daniels and the General have powerful friends." After a series of clicks, all Sara heard was the buzz of a dead phone line.

She gulped and looked over at the Commandant. Instead of having his back turned to her, he was staring at her. Had he been listening?

CHAPTER 27: Lt. Steve Nasi on a ship in the Persian Gulf

Nasi guided the jet boat toward Khasab, expecting to hear the dock landing ship would pick him up any minute. The minutes passed. Something was wrong. He was a desert kid; piloting a jet boat in high-traffic areas of the Persian Gulf wasn't his idea of fun.

"Ready for pick up?" It was Meyers's voice.

Thirty minutes later, Sarge helped Souri as she stumbled from the jet boat. Kumari whined, "Where's my jet boat?" Nasi thought it sad that Kumari forgot to ask about his daughter, but he focused his attention on Meyers.

Meyers let Nasi complete five sentences of his report before he grabbed Kumari by the scruff of the neck, motioned to the sergeant to follow with Souri, and shoved Nasi into a small compartment. "Write up your report."

The next twenty minutes were long. The compartment was small, had no port, and contained only a table, three chairs, and a computer tablet. He opened the door, watched a helicopter land on the deck, and worried as he typed his report. He felt better when Sarge ambled into the compartment and secured the door.

"For a guy who doesn't like sailing, you did all right. You impressed Kumari. The interrogators can't shut him up, but you and I pulled everything important. Now, Souri is another story. Not talking. Keeps saying, 'I want to talk to Sara.' Capt'n is losing patience."

"Should I be there?"

"Capt'n likes his moment of glory. Wants to look good when the Commandant arrives. Thought you might want to know what happened to the boat with the two Omani soldiers disguised as fishermen. They left two channels open on their radio throughout their rendezvous. Either those two guys deserve Oscars for their performances or they've bribed Iranian guards before. They told the guards some type of local fish on the north shore Qeshm was their father's favorite, and he was ill."

"Bet the guards didn't buy the routine."

He shrugged. "They were a bit surly. The Omanis must have pointed to a case of Jack Daniels black label and asked the guards whether they'd like four cases. Evidently, the Omanis convinced Meyers to fly in booze from Al Udeid before they agreed to this rendezvous. Within five minutes, the guards stormed off the jet boat, I assume with the booze. The Omanis radioed they'd keep up their disguise as fishermen and pilot the boat to Khasab in Oman. Funny thing, Meyers had five cases delivered to the ship."

"Scary how well Meyers can manipulate people."

Sarge smiled. "Expect, he hopes the Commandant notices and promotes him, but then the Commandant would have to figure out what to do with the Major."

Nasi sighed. "How about retire him? Back to my main question. Why was Meyers short with me this time?"

"The Capt'n is worried. Remember the small waterproof packet in Daniels's shorts?"

Nasi smirked.

"Yeah that package. Bet you forgot about the list of numbers in the packet. Intelligence reviewed the list of numbers and asked me lots of questions." Sarge shook his head. "How should I know? All I did was find it."

"So, what did they decide?"

"Think it's a list of coordinates — addresses. One appears to be for a café in the port of Qeshm. Another one is way in the middle of Iran in the Kavir Desert. I guess close to the city of Yazd. The last one also appears to be on the island of Qeshm. Satellite photos of the spot suggest it's a decrepit building in the village of Tabl on the north shore of the island. Close to where you picked up Souri."

"When does the fabled Sara arrive?"

"On her way from Al Udeid now. Problem is she says she wants to be helpful, but she won't go into Iran. Evidently, the Commandant never mentioned the possibility to her directly. She guessed. Smart woman."

"So, one of us dresses as Sara."

The sergeant grinned. "Sara is about five-eight, blonde. It won't be me."

The door flew open. "Drat, uncooperative woman. Here's what the interrogators learned that you missed. Souri's been to Iran several times over the last five years with Robert Daniels. Seems he put on a chador, and they traveled as two women."

"But that's not enough. Does he wear women's shoes?"

Meyers eyed Nasi. "Why did you ask that?"

"I've learned to identify Qatari women by their shoes. The young ones seem to try to wear distinctive ones. Bet most Iranian men, at least young ones, notice shoes."

Sarge snickered. "Didn't know you had a foot fetish."

"Let's not waste time." Meyers sat down and scanned Nasi's report. "You could have pulled more from Souri. Here's what you missed."

"Captain, give me a break. I was kinda busy piloting the boat and all on this mission."

"Souri said they usually went to Bushehr and Shiraz. She carried at least part of the documents that Farideh gave them and spoke to strangers. She said Robert Daniels's Farsi wasn't good," He looked at Nasi. "Like yours. This time, he instructed her to meet him and Farideh in the port of Qeshm at a café. The one on Daniels's list of numbers."

Nasi decided he'd done a pretty god job of interrogating her. He hadn't missed much, but decided it wasn't wise to say that to Meyers. "So, what did she do when Robert Daniels didn't show?"

Meyers scratched his head. "Actually, she's a pretty cool character. Waited in the café reading a book until a woman approached her and said she was leading an eco-tour to the mangrove forests along the coast. The woman was unnerved that Souri was alone. She expected two women would be waiting for her."

"So, how did Robert Daniels send the tour guide when he never got into Iran.?"

Meyers shrugged. "No idea."

"Capt'n," drawled Sarge. "This is fascinating, but cut to the bottom line."

Meyers straightened in his chair. "Be thankful you missed Souri's gripes about her night in an inn in Tabl. Here's the bottom line. One of the people on the tour was a man Souri knew as Yousef, Farideh's son."

Nasi tapped his fingers on the table. "So, Yousef or F probably sent the tour guide to get Souri and Robert Daniels from the cafe. What's the bottom line?"

"You pulled it from Souri already. Farideh won't appear until she sees Sara. Doesn't seem to trust Souri or Daniels."

Nasi nodded. "Souri had reason to be pissed. But we're left with the big questions: How will Sara or anyone recognize Yousef or even Farideh? Is Sara supposed to meet Farideh at one of the sites on Daniels's list. Aren't we going to have trouble meeting the deadline?"

Meyers jumped to his feet and paced, or more correctly minced his way around the table. The compartment was too small to take two normal steps in any one direction "Good questions."

Nasi leaned forward with his hands supporting his head and his elbows braced on the table. "What about Daniels's promise to speak to the General?"

Meyers grimaced. "I suppose I might as well admit the problem. The General told Daniels he'd face a court marital for killing Mickelson. Daniels replied, 'If I do, you'll be sorry,' and refused to talk more to the General. The Commandant suggested I have a chaplain talk to Daniels."

Nasi smirked. "I'm all ears."

Meyers sat down. "Afterwards, Daniels was civil, except when he spoke about the General. He guessed about F's delivery. Admitted he wasn't sure anymore who F was. Claimed to have no idea why Sara was mentioned in emails. When we told him Yousef's message to Souri, he exploded into curses, but wouldn't explain his anger. The interrogators don't think he knows F's intentions, but are sure he knows plenty about her and the General's pasts."

"Capt'n, what's next?" Sarge leaned back on the back two legs of his chair and with his hands outlined the shape of a woman as he leered at Nasi.

Nasi groaned. "After Souri talks to Sara, I have the funny feeling, I'll have to impersonate her and go to Tabl."

Meyers looked down. "What size shoe do you wear?"

Sarge doubled up with laughter.

Nasi stood. "I hate to think what the Iranians do to men who impersonate women. Tell them no red shoes, something practical but pretty, like a T-strap." He paused, "Wait. I forgot. Souri said Farideh's son had blue eyes. Any possibility Daniels was his father?"

CHAPTER 28: Sara with six hours left

Whomp, whomp, whomp. Sara ducked her head as she entered the helicopter waiting to take her and the Commandant to a dock landing ship as close to Qeshm Island as possible without being obvious to Iranians.

The Commandant's nose was buried in apparently new files, and he hardly nodded to her as she climbed into the helicopter. Sara didn't feel like talking either. She needed to think.

She hoped she'd sounded upbeat when she talked to Sanders a few minutes before the plane landed at Al Udeid. As she handwrote a note to Sanders, she thought of Bug. She could offer apologies to Sanders for this mess; she couldn't to Bug who always lost his appetite when she was away for more than a day.

This rendezvous had made her re-evaluate what was important to her. It wasn't her past, and it certainly wasn't the prestige, whatever that was, or excitement of participating in a raid into Iran. However, a lot of people — Sanders, Inge, Susan, Mary, FBI agents, Marines in the Persian Gulf — had risked or lost their lives to get F and her secrets out of Iran. She owed them something. She guessed her full cooperation.

On the plane, the Commandant had allowed her to watch as off-screen interrogators questioned Daniels with his head covered with a black bag. Daniels gave evasive answers to several questions but stated his opinion of the General clearly. "He's a goof up. Always has been. There would have been no Iran Contra mess if he hadn't screwed up communications with the Hezbollah militants and so-called members of the Iranian Revolutionary Guards. And we wouldn't need to rescue F, if he hadn't lied repeatedly." After those comments, the Commandant mumbled a few words and switched off the live transmission of the interrogation.

Now in the helicopter, Sara pondered Daniels's comments. His voice timbre and thoughts were not those of the young man she'd known as an undergrad. She figured Farideh had changed too. Surely, nothing she remembered about Daniels or Farideh was relevant.

She decided dread and regret were not good ways to prepare for the next six hours. She sealed her note in an envelope and addressed the envelope to Sanders and Bug.

Next, she watched the dolphins or porpoises, she didn't know which, frolic in the water below. Slowly, she felt a bit of optimism. She prayed she could be useful without actually participating in a raid on Qeshm. No one had defined what the extraction of F from Iran entailed, but she assumed it included a raid on Qeshm Island. Later, she saw convoys of tankers and other ships queue up before they passed through the Strait of Hormuz. She knew she would soon be faced with a hard decision.

Upon landing, the Commandant rushed away with several men in fatigues. A young man with a deep tan and bleached blond hair greeted her. "Hi, I'm Nasi from New Mexico. Did they tell you Sarge and I rescued Souri?"

The sergeant touched the brim of his cap. "Pleased to meet you Ma'am." He eyed her. "You've had a hard forty hours."

She pulled at her hair. "I'd hoped..."

"You look better than we expected for a woman of your age." Nasi blushed. "I mean... er... you look fine." He looked down and seemed to study her shoes, while the sergeant rolled his eyes.

"You two also captured Robert Daniels. I'd like to talk to him, but first tell me about him. The man with the black bag over his head on the screen wasn't the young grad student I knew in Madison."

Nasi stopped pushing her down a passageway. "The fingerprints match."

"Not what I meant. I knew an inconsiderate know-it-all, who knew nothing. This man was world-weary, sophisticated. He'd even lost most of his Boston accent."

Nasi nudged her forward. The sergeant grunted. "People change."

"That's what I'm getting at." Sara stopped, blocking the claustrophobic hall, and looked at the two men. "I'm afraid my conversation with him will be as useful as the kind you have at a thirty-year class reunion. Tell me about him."

The sergeant chuckled. "Nasi has no idea what you mean. He's too young to have endured a class reunion. Think of George Clooney in the movie *Syriana*. A man gone to seed, and angry for a reason."

"I heard his comments on the General."

Nasi leaned toward her. "We didn't. What did he say?"

"Not in a hall."

Nasi scratched his head. "We're to keep you busy for twenty minutes before you see Souri. No one said you couldn't speak to Robert Daniels."

Sarge shook his head. "Capt'n won't like this."

Nasi winked. "That's why we won't ask for permission." He paused. "You see, Ma'am, I'm going to have to impersonate you when we try to extract F. Anything I learn about F or you could be helpful. I'll watch through the mirror as you and Sarge talk to Robert Daniels. And I'll see how the professional interrogators react to your questions. Maybe learn a few of their tricks."

Sarge clicked his tongue. "Ma'am are you sure? Daniel Roberts could be hostile, even nasty."

Sara wasn't sure of anyone or anything at this point, but she liked these two men. Somehow, they seemed more open and trustworthy than the senior officers who hid their emotions well.

***

Sarge removed the black bag form Daniel's head. Daniels squinted. "Little Sara, all grown up. Stand up. Let me see how you've aged."

Sara stifled a gasp as she gazed at the man seated at the other end of the gray metal table. His eyes were red and crusty, and his face looked swollen on one side. Obviously, his capture and interrogation had been rough, but the chronic effects of aging shocked her more. His curly red hair was white and pulled into a ponytail. His once pale skin had been baked in the sun too often and looked like badly worn leather. More red than tanned.

She decided direct, honest questions, not bluffs, were the best way to handle him. Before she sat down, she said, "Are you the father of Farideh's son?"

Daniels shrunk in his chair. "I wish. When she was young, Farideh would have made any man proud." He said even more softly, "You remember."

"I remember your crude passes. Who is?"

"Her husband."

"First lie. Timing isn't right."

Daniels rose from his chair. Sarge in one fluid move clamped his hand on Daniels's shoulder and slammed him back into the metal chair.

She looked at the mirrored wall and imagined Nasi snickering. She wondered what the professional interrogators were thinking. She guessed it didn't matter. If she got answers from Daniels, it would be because Daniels was curious about her, not because of her interrogation skills. "How many people are F?"

Daniels with handcuffs around his wrists raised his hands to scratch his right eye. "You were mission oriented, no sense of humor, as an undergrad. Old Doc spotted your… your potential early on."

"F?"

"Told them." He motioned with his hands towards a mirror. "Don't know."

"Guess."

"Farideh and one or two other women scientists. Now probably her son."

"Why was I named?"

He stared at his bleeding handcuffed wrists. "Stumps me. She should have come out with Souri. Two cats never liked each other. Told the General at the start that they wouldn't work together."

That was an intriguing comment, but she didn't have time to waste and had to keep him focused. "Again, why me?"

"All I can figure is you're the only one left with all your marbles. Though if you're thinking of going to Qeshm, I'll doubt your sanity. Couldn't be chicken-shit Olsen or cuckoo Elvira." He shook his head. "But it's more."

"Let's get back to what you know. What names does Farideh's son use?" She slid a pencil and pad of paper to him. "All his aliases. We know he's been to Beirut…" She started to say two times, but she decided not to reveal how little she knew. "We know he's been there several times using different aliases." As he wrote, "In return for your cooperation, what do you want most?"

He paused and wrote more. "I want Farideh to be safe."

Sarge grabbed the page and snorted as he stood.

Sara suppressed a gasp as she looked at the last name on the list. "Isn't that one of your aliases? The one as a Lebanese businessman. Why?"

He looked at the mirror. "See guys, what you could have learned if you asked nicely." He looked at her. "I'm married to Farideh, at least according to an official paper filed somewhere in Iran."

Sarge, who was standing behind Daniels, rolled his eyes. "How did the big wigs miss that?" Someone in the observing room knocked on the mirror.

Sara suppressed a giggle. "I'll bite. How?"

"The General worked for Ollie North in the early eighties. You know, setting up the Iran-Contra trade. He went to Iran, looked up Farideh, got her pregnant, and..."

Sara couldn't believe what she was hearing, but she remembered the General had blue eyes. Danny's were brown.

He looked over at the mirrors. "Guys, forget your heavy-handed questions. I don't know the details, and I don't think the General will tell the same story as Farideh. He played you, too." He sighed as he looked back at Sara. "I received a call from the General to get my butt to Tehran in eighty. Told to come as a Lebanese businessman, Nazir Malouf." He shook his head. "The General, all starched and proper, informed me he couldn't divorce his wife. And he couldn't bring Farideh out of Iran."

The General was more of a jerk than she'd thought. "But if Farideh was pregnant and unmarried, I assume her husband had been executed by then, she'd be stoned to death for adultery."

He stomped his handcuffs on the metal table and blood trickled from his wrist. "Yeah, I was single, and... you know... I wanted action with Farideh. The General knew it, too. I guess everyone did. I married her. The General put me on a plane to Beirut and promised she'd follow in a few weeks after he cleared the paperwork. Bastard never intended to get her out. Later, he bragged how he'd created the perfect mole. He strung her along with promises that he'd get her out as soon as she passed the right datar to him."

Sara noticed Daniels for a second had slipped into his old Boston accent and said datar, instead of data. "Is that how he kept you in line, too?"

His head snapped up. "Yeah, through guilt. No... I don't know... hope. I went in every year or two with gifts as her estranged husband. She sent stuff out with me. Made the General look like a genius on the Middle East. The General didn't like talkative loose ends like Mickelson or nervous one like Doc. So, he promised he would get her political asylum in ninety-five if we performed a couple of services. I took care of blabbermouth Mickelson, but Farideh failed to kill Doc. The General reneged on his promise, but gave her a second chance in ninety-nine. Had her take the horrible trip from northern Iran to Van, Turkey with the Kurds and then fly from Ankara to Beirut. She had no intention of hurting Doc, but he was so frightened when he saw her that he had a heart attack. Didn't satisfy the General — the bastard." He beat his cuffed wrists against the table and repeated, "bastard" over and over. Each time he said the word louder.

Sarge held up one finger. She had to leave in a minute to learn what the Commandant and Meyers had decided. "If I go to Qeshm, how will I recognize her? I assume time hasn't been kind."

"Scar on right cheek. Limp."

"How about the son, I'll use the name Yousef because that's what Souri called him?"

"As I suspect you know, average height, thin, black hair, but with blue eyes. He's squirrelly, but you can focus his attention with key questions. I used: Where do you buy the best ice cream in the world?"

She stared at him.

"The UW Dairy Store. Who's the biggest liar?"

Sarge signaled Sara to go. She stood. "I don't know the last answer."

"You do." Suddenly, she did. "Danny, I'll tell Farideh you love her." She thought of the awful photos. "You love her in your own way."

He swayed back and forth and held up his right hand in a wave as he whispered something over and over.

Sarge grabbed her arm and bustled her out of the room. "They pushed another one too far. Now we'll never get answers from him."

"Maybe not."

CHAPTER 29: Too late to turn back

As the jet boat lurched over the water, Sara felt her stomach contents pitch back and forth. She was glad she'd taken Dramamine because the combination of the erratic motion, fear, and the blanket of heat about her were nauseating. She looked over at the two black shrouded figures next to her.

"I thought piloting a jet boat was rough. This is worse." Nasi pulled the black robe up to his knees and fanned himself with the lower part of his chador. "Glad they modified these chadors so we didn't have to clutch them to keep them closed. But I wish they would have let me wear only swimming trunks under this costume." He pulled the fabric over him arms up to his elbows and flapped his arms like a bird on take-off.

She looked down his hairy legs to his feet, which were encased in black patent leather women's dress shoes. She had laughed when he admitted he bleached his hair prior to her arrival because he figured he'd have to impersonate her and thought blonde hair was better than a wig. The black fabric bows on his shoes and his freshly bleached blonde hair were sources of laughter on the ship when they departed. The only sources of merriment.

The other black figure was a Navy petty officer of Iranian extraction. Her lips puckered as if she'd tasted a rotten piece of fruit as she eyed Nasi's legs. "Behave like an Iranian lady."

"Afari, no one can see me."

***

As they bickered, Sara replayed the last hour in her mind. The meeting with the Commandant had been brief. Meyers had claimed Souri, under intensive questioning, never changed her story. She repeated over and over, "If Yousef sees Sara in Tabl, he'll believe this isn't another American trick. F will go with Sara. The nuclear secrets will be delivered to someone, who isn't under the General's command, when F is satisfied about her and Yousef's safety. If someone under the General's command arrives, the deal is off."

Sara had insisted on seeing Souri to ask a couple of questions. Mainly, "Why me?"

Souri had been hardly recognizable. When Sara had seen her ten years before at a conference, Souri looked trim in a maroon suit and stylishly coifed hair. Today she had deteriorated to being a heavy woman with her gray hair plastered to her head. She had blinked twice, as if Sara's question had surprised her. "You must know. Yousef said he spoke to you in Beirut." The collective sigh from the interrogators had been intimidating.

Sara had gasped. Yousef must have been been on the American University of Beirut campus in ninety-nine. But where? He'd been a teen then. She'd met many, dark-haired, thin male students. Which one? She decided it was a waste of time to try to guess which one. "Why didn't F go with you?"

Souri had groaned. "We never got along. Farideh knows I must do what Robert Daniels wants or the picture goes to my husband. And Daniels does what the General wants. And F doesn't trust the General."

Sara had insisted the Commandant give Nasi a letter stating he had relieved the General of his command. It appalled her how easily the Commandant had agreed and then said, "The document is meaningless." She didn't have time to ask whether it was meaningless to F or to him. She was too busy scribbling another note.

When the Commandant handed Nasi a copy of the letter, Nasi had carefully wadded it into the pocket of his shorts before he pulled a folded chador from the pile on the table.

Souri had shaken her head and muttered, "Waste of time," as she was led away.

Sara had eyed the remaining mound of black on the table. "Okay, I'll do it, but Joe, you must sign this." She had handed the Commandant the page she'd written. It was a pledge to negotiate for her release from Iran immediately if she and Nasi were captured. Then, she'd realized the pledge couldn't be faxed to Sanders and Ulysses Howe, as she'd planned, because it might tip off the Iranian police. She felt like someone had punched her in the gut as she'd looked around the tiny compartment.

The Commandant had looked amused as he signed the page.

Meyers had swallowed another pill. "Hurry, time is running out."

Sarge had looked at the ceiling.

She'd decided that he was her best bet. "Please deliver copies of this to both senators at Al Udeid and fax it to Ulysses Howe and

Sanders, if I'm not back in four hours. Thanks." She'd handed the page to the startled sergeant. "Remember, I'm counting on you."

***

Sara came back to the present when she felt a page wadded up in a handkerchief pinned to the waistband of her skirt. It was a copy of the letter Nasi carried. She was pretty sure no one today had given her a full, honest answer. "Please Lord, don't let me be part of another hoax by either side," she whispered.

CHAPTER 30: Two hours to the deadline

Nasi pointed ahead to the shore of Qeshm. "Our pilot stays with the boat. We may need a fast get-away." He pointed to fishing gear by the pilot. "Hopefully locals will buy his story of being hired by two elderly sisters and their niece." He pointed to Sara, himself and lastly Afari. "They plan to escort their cousin to the Emirates for medical care. The pilot figured this trip would give him a chance to get in some fishing."

"Who came up with that story?"

"Meyers. Not his best cover story. So, he also gave the pilot Iranian rials, Omani rials, Qatari riyals, and Emirate dirhams to bribe any police. Never know which they'll prefer."

Sara, for a moment, was glad she wore a chador. No one could see her face. "We'd better pray the locals aren't nosy."

Sara thought as she sat under the blazing sun on the jet boat, how good it would feel to wet down the chador. But as she tramped on the beach with the wet robe slapping against her legs, the chador felt twice as heavy as before. She'd never jumped from a bobbing boat into shallow water before. She fell and turned her ankle when she stepped on a rock, which turned out to be a turtle. The wet black fabric was like a magnet for sand and mud. Her ankle hurt, and the poor turtle would probably die from injuries. Not a good start.

She gazed at Nasi and giggled. He was taking mincing steps in the black flats, which were at least two sizes too small. "Our disguise is perfect. We look too pathetic to be dangerous or even interesting."

Afari, who had alit from the boat gracefully, managed to keep her chador from dragging in the mud and sand. She waved toward a grove of mangroves and in a lilting soprano said. "Do you need to rest?"

"No, if I sat down and thought, I might race to the boat and demand to go home. I'm glad to pretend to be hard of hearing, so I don't have to answer questions, but I don't think Nasi's falsetto sounds like a woman's voice."

Afari sniffed. "And the falsetto turns his so-so Farsi, into something atrocious. I'll do all the talking."

J. L. Greger

"Yeah, the two old ladies are guided by their dutiful niece." He emphasized the last two words. He shielded his eyes from the sun with his hand. "According to the satellite shots of the third address on Daniels's list, we follow that row of date palms," He pointed past the mangroves. "to the main street of Tabl and then cut back south a block. Wish we had street side views. Knowing the roof is damaged won't help us much. It should be the fourth building on the side path."

Sara eyed a dhow moving toward the shore. "We'd better speed up, so we don't have to answer questions."

"Yeah, we're only a half-mile from the town now. Let's follow the row of date palms."

Sara soon found herself panting to keep up with Nasi and Afari. She felt like she was being steamed alive in the wet chador in the sun. Near the first building, which appeared to be bricks covered with mud and stone, a couple of goats swatted flies with their tails in a stone enclosed pen. Nasi guided her toward the right, and they walked behind the complex onto a rougher path.

"Watch where you're walking, but look for roof damage. It should be the fourth structure on the left."

Sara snorted. "Wish the Commandant had to do this."

"Shh." Afari grabbed her hand. "If someone heard your voice, we'd be in trouble."

Sara recognized Afari was right, but she felt annoyed. Maybe frustrated was a better descriptor of her feelings. She shook her hand free.

Nasi gazed at the rooftops, while Afari walked ahead and looked for signs on buildings. Sara watched the first man they passed. He was gray-haired and bent forward on his cane. He spoke as they passed and nodded when both Afari and Nasi said, "salaam" softly. Similarly, a band of boys, about eight to ten, yelled boisterously as they ran by the trio. Sara thought their lack of interest was a good sign, but she wondered what they yelled. It could be "police, police," for all she knew.

In front of a sign on a particularly decrepit building on a small rise, Afari stopped. The mud no longer covered all the bricks and stone. The wood door was badly cracked and there was no glass in the small window. Nasi nodded as he looked at the roof. Sara resisted the urge to turn around and run to the boat. However, that didn't stop her from almost vomiting. The chador made her feel claustrophobic, and it stunk of stale sweat.

Afari climbed two steps to the door and knocked. No one answered. She rapped again and spoke in Farsi. Nasi pushed Sara behind Afari and shielded her from behind.

Sara thought she heard shuffling on the hard floor inside the building. She expected to see the skeletal hand of an old woman with a cane, instead a young man stood, actually bounced up and down, with his arms spread to the two doorjambs. He was moderate height, thin, and dark haired with blue eyes. She didn't think she'd ever seen him before but guessed he must be Yousef. She suspected blue eyes weren't common in Iran.

Sara peered past him. Two walls of the room were covered with bottles of herbs and powders. The aroma in the room was heavy. Sara identified the predominant scents of rosemary and sage. The owner was some sort of herbalist, but no clients were visible.

She tottered from side to side and raised her right hand in a wave and hummed "Varsity," the Wisconsin alma mater song.

Afari looked at her in alarm. Nasi grabbed her other arm to stabilize her. The man stopped bouncing. He also swayed from side to side in the doorway, waved his right hand, and said, "Varsity." He motioned them inside, closed the door behind them, slid a wood bar across the door, and closed a decrepit wood shutter over the window.

Good sign. Danny had given her the password — the University of Wisconsin song "Varsity" and wave — evidently. Sara looked around the dimly lit room. Even with more lights, the room would be dingy. She thought she heard a noise from behind the heavy, brown paisley curtain across the back of the room. Could it be the police? Time to get her guts up. "Who makes the best ice cream in the world?"

"The UW-Madison dairy store." The man moved swiftly to the back of the room and parted the curtain. A black figure was bent over more jars and boxes. She clutched her chador tightly so as to hide her face. Another black figure was seated on a small wood bench. This woman allowed her chador to fall loosely from her head but the lower part of her face was covered with a veil.

A raspy woman's voice came from the figure examining a jar of oil. "Show me your face."

Sara didn't recognize the voice. She remembered Robert Daniels's last clue. She said, "Who's the biggest liar?"

The young man spoke. "You talked to Daniels. Are you working with him?"

"He's under arrest for killing Mickelson in Beirut." She fumbled with the wad pinned to her waistband. She pulled it out. "First your answer."

The veiled woman spoke. "You know the answer — the General." Sara didn't recognize her voice either.

Afari emitted an "eek." Obviously, she hadn't been well briefed.

Sara smoothed the page, damp with sweat. "The U.S. Marine Corp Commandant has removed the General from his command." She stepped forward to hand it to the first woman and stopped. "Are you F?"

The woman waved her hand.

"Are you Farideh Hossein?"

The woman grimaced. "Let me see your face and hair."

Sara pulled her chador open and lowered the fabric from her head. She immediately felt cooler and maybe less nauseated.

The woman eyed her for a second and then turned Sara around so the woman on the bench could also see her briefly. After the veiled woman nodded, the standing woman pulled Sara around to again look at her. "I can see a bit of the bright undergrad in Doc's group."

Sara wasted no time. "It's you turn now. Let me see your whole face."

The standing woman shrugged. "I doubt you will recognize me." She dropped the chador from around her head.

She had a prominent mole near her right eyebrow. Her long gray hair was pulled back from her pale sunken cheeks.

Sara couldn't identify her. She was sure Farideh didn't have a mole on her face when she was in graduate school at the University of Wisconsin. But the woman and the young man had answered the questions correctly. "Let's go."

The woman grabbed Sara's arm. Her black eyes focused on Sara's eyes. "Can you see any of Farideh in me?"

Sara couldn't lie but didn't want to admit the truth. "I believe you're part of F." She had an idea that might flush out the truth. "You know Danny, in his own way, loves Farideh."

The woman coughed and looked bored. Sara thought this further supported her belief — this woman wasn't Farideh.

The woman after ten seconds said, "All three of us here are F. There is one more in Tabriz. We three here must go."

Nasi stepped forward "Do you have the documents?"

A rap on the door.

Sara froze. Afari and Nasi both reached through slits in their specially designed chadors, which remained closed even when not clutched shut. Sara was sure both had reached for their guns. She again realized that she wasn't cut out for this type of adventure. She felt safer with her hands free and without a gun.

Yousef, who had stared at Sara and occasionally pulled a strand of her blonde hair during the previous conversation, sprang into action. He pushed Sara, Afari, and Nasi further into the small back room and drew the curtains closed. She could hear him drag furniture across the stone floor on the other side of the curtain.

The veiled black figure, who was taller than the first woman when she stood, picked up a cane and pulled at the wood bench. As she moved the small bench, a slot on the floor appeared. The woman pulled at the slot to lift a trap door and then descended several stairs. She stopped to light a candle stored on a shelf by the steps and motioned for Sara to follow.

The first woman shoved Afari forward so hard that she stumbled into Sara who had already descended the stone steps into what seemed to be a cave. The second slightly taller woman darted across the packed dirt floor of the cave as fast as she could. She was bent over her cane because the ceiling was low, probably about four feet above the dirt floor. She placed the candle in a rack and struggled with a piece of wood on the ceiling twelve feet away.

The four women crouched in the four-foot wide tunnel while Nasi stood on the last step holding the trap door open. Sara dreaded the feeling that would enfold her when he closed the door. This room was like a large grave. She stifled her urge to scream, but couldn't stop herself from gasping for air. The candle gave only a speck of light.

The taller, veiled woman said, "Help. It's heavy."

Sara roused herself and backed under what appeared to be another wood door. She and the taller woman squatted, raised their hands, and pushed upward. Sara guessed that short desperate people had built this tunnel.

Light streamed in at the front edge of the overhead door. Good. "Afari, help push."

Afari ignored her. The first woman elbowed Afari aside. She also squatted, and pushed upward. Little by little the light increased as the three women not only lifted their arms but shoved to the right.

When the space was wide enough, the veiled woman stepped on a large rock and then onto a rock shelf. She raised her leg to the ground above and but couldn't lift her body. Sara gave her a boost, and the woman frantically clawed at the dirt and the rocks on the ground. She fell back against Sara. Then the first woman and Sara squatted behind the fallen woman. Together they shoved her upward. She crawled out. Sara handed up her cane.

Sara heard no alarming noises. Nasi had closed the other trap door. The tunnel was dark and dank. She had no choice but to try to climb out of the pit.

She stepped on the big stone. It shifted under her weight. She teetered before she resumed her balance and stepped on the rock step. Sara bounced a bit, but her thigh muscles weren't strong enough to lift her to the ground over two feet above. She heard rustling behind her, and she felt a big hand on her rear as Nasi pushed her up. She struggled out. She was behind a stone wall in back of the building and in the middle of a grove of fig trees. Sara could hear a man speaking and Yousef screaming at the front of the small decrepit building.

She looked around. The veiled woman was already hobbling in the right direction — toward the jet boat. Nasi whistled and then whispered in Sara's ear. "Don't wait for anyone. That's our job. Tell the pilot to send backup, if he hasn't responded already to my alert."

Sara pulled her chador up around her head and walked rapidly. She wasn't in good enough condition to run a half-mile in the heat with a chador on, but she usually walked a mile in less than thirteen minutes. She figured she could reach the boat in less than eight minutes.

As she sped by the veiled woman, she looked back and saw the other woman had also exited the tunnel and was hobbling forward. Nasi was circling around the wall toward the front of the building. Afari wasn't in sight.

When she reached the house with the goats, where the side path merged with the larger path at the edge of the village, she heard a gunshot and then another. Bad sign. The veiled woman was two hundred yards behind her. The other woman was three hundred yards farther behind. Neither of them looked back. Both walked rapidly, especially for women with canes.

Sara raced along the row of date palms toward the mangroves near the shore. Occasionally, she looked over her shoulder. The women were following. Nasi and Afari weren't in sight. When the path under the date palms ended by the mangroves, she spotted the jet boat.

She choked. A dhow bobbed in the water next to the jet boat. A dark-haired man in a gray robe stood on the dhow and yelled at the pilot. She guessed in Farsi. Better not wave at him until she could assess the situation.

She raised her chador, as she'd seen Afari do, and raced across the sand. The pilot beckoned her forward.

"The two… women from F are… behind me." She gasped for breath. "Nasi needs help. Someone came to the front door." She gasped again. "I heard two gunshots when I was about five or six football-fields away from the building, but Nasi had told me to keep going no matter what."

The pilot held up four fingers and pointed toward the village. In response, four men in dirty white robes jumped from the dhow and ran up the beach toward the mangroves. Although they had black hair and dark skin, the men were too muscular and tall to resemble most Iranians. They jogged like professional athletes.

The pilot spoke into his radio. "Lara here. Door out." He looked at Sara. "What else?"

She gave him more details, rather than wasting time to ask him about his strange message.

He condensed her comments into: "Go to funnel between ball and hop."

"What?"

He smirked. "No way to be sure our messages aren't intercepted by Iranian police. We're using a limited code based on rhymes. Dumb but might confuse some listeners."

"How did Nasi signal you?"

"Whistled into his radio." He pointed towards the date palms. Two of the men were returning. They had hoisted the women on their backs and were jogging across the sand toward the jet boat. The other two weren't in sight. "Hope the reinforcements get there in time."

The man who had waved to her from dhow approached. "I'm Jim."

"What?" She felt like crying as she looked back and forth between the pilot and Jim.

The pilot put a hand on her shoulder. "Nasi didn't tell you about the backup dhow because… Meyers thought it would increase your stress. Jim will take you and the two ladies. How many more are coming?"

"Yousef, Nasi, and Afari."

"Do you have the documents?"

"The women said that we'd get them when they were safe."

"Aha, pull a bluff. Documents now, or they don't get on the dhow."

The men dumped the women on the sand. The two seamen jumped on the dhow and pulled at ropes to unfurl the sails. The pilot helped the ladies to their feet and brushed sand off their chadors.

Sara picked up their canes. "Ladies, the pilot says you can't leave on the dhow until you give me the documents."

The first woman turned and stepped toward the dhow. The veiled woman removed her veil. She had a scar on her right cheek More importantly her smile was Farideh's smile. "You have them."

Sara, mouth agape, stared at her.

"They're rolled in the canes." Farideh grabbed one and unscrewed the hook. The tube was filled with rolled papers.

CHAPTER 31: Lt. Steve Nasi is running out of time

Yousef waved his arms and screamed at two uniformed Iranian police officers in a frantic, high-pitched voice. Nasi usually understood Farsi as spoken in Oman and the Emirates, but Yousef's screams were difficult to interpret. He seemed to be saying, "Go away. Only me here."

The officers, with their backs toward Nasi, had their guns in the holsters, but their stances with their arms akimbo and legs spread suggested they were ready for action. Luckily, both were shorter and lighter than Nasi.

He adjusted the strands of fishing lines in his hands. He could easily garrote them without a sound. If Sarge, not Yousef, was distracting the officers, this would be a piece of cake, but Yousef was unpredictable. Afari was nowhere in sight and way too jittery. One policeman took a step backward. He was ready to pull a gun.

Nasi slid forward and tightened the two loops of fishing line around the man's throat before he made a sound. Nasi motioned to Yousef to keep screaming, so the other officer would continue to focus on Yousef. Instead, Yousef's jaw dropped, and he stammered. The officer stepped forward but hadn't turned yet, as Nasi let the first policeman's body slide to the ground.

Afari strode out from the behind the building. Nasi was relieved. The diversion would give him time. Wait. Her gun was out.

The policeman instantly reached for his gun. She fired and missed the officer, but nearly hit Nasi as he strangled the second policeman. During the commotion, the officer discharged his gun.

Nasi feared the whole village would be there in seconds. "Afari, move the police car down the path. Curse loudly that the car keeps backfiring. Might explain the gunshots. If we're not behind the wall in five, go to the boat." He hadn't bothered to use Farsi.

He hauled the still kicking body of the second officer toward the door. "Yousef, hold the door open."

Yousef held the door open and scanned in both directions, as Nasi heaved both bodies inside. Nasi pulled Yousef inside. "We'll hide them in the tunnel."

Yousef acted as though he'd experienced tight escapes before. He suddenly wasn't spastic. He opened the trap door, pulled the wood bar across the front door, and closed the shutter on the window. He drew the curtain across the room as Nasi toted the second body down the steps into the cellar.

Nasi peeled off his chador, kicked off his black women's shoes, and put on a pair of leather sandals and cap that he'd strapped around his waist. Ostensibly he was an Iranian fisherman. Granted a strange one.

Yousef lit a candle, closed the trap door, and jumped over the bodies as he raced behind Nasi to the partially open back exit. They emerged beyond the wall, but Afari was nowhere in sight. He knew Meyers had assigned Amari to this mission because they needed a woman who spoke fluent Farsi, but she wasn't up to this assignment.

He grabbed Yousef's arm. He didn't want him to freak out and run in another direction. They walked down the rocky path by two other buildings rapidly, but Nasi hoped not so fast as to attract attention. Several boys, playing some sort of tag, ran past them as they reached the main path. The boys only glanced at them. Good. He hoped Afari had already reached the boat.

Two men ran down the path lined by olive trees toward them. He heard a police siren close by.

Oh, no. Were Yousef and he trapped? Doubtful, the runners weren't in Iranian police or military uniforms. Then he recognized them. "Afari?"

Both men shook their heads. He shoved Yousef toward one. "Take him to the boat."

He tapped the arm of the other, who carried a soccer ball, obviously one of Meyers's props. "Smith, we look for Afari." They trotted back toward the village. No one was out. The quiet was eerie, but the heat was brutal. They saw a black blob where the two paths merged. It wasn't there a couple of minutes before. Too obvious. This was a set-up.

Both men jogged in place. Smith threw a soccer ball at him. Nasi kicked the ball toward the black blob. The ball didn't explode when it hit the blob. Smith nudged the black blob as he picked up the ball. He held up a bloodied finger. "Wounded."

"Where?" Nasi stayed at a slight distance and scanned their surroundings. No one was in sight but he could hear sounds emanating from the houses he'd passed earlier.

Smith pulled at the chador to reveal the woman's face. "Afari." He reached under the chador. "Chest wound. Too weak to walk."

Nasi and Smith made an arm sling and lifted her. Afari could barely put her right arm around Nasi neck. Her left arm hung limply. Nasi grimaced at the red spot on the ground. This was a significant wound. Time was of the essence. They raced back along the path, not worrying about their cover.

When they reached the mangroves. He saw the dhow in the far distance sailing. A man in a dirty white fisherman's robe paced in front of the jet boat. When he saw them, he sped across the sand.

"Bad gunshot," was all Nasi said before the man raced back to the jet boat.

The jet boat roared into action as soon as the two men loaded Afari on board. As the boat zoomed from shore, Nasi cut the black robe from Afari's left shoulder. The man who'd been waiting on shore ripped off his own robe and tore it into strips. He wadded the strips and applied pressure to her shoulder at the site where blood was oozing.

"Medic?" asked Nasi.

The man nodded and yelled to the pilot. "Make time or we'll lose her. I don't think the bullet hit an artery, but she's lost a lot of blood." He turned to Nasi and pointed at Afari's chador. "Take the black rag and prop her feet up. Then take over applying pressure."

Nasi lifted her feet and bent over her as he pressed on the wound. "Afari, when were you shot?"

"Stray bullet... second officer." She gasped.

The medic pulled an i.v. line with a bag of saline from an iced beer cooler, which Smith pulled from under the seat. "I like working for Meyers. Thinks of all contingencies." The medic inserted the needle into Afari's right arm. "She's thirsty."

Smith poured water from a thermos onto a relatively clean piece of cloth. Nasi pressed it to her lips. He leaned over her. "Why didn't you tell me?"

Afari's eyelashes fluttered as she partially opened her eyes. "Must... move... car."

Nasi felt guilty for his earlier negative thoughts. She'd proven she was tough. Suddenly, he jerked upward. "Where's Yousef?"

J. L. Greger

The pilot yelled over the roaring jet boat motor. "I sent him and two crewmen on with the women. Thought he made their trip seem more plausible."

The medic checked the i.v. line and touched her left arm. "Better let up a bit."

The pilot groaned. "I see an Iranian shore patrol ahead." He altered his course and a spray of water hit them. "They've stopped the dhow."

CHAPTER 32: Sara with only minutes left

Yousef yammered about his escape as the pilot of the jet boat shoved him on the dhow. The pilot ignored him and said to Jim on the dhow, "Don't attract attention by using the auxiliary diesel engine hidden in the subdeck of this baby until you're out of Iranian waters. The medic and I will wait for the three others."

He and the medic shoved the dhow from shore after two other crewmen, who actually looked like Iranians, jumped aboard and helped the two rescuers finish raising the lateen sails.

As the sails billowed in the breeze, the pilot yelled almost as an afterthought, "Make them practice their lines."

Sara watched as the jet boat with the pilot and the medic on the shore faded from sight. She wondered what would become of Nasi, Afari, and the other men.

She didn't have time to worry because Jim distributed passports immediately. He changed the story slightly from the one Nasi had outlined. Two women, Sara and Farideh, and their nephew, Yousef, had come from Doha to take their sick cousin, the other woman, from Iran to Doha for treatment. She was too ill to wait for all the required papers to clear through proper channels. Hence, they'd hired Jim and his crew.

Sara recognized she was the weakest part in the scenario, but Jim and the two rescuers didn't look like Iranian fishermen and might also raise suspicion. However, they spoke Farsi. Farideh even complimented them on their accents. Sara, on the other hand, hadn't had time to dye her hair, her skin was white, and she spoke no Farsi. The deaf and dumb routine could only go so far, and would fail if she had to remove her chador.

The dhow's movements were less jerky than those of the jet boat, but almost as nauseating. Sara roamed the dhow looking for the most stable spot and finally settled under the wooden shelter in the center of the dhow next to the woman, who now was using the alias of Ramina and was supposedly ill with cancer. Sara noted Farideh and

Yousef continued to ramble about the dhow, but seemed to avoid each other. Ramina, with her head lolling back, snored noisily.

Sara poked Ramina. "Excuse me, I thought Farideh would be more worried about her son, Yousef."

The woman jerked forward and opened one eye. A look of disgust spread over her face. "You Americans are dumb sometimes. Yousef isn't Farideh's son."

"Who is his mother? The other woman you mentioned?"

Ramina shook her head. "So many useless questions. Yousef's mother died many years ago. Farideh raised him."

"Why did the other woman remain in Tabriz?"

"Someone had to send the emails from Tabriz to confuse the police. She was dying from cancer anyway. Getting shot would be kinder than the death she's apt to have from cancer."

Sara sat and thought for several moments as she watched waves lap up on the side of the dhow. "Does Farideh have a son?"

Ramina closed her eyes. "Ask her."

Sara thought for a moment more. "Excuse me, why was I named in the emails."

Ramina kept her eyes closed. "Ask Farideh." She snored almost immediately.

Sara doubted anyone could fall asleep so quickly, so she spoke again. "When did you meet Farideh?"

Ramina kept her eyes shut. "In prison."

"When did you start to work with her?"

This time the woman squinted at Sara. "Both my husband and I were imprisoned during the Iranian Cultural Revolution. He was weak and agreed, as a geologist, to search for uranium. I worked as his assistant, even though I had earned a doctorate in chemistry. At first, I worked in a lab at the University of Tabriz and analyzed samples that he and other geologists collected throughout the northern mountains. I liked it there. One of my grandmothers was a Kurd, and I became friends with several people, including Farideh, who thought as I did about Iran." She shrugged. "My husband found nothing useful. We were transferred."

Sara was still waiting for the answer to her question, but decided patience would yield better results than asking more pointed questions. "Where was your next assignment?"

Ramina spit into her handkerchief. "Yazd Province. Miserable area. Should be called the oven. They brag about their qanāts, nothing but big water ducts with windcatchers."

Sara must have looked confused, Ramina continued, "Qanāts is a fancy name for our underground aqueduct system, which reduces evaporation of water. With wind tunnels, they also cool buildings."

Sara usually would have enjoyed learning about Yazd, but now she wanted to understand the operation of F. "What did you do there?"

"I processed uranium ore to produce yellowcake, a raw material for nuclear grade uranium."

Ramina convulsed in a coughing fit. When she spoke again, her voice was hoarse. "About twenty years ago, my husband was killed in a mining accident in the Kavir Desert, not far from Yazd. He was convinced there was high-grade ore in the area, but he never found it. No matter, he was dying anyway from exposure to radiation. Probably why we had no children. He'd been ill a long time." She hacked more. "Maybe my fault too. I didn't want a child, like Yousef. He was never normal. Many of the children born to women in prison were... slow,... emotional, how you say it... odd." She pointed her index finger and circled it around her ear.

Sara noted Ramina stated the facts without emotion. "I'm sorry."

The woman shrugged. "I continued my work, but at a slow pace. Once or twice a year, I was sent to report on our progress to the physicists and engineers building nuclear plants... and devices in Tehran." I always saw the physicist, now dying in Tabriz, and Farideh." A smile flitted across her face before she coughed uncontrollably.

"You liked them."

"None of us who spent much time in prison are likable, but I respected both women. One was a talented nuclear engineer. Farideh investigated morbidity and mortality of personnel in the nuclear industry. In prison and afterward, we made decisions." She shrugged. "And had to live with our choices."

Another coughing jag. This time she spit blood into a wad of cloth.

"You're ill. Is that why you decided to leave Iran?"

"We're all ill. None of us could work much longer, so F would," she waved her hand, "cease to exist. Then too, they found a rich source of high-grade uranium in the Kavir Desert, near the old Saghand mines and not far from where my husband was killed. The yellowcake production plant at Ardakan will double its operational capacity soon, secretly of course, to process the newly found uranium. And Yousef wanted out of Iran." She hacked more bloody gunk. "It was time to go."

Sara was basking in the satisfaction of having learned many of F's secrets when she heard a honking noise, gunshots, and a voice over a bullhorn.

Ramina's eyes almost bulged out of her head. Yousef and Farideh raced toward them. She felt the dhow slow as crew members lowered the sails. She heard Jim respond in rapid Farsi.

Farideh whispered, "The Iranian police threatened to sink our dhow, if we didn't stop."

Yousef rocked back and forth and yammered louder and louder. Ramina slapped him across the face and uttered a few words. He immediately stopped moaning but continued to shake. The three women pulled their chadors over their faces.

As two Iranian police boarded the dhow, other officers on the police boat trained their guns on Jim. The two crew members on the dhow, who looked like Iranians, spoke first to the police officers. The officers pushed them aside.

Jim stepped forward and pointed to the women as he spoke. He motioned for the crew members to get a box from the cabinet at the front of the boat.

Sara noticed the voices of the police became louder, even though Jim's tones hadn't changed.

While Yousef hiccupped, Ramina rose unsteadily. She coughed as she shuffled toward the lead police officer. She braced her legs and made loud hacking noises before she shoved the rag with bloody mucous toward him. He retreated a step.

As she tottered back to her seat, Yousef charged toward the edge of the boat. The second guard raised his gun and shouted. Yousef stopped and vomited on the deck. The guard turned away in disgust.

The crew, under Jim's direction, pulled two cases of Jack Daniels black label whiskey from the cabinet. The lead officer spat on the deck. Sara assumed he was more religious and honest than the Iranian patrol guards encountered by the two Omanis whom Sarge had talked about.

Jim pulled a box labeled with red crescents from the cabinet. The guard rummaged through the box and pulled out syringes, needles, bottles, and vials. The lead officer waved for another guard to board the dhow. While the third man carried the box back to the patrol boat, the lead officer stomped over to the three women and Yousef.

Sara was glad her face was covered with her chador. She recognized she'd no acting talent and often smiled when she was nervous. Now no one could see her face. She was also glad Jim had handed her dark makeup to apply to her face and hands at the start of the trip. However, she was worried the sweat running down her arms and from her scalp would create white streaks on her hands and face. Nothing she could do about it now.

The lead police officer spoke in a conversational manner to Ramina. Sara thought that was good sign.

Ramina hacked red gunk onto the rag in her hand and gave a four-word reply.

He barked at Yousef, who allowed drool to drip from his mouth before he spoke. Sara couldn't understand Farsi, but she thought he was stuttering.

The lead officer pointed at Sara. The tone of his voice sounded like a question.

She patted the chador over her ears, being careful to keep the chador over most of her face.

He seemed to say the same phrase again, but much louder.

She shook her head and shrugged.

His face became red.

She suppressed her urge to vomit. Maybe, he'd not seen her shrug. She lifted her hands with palms upward to her face and shook her head more.

The second guard moved toward the group.

She wondered why Ramina or Farideh didn't help. She patted Farideh's head with one hand. Finally, Farideh leaned forward and said something. Sara sighed internally, but she still felt nauseated.

The officer snickered as he pointed back and forth at Yousef and Sara, made a circular motion with his hand, and pointed again at Yousef and Sara. Yousef panted like a dog in hot weather. Farideh continued to speak rapidly, but her voice sounded calm, at least to Sara.

Sara assumed Farideh called Sara deaf and dumb with an emphasis on dumb. Jim had suggested during the briefing at the start of the trip that such a description was the only way to cover for Sara's inability to speak or understand Farsi.

The lead officer barked a command.

Both Farideh and Ramina pulled out their fake passports. Sara reached into the purse, hanging on a long cord around her neck, and claimed her passport, while Farideh spoke sharply to Yousef. He stood and drew his passport from the back pocket of his jeans and lurched forward.

The second guard drew his gun as Yousef approached. Farideh screamed. This time Yousef retched into the water, not on the deck. He staggered back to the wood bench.

The lead officer quickly handed all the passports back to Farideh. He stalked back to Jim, who had two more boxes labeled with red crescents at his feet. Sara assumed these were filled with medical supplies, too. The lead officer looked into the wooden cabinet. She surmised he wanted to be sure it was empty. He waved for the third guard to again jump onto the dhow. As his two assistants carted the boxes onto the patrol boat, the lead officer appeared to lecture Jim who hung his head and shuffled his feet.

Sara felt sweat trickle down her face, but she didn't wipe it lest she remove her dark makeup. Yousef hiccupped, and Ramina hacked and spit. Farideh chanted softly. Sara decided it was time to pray harder than before.

The lead officer climbed across the rope ladder between the two boats. Jim untied the ladder from the dhow. The crew wasted no time. They lifted the three lateen sails as the patrol boat zoomed away.

Sara needed to use a bathroom, but there was none on the dhow, only a lidded pot in the closet. She staggered forward.

Jim met her at the closet. "That was close. I know why F succeeded in outwitting the police for more than thirty years. Those two women are good. The patrol captain was afraid Ramina would infect him with something fatal. Farideh convinced him that you and Yousef were weak-minded and needed her constant attention. So, she'd brought you along because you were incapable of remaining alone in Doha."

Sara shrugged. "I'm sorry I couldn't do better, but everyone covered for me. Yousef is a pretty good actor."

"I doubt he was acting. And as usual, Meyers gave us the right props. The officer was insulted by the booze but almost grateful to get the medical supplies."

Sara grabbed the chamber pot. "There are two things good about a chador. It hides your face when your emotions might give you away, and you don't need a private bathroom."

He laughed. "Hope the patrol ship doesn't stop our jet boat They sent one of those stupid rhyming messages as we were stopped. 'Pan gown.' I wonder who was wounded."

CHAPTER 33: Deadline

The three women wadded up their chadors as the dhow approached the dock loading ship. They bet how far they could throw them before Jim snatched them. "Never know, when we'll need them again."

A large bag of rope netting was lowered from the ship onto the dhow. Yousef jumped into the middle of it before the women grasped the implications, but after a few seconds they clambered over the snakes of cords and knots. Jim gave a signal. The rope sling snapped upward, and Sara felt herself sway back and forth as they were lifted like cargo onto the dock loading ship. Demeaning and scary in one sense, but exhilarating in another. For the first time in almost two days, she felt safe.

Sarge and Nasi were on the deck. Sara wasn't surprised that the dhow was slower than the jet boat. "Jim got the message 'Man down.' Who was injured?"

Nasi blanched. "Afari is in surgery now."

Sara gasped, but she was determined to complete her last mission. "Guys, this is Farideh. We've got to talk to the Commandant pronto. I've got valuable info. Where is he?" She grabbed Nasi's arm. "Any news on Sanders?"

He grinned. "Doing fine, but worried about you." His smile disappeared. "The Iranian news agency reported a well-known woman physicist was shot and killed by an unknown assailant at a café in Tabriz. They claimed the culprit was an Israeli terrorist." He stared at Farideh. "I'm so sorry. It was the café where the first email came from."

Farideh choked, only a bit. "We expected they'd identify her. I'm sure it was our own police who executed her."

Sara whispered to Nasi, "Get us off the deck and to the Commandant."

He nodded and led the women down a flight of stairs, while Sarge rounded up Yousef who was waving to the flight crew on the deck.

Suddenly Sara stopped in the middle of the steps. "One thing I don't understand. The chatter on the Web predicted pretty accurately when F, or at least one member, would be killed. How could they know that thirty-six hours ago?"

Farideh and Ramina giggled like schoolgirls. "We — F — planted the message." Farideh paused, "We thought Americans responded well to deadlines, and we suspected the General would try to slow our rescue. However, we hoped there'd be other announcements from Iran about the time of our deadline."

Sarge pulled his headphone from one ear, but kept one hand around Yousef's shoulder to keep him from bounding off. "We received a report of a small earthquake north of Yazd an hour ago. Near a location that Daniels identified as important. Know anything about it?"

Farideh beamed. "Have your satellites check the yellowcake processing plant at Ardakan. Yousef set the timers two days ago. He wanted to level the place, but that quantity of munitions was apt to be discovered."

Nasi was already texting.

Farideh motioned to Ramina. "She convinced him to reduce his expectations, but make it large enough to stop the plant's operation for a month and to trigger a visit by an international inspection team. The complete layout of the plant, including the new secret addition, is in the documents rolled into the canes. We assume they'll rebuild the destroyed section if international authorities don't monitor the plant closely."

Nasi stopped texting. "Did Robert Daniels know about the addition to the plant?"

"No, he was trying to identify the location where they recently found a high grade uranium ore, but he had incomplete data. Among the documents in the canes, you'll find more detailed maps for the mine and chemical analyses of the ore."

"Wow, guess those canes… and you were worth all our efforts." Nasi resumed texting.

Farideh frowned. "Any news from the Rudan Nuclear Conversion Facility in Fasa?"

Sarge choked. "Like what?"

"I rigged a bomb to go off there," she shrugged, "but I'm not as good with explosives as Yousef. The engineering plans for that facility are in the canes, too. The international inspections teams should find the plans useful."

Sara tugged the sleeve of Nasi's shirt again. "Lead us to the Commandant. We can talk as we walk."

Sarge shook his finger at Nasi, who whistled as he led the way down a narrow corridor. Nasi stopped in front of a closed door with a guard posted. He whispered to the guard and managed to move him slightly away from the center of the doorway, but the guard kept saying, "No."

Sarge looked nervous and seemed to want to distract Farideh. "Why Rudan Nuclear Conversion Facility in Fasa? Fasa is almost five hours south of Yazd."

Farideh looked back and forth between Sara at the door and Sarge. "Iran secretly expanded its capacity to convert yellowcake into weapons grade uranium hexafluoride in Fasa. The new ore from Yazd would be processed in Fasa. We sent the message out several times, but someone intercepted it each time. We — F — decided, with three of us ill, our last act would be a defiant one."

Sara wasn't in the mood to be distracted and figured Nasi suspected what she would do. She knocked on the door and slid it open. As expected, the Commandant, Meyers, the two senators, and a couple of other apparently senior officials, at least their hair was gray, sat around the table. "Gentlemen, you owe this lady, Farideh, your time. Seems we got a few things wrong in Washington and on the flight over here." Sara grabbed Farideh's hand and pulled her inside the room.

All the men stood. The Commandant offered the women chairs next to him. "Nasi already texted us messages."

Meyers left the room. Sara could hear him say, "Nasi, I told you..." before the door was slid shut.

Sara spoke before she sat down. "The snapshots, at least of Farideh, were taken by the General. He, not Daniels, wrote the threat on the photo."

No one seemed surprised, but they studied her intensely.

"You've got to find her son, now a man, before it's too late."

The Commandant cleared his throat and sat. "I thought the handwriting on the photo looked familiar. Shortly after you departed, I found a sample of the General's handwriting and requested an investigation of the General's travels during the eighties. We were talking about what to do with the General and the Major when you barged in."

The northern senator said, "A court martial is in orders for the General. He's spent the last thirty years covering his mistakes and peccadillos. We agree that he, not Robert Daniels, took the questionable photos of women. FBI auditors also pointed DOD auditors toward a whole slew of shortcuts by defense contractors with coverups by the General."

The southern senator looked at his colleagues. "Y'all know we have to be careful because the publicity on a court-martial would hurt a lot of innocent people and damage our activities here. The Major is easier. We think the General kept him around because he was too incompetent to recognize the General's schemes. His dismissal papers are being processed as we speak."

"Farideh's son?" Sara thought about making a threat to go to the press, but hoped it was unnecessary.

The Commandant looked smug. "Farideh, when did you know the General and his wife adopted your son?"

Sara gasped. Ramina had told the truth — at least partially.

Farideh shrugged. "About fifteen years ago, when I saw a picture of the General with his blonde wife and black-haired son on the Web. Until then, I was terrified to please the General. Afterwards, I stayed in Iran because Yousef and the others in F needed me."

"We're puzzled. How did you hide from Robert Daniels the transfer of the child to the General?"

"Daniels wasn't the only one who used the Kurds. I moved with Kurdish groups from Tabriz north to Van in Turkey where the General was waiting when my boy was about six months old. I prayed the boy would be safe. When I returned to Tabriz, I adopted Yousef because his mother had died. She'd also been raped by the General. Only the other members of F knew."

The Commandant stood. "I think you can leave now."

Sara remained sitting. "Farideh and her friend both have cancer, probably from continued exposure to radiation. They served the U.S. well and deserve free treatment."

The southern senator nodded. "Ma'am, we agree. Jim radioed us from the dhow. Physicians at the National Institute of Health are prepared to treat them."

As the senator spoke, Farideh moved restlessly in her chair. When he paused, she stood. "I'm not a servant of the U.S., but a proud Irani. However, those in power in Iran have made bad choices. Thank you for finally recognizing at least one of your generals was evil, too."

The senators were now the ones wiggling in their chairs. Even the Commandant looked relieved when Meyers entered carrying two canes. "Fires swept Fasa nuclear conversion plant about an hour ago." He looked at Farideh. "Nasi tells me we can thank you." He handed the canes to Farideh. "Please accept these as mementoes of your service."

Farideh stroked the canes, almost lovingly.

Meyers touched her shoulder. "Do you want to see your husband Robert Daniels before you leave?"

Farideh blinked back tears. "No, he loves a woman who doesn't exist anymore. I let him think Yousef was the General's and my son. Kept him from asking questions and doing something foolish." She wiped the tears from her eyes. "Forgive my Danny. He was under orders, always. He obeyed the General to protect me."

The Southern senator looked at his northern senatorial colleague and then at Farideh. "We all may be slow, but we figured out during the last three hours that Robert Daniels was a valuable asset here. We think Yousef, with his unique talents, should stay here, too, for the time being."

Meyers interrupted, "Sir, the helicopter is ready to take us to meet our flight from Al Udeid to Washington. Will you be joining the rest of us on the flight to Washington?"

The Commandant coughed. "Meyers, I know you're eager to start your new assignment as director of Marine intelligence in the Middle East in Washington. You'd better impress the senators during this trip because you'll be reporting to their committee."

Both senators chuckled.

The Commandant turned to Sara. "If you don't mind, you and I won't leave Al Udeid until late tomorrow. Sanders and Bug are fine. I have business to finish, including unraveling the last, I hope, of the General's schemes and correcting a few of your misconceptions. You and Nasi have the same problem — too impatient to work within a bureaucracy."

Sara reddened.

"Speaking of Nasi. He and Sarge want to show you around Qatar." He coughed. "They may try to talk you into another mission."

Sara blanched. "I can't." She turned to Farideh. "One last question. Why me?"

Farideh looked down. "Many reasons. You were the last one from Madison. I'd followed your career, easy to follow a fellow epidemiologist."

"That's all?"

"It was obvious you'd defied authorities several times in your career and now had contacts. I suspected, or maybe hoped, you wouldn't give in to the General when he hindered my escape from Iran."

Sara hugged Farideh. "Good luck."

Farideh walked to the door and turned. "Do you remember the teenager in ninety-nine who asked you if you were staying at the president's house at American University of Beirut?"

Sara nodded.

"That was Yousef. He always says, 'Photos lie' when he looks at old photos of me. He only trusts those he's met and who were pleasant to him. You met his criteria. He chose you because he said, "I saw her in Beirut.""

CHAPTER 34: One last adventure

"Guys, are you sure this memento is worth the effort?" The heat was terrible but not as bad as when wearing a chador.

The jeep rumbled to a stop in the middle of a deserted highway in the middle of a sea of sand. Nasi jumped out with a bag of tools and a stepladder. Sarge chuckled. "What a waste. Nasi understands the people in this part of the world better than most officers, but he has no... discipline. Not cut out for the military."

"Perhaps two months in Washington in preparation for his new assignment here will mature him. Responsibility does that... Especially, if his girlfriend says yes."

The sergeant shook his head. "Met her when she visited him. She's too smart to say yes, without conditions."

Nasi threw the supplies in the back of the jeep, but lovingly held a triangular metal sign, white with a red border. The profile of a camel in black was in the middle. "The epitome of Qatar. Old and new colliding literally. Cars really have hit camels that wandered onto the highway. A lot worse than hitting a deer." He rubbed dust off the sign. "Don't you think it's the perfect gift for my girl?"

"Huh." Sarge's eyes bulged. "You aren't ready to get married if you think your girl wants a sign. I thought you were collecting this memento for Sara. You need to be looking at engagement rings."

Nasi's eyebrows almost met in the middle as he frowned. "Seemed too pushy, but I, actually we, looked at rings when she visited two months ago. She thought the selection was better in Doha than in the States, at least New Mexico."

Sarge coughed. "Now that was a hint."

"Guess... you're right, and Sara deserves a memento." He handed her the sign. After a few more seconds of self-pity, he brightened. "Now, who's up for a camel ride?"

Sara blinked. She admired the spontaneity of the young, but wasn't prepared for this rapid transition. She thought a second. "Haven't they warned you about MERS? Camels are believed to be the reservoir

J. L. Greger

for the virus that causes the Middle East Respiratory Syndrome. The mortality rate is over thirty percent for patients with MERS."

Nasi looked like a five-year-old who'd been disciplined. "So, that's not a good idea either?"

Sarge clicked his tongue. "You've spent too much time looking at women's shoes and not enough time talking to real women. Sara wants to talk to Sanders."

Sand flew in all directions as Sarge made a wide U-turn in the jeep and raced back to Al Udeid. Nasi cranked up the radio.

Sara was thankful the noise level prevented conversation and gave her time to think about her future with Sanders. During the last three days, she'd learned a lot about the knots that bound couples together and those that separated them. She didn't expect the giddy highs that Nasi and his girl anticipated, well not really... But she didn't want to face regrets, like Farideh and Robert Daniels, for things not said or not done. That meant Sanders and she needed to add more playfulness to their relationship and to discuss formerly taboo subjects without violating national secrets. Maybe, the perfect place for the camel sign wasn't her office, but in his bedroom along with that red chemise she'd left there so long ago, actually less than sixty hours before.

As soon as they delivered her to her quarters at Al Udeid, Sara called Sanders. "Honey, I'm coming home. We've got to talk. And I don't ever want to hear again: I saw you in Beirut."

SCIENCE AND HISTORY BEHIND THE STORY

Both historical facts and tidbits of science abound in this novel. These references may add authenticity to *I Saw You in Beirut* for the curious.

• During the two hundred and fifty years before 1810, miners and refiners released over two hundred thousand metric tons of mercury into the air as they processed over one hundred thirty thousand metric tons of silver in Latin America. (Robins NA and Hagan NA. Mercury production and use in colonial Andean sliver production: Emissions and health implications. *Environmental Health Perspectives* 2012; 120: 627-31). Much of the mercury vapors recycled into soil and water around silver productions areas, such as Potosí. Thus, the pollution concerns in Bolivia mentioned in Chapter 1 are real.

• One of the largest accidental incidents of methylmercury poisoning ever occurred in Iraq in 1971 and 1972 and is mentioned in Chapter 2. (Bakir F, Damiuji SF, et al. Methylmercury poisoning in Iraq. *Science* 1973; 181 [issue 4096]; 230-41).

• The dissertation research of the fictional Doc Steinhaus was based on actual research. Scientists found zinc deficiency caused stunted growth and lack of sexual development in rural villagers in Iran and Egypt. (Halstead JA, Ronaghy HA, et al. Zinc deficiency in man: The Shiraz experiment. *American Journal of. Medicine* 1972; 53: 277-284). These villagers not only consumed low levels of zinc, but also ate a diet poor in protein and iron with high levels of phytate (an organic compound that reduces the absorption of minerals) and practiced geophagia (deliberate consumption of soil and clay). At first, scientist thought geophagia was the cause of the growth retardation.

• Originally the research on zinc deficiency in Iran was led by Dr. James A. Halstead, mentioned in Chapter 10. He was married to

Anna Roosevelt, the daughter of President Franklin Roosevelt. (Smith JC and Swenseid M. Biography: James A. Halstead. *Journal of Nutrition* 1988; 118: 421-4).

• After World War II, a variety of agencies, including the United States Agency for International Development (USAID) and the Peace Corps, private foundations, and universities were involved in scientific research and development projects in Iran. (Ehsani-Nia S. Go forth and do good: US-Iranian relations during the cold war through the lens of public diplomacy. *Pennsylvania History Review* 2011; 19 [issue 1]: article 5). The research of Doc Steinhaus, Howard Baum, and Mark Olsen in Iran are realistic examples of these activities.

• Sara's experiences as a consultant at universities in the Middle East are based on actual experiences of professors, including myself. I actually had a youth on campus ask me if I was staying at the university president's house when I was a consultant at the American University of Beirut. The security officer was alarmed when he learned of my encounter.

• American universities have partnered with several countries in the Middle East during the last thirty years to create modern campuses. For example, Education City in Doha, Qatar is a partnership of the Qatar Foundation for Education, Science and Community Development and six U.S. universities, including Weill Cornell Medical School (http://www.qf.org.qa).

• The involvement of U.S. agencies in science and development in the Middle East continues. One example is the State Department program called the Iraq Science Fellowship Program. (Stone R. Throwing a lifeline to a one-time Arab science power. *Science* 2015; 347 [issue 6219]: 223). Iranian scientists are now eager to increase contact with scientists worldwide (Stone R. Unsanctioned science. *Science* 2015; 349 [issue 6252]: 1038-43).

• The nuclear power plant in Bushehr, the uranium enrichment facilities in Fasa, and the Saghand uranium mines in Yazd province, mentioned in this novel are actual sites and are subject to international inspection. (Nuclear power in Iran. http://www.worldnuclear.org/info/Country-Profiles; Stone R. Iran deal would transform its nuclear infrastructure. *Science* 2015; 348 [issue 6231]: 164-5).

• Middle East Respiratory syndrome, better known as MERS, has been a hot topic in virology research during the last couple of years. As mentioned in Chapter 34, camels appear to be a reservoir for the MERS virus. (Enserink M. Mission to MERS. *Science* 2014; 344 [issue 6189]: 1218-1220).

THE END

ABOUT THE AUTHOR

J. L. Greger is no longer a biology professor at the University of Wisconsin-Madison, instead she puts tidbits of science into her thrillers and mysteries: *The Flu Is Coming*, *Murder...A Way to Lose Weight*, *Ignore the Pain, Malignancy*, and now *I Saw You in Beirut*. Besides writing, her favorite activities are spending time with Bug, her Japanese Chin dog, and traveling to exotic locations. She incorporates both of these activities into her novels. *I Saw You in Beirut* includes several of her observations while consulting on scientific and education issues in the United Arab Emirates and Lebanon in the nineties. And of course, Bug is a character in all the books in the Science Traveler series.

Her website is: www.jlgreger.com.